WOMEN WRITING

WOMEN WRITING

An Anthology

edited by Denys Val Baker

St. Martin's Press

New York

Introduction and organization copyright © Denys Val Baker
  1978,1979
Lilacs, copyright © Mary Lavin
A Romantic Hero, copyright © Olivia Manning
Mice and Birds and Boy, copyright © Elizabeth Taylor
Man With No Eyes, copyright © Fay Weldon
Each Other, copyright © Doris Lessing
Blue Lenses, copyright © Daphne du Maurier
The House of my Dreams, copyright © Edna O'Brien
Here and There in the Wastes of Ocean a Swimmer was Seen,
  copyright © Penelope Mortimer
A Member of the Family, copyright © Muriel Spark
Another Survivor, copyright © Ruth Fainlight
The Elephant Man, copyright © Susan Hill
Fixing Pixie Loveless, copyright © A. L. Barker

All rights reserved. For information, write:
St. Martin's Press, Inc.,
175 Fifth Ave., New York, N.Y. 10010
Manufactured in the United States of America

Library of Congress Cataloging in Publication Data

Main entry under title:

Women writing.

Edition for 1978 published under title: Twelve stories by
famous women writers.
  CONTENTS: Lavin, M. Lilacs.—Manning, O. A romantic
hero.—Taylor, E. Mice and birds and boy. [etc.]
  1. Short stories, English—Women authors.
I. Val Baker, Denys, 1917-
PZ1.W6847   [PR1286.W6]   823'.01   79-4842
ISBN 0-312-88787-6

CONTENTS

ACKNOWLEDGEMENTS

Lilacs by Mary Lavin first appeared in *Tales From Bective Bridge* (Michael Joseph, 1943); *A Romantic Hero* by Olivia Manning first appeared in a book of stories of that title (Heinemann, 1967); *Mice and Birds and Boy* by Elizabeth Taylor first appeared in *A Dedicated Man* (Chatto and Windus, 1965); *Man With No Eyes* by Fay Weldon is newly published; *Each Other* by Doris Lessing first appeared in *A Man and Two Women* (MacGibbon and Kee, 1963); *Blue Lenses* by Daphne du Maurier first appeared in *The Breaking Point* (Victor Gollancz, 1959); *The House of My Dreams* by Edna O'Brien first appeared in *A Scandalous Woman* (Weidenfeld and Nicolson, 1974); *Here and There in the Wastes of the Ocean a Swimmer was Seen* by Penelope Mortimer first appeared in *Boston University Journal*, 1970; *A Member of the Family* by Muriel Spark first appeared in *Voices at Play* (Macmillan, 1961); *Another Survivor* by Ruth Fainlight is newly published; *The Elephant Man* by Susan Hill first appeared in *The Albatross* (Hamish Hamilton, 1971); and *Fixing Pixie Loveless* by A. L. Barker first appeared in *Femina Regal* (Hogarth Press, 1971).

WOMEN WRITING

INTRODUCTION

This book is not intended to propagate the idea of women writers as a breed apart but rather to reflect and pay homage to their quite dazzling array of talents in the field of contemporary literature. Certainly recognition has been delayed by a kind of inevitable rear-guard action of predictable male chauvinism but today there can be little doubt that the position of our leading women writers is so secure that—well, mere male writers must indeed look to their laurels. In particular women seem to excel at that most difficult of art forms, the short story, and in this volume is presented a representative selection of work in this field by some of our most outstanding women writers.

First, though, it may be interesting to consider, very briefly, the historical background. When writing became a money-making profession it was the men who took charge, and for many centuries at that. In England the first woman really to break this monopoly and earn her living by her pen was the playwright, Mrs Aphra Behn, who flourished during the reign of King Charles II, writing a series of lively and rather bawdy plays which later earned her the description 'the female Wycherley'. Appropriately enough for such a doughty pioneer when she died in 1689 she was buried at Westminster Abbey, accompanied by a tombstone epitaph which declared: 'Here lies a proof that wit can be Defence against mortalitie.'

After Mrs Behn had broken the ice a number of other women playwrights made their mark, notably the Duchess of Newcastle and Catherine Cockburn, but it was really during the eighteenth century that women writers began to proliferate. This was the period when a wide range of women's magazines began to appear, such as the *Lady's Magazine*, the *Female Tatler*, the *Matrimonial Magazine*, the *Lady's Museum* and even, in rather obvious imitation of Addison and Steele's more famous publication, the *Female Spectator*. Some of these magazines began serialising women's novels, the first example on record being *Sophie*, by Charlotte Lennox, which appeared in the *Lady's Museum* in the 1770s. The author was by no means a nonentity and indeed Henry Fielding described another of her novels, *Adventures of Arabella*, as entitling her to the rank of 'a woman of genius'. Fanny Burney, author of *Evelina* and *Cecilia* belongs to this period—it was, indeed, the time of 'the Blue Stockings', a group of lady novelists whose earnings would compare favourably with anything today (such popular authors as Lady Elizabeth Montague and Hannah More earning up to £2,000 from a single novel). It was also the period when women writers began to widen their scope—ranging from the impressive Gothic novels of Mrs Ann Radcliffe to the romantic books of Elizabeth Inchbald (whose *A Simple Story* is claimed to have influenced the later *Jane Eyre*), from the passionate Irish tales of Lady Morgan, who became the first woman writer to be granted a Civic Pension (£300 a year, a fair sum for those days) to the 'Byron of Modern Poetesses', Caroline Norton, and from the somewhat superior novels of Mary Russell Mitford to the even greater works of genius penned by a perceptive young lady called Jane Austen.

From Jane Austen onwards the status of women writers became firmly established so that by the time the incredible Brontë sisters burst upon the literary world in the nineteenth century there was no turning the inevitable tide ... after all *Wuthering Heights* is one of the great English novels.

While there is no space here to continue the list of names and achievements more fully—think, for instance, of the industrious Mrs Trollope, supposed to have written more than a hundred novels!—tribute is due to the Victorian and Edwardian period of the grand novelists, double and even treble deckers some of them, national and international figures such as Ouida, Mrs Humphry Ward,

2

Marie Corelli, Mrs Belloc Lowndes. Later, as we entered the twentieth century so women novelists of even greater literary powers began to appear: Dorothy Richardson, the true instigator of the stream of consciousness style, Virginia Woolf, Vita Sackville West, Katherine Mansfield, Rebecca West, Rose Macaulay.

Between the wars, women writers conquered new fields—a typical example being the detective novel, where writers such as Agatha Christie and Dorothy Sayers reigned supreme—and since then the expansion into all spheres has proliferated. Today the list of truly original and often quite dazzling performers is almost embarrassingly long: Mary Renault, Iris Murdoch, Daphne du Maurier, Mary Lavin, Nina Bawden, Brigid Brophy, Muriel Spark, Edna O'Brien, A. L. Barker, Beryl Bainbridge, Olivia Manning, Margaret Drabble, Doris Lessing, Elizabeth Jane Howard, Penelope Mortimer, Maureen Duffy, Fay Weldon, Bernice Rubens, Rosalind Wade, Christine Brook Rose, Jean Stubbs, Susan Hill, Jean Rhys—to name but a tiny percentage. It is truly a delight to read the richly imaginative, perceptive, liberated and very professional work of such superbly gifted writers.

This delight will, I hope, be shared by the readers of this first ever anthology of short stories by women writers of today. Selection has not been easy but for this first volume I have aimed for as wide a variety of stories as possible within the inevitable space limitations. There is wit, comedy, nostalgia, irony, drama, poetry, delicacy, sometimes a touch of the macabre, often a powerful sense of narrative, and always, I think, the feeling—dare I say it!—of very feminine imaginations at work. Happy reading!

Denys Val Baker

NOTES ON CONTRIBUTORS

Mary Lavin

Ever since with her first volume of short stories, *Tales from Bective Bridge*, in 1943 when she won the James Tait Black Memorial Prize, she has been recognised as one of the main figures of Irish literature—as witness many subsequent collections, notably *In the Middle of the Fields*, *Selected Stories*, *At Sallygap*, and *The Great Wave*, which won another award, the Katherine Mansfield Prize for 1961. Recently Constable's have begun issuing her stories in a collected edition. She still lives in County Meath, Eire, and was President of the Irish Academy of Letters, 1972–1973. She had three daughters by her late first husband, and in 1969 married again, to Michael MacDonald Scott.

Olivia Manning

Author of twelve novels and two volumes of short stories. Her best known works are the three novels which comprise what is known as 'The Balkan Trilogy'. Her new novel, *The Danger Tree*, out last year, continues the trilogy into Egypt.

Elizabeth Taylor

Sadly a posthumous contributor to our volume, she was, until her recent death, undoubtedly one of the most gifted of all English writers, among her novels being *Palladian*, *A View of the Harbour* and *The Wedding Group*. Like so many women writers she first made her mark with short stories, many first published in the influential *New Yorker* magazine—and interestingly enough, her work has always been even more popular in America than at home. Among several volumes of short stories was *A Dedicated Man*, from which our selection was taken. Married, she lived a quiet life for many decades in the village of Penn, near High Wycombe, Bucks.

Fay Weldon

Born in England and reared in New Zealand, returning to the mother country and obtaining an M.A. in psychology before taking up a new career as a writer—initially making her mark with a number of successful radio and television plays, and then with three remarkable novels, *Female Friends*, *Down Among the Women* and *Remember Me*. Of the first of these Philip Oakes in the *Sunday Times* commented: 'The novel that has remained painfully and comically in my mind all year is Fay Weldon's *Female Friends* ... it is precise, compassionate and murderously funny. What's more, in the last resort it's optimistic.'

Doris Lessing

Best known for her earlier sequence of novels based on her early life in Rhodesia—*Martha Quest, A Proper Marriage, A Ripple from the Storm, Landlocked* and *The Four Gated City* (published under the general title of 'Children of Violence'). Doris Lessing has since written several dramatic and experimental novels, such as *The Golden Notebook* and *Briefing for a Descent Into Hell*, as well as a collection of short stories, *A Man and Two Women*, from which this story is taken. The *Sunday Times* described her quite simply as 'the best woman novelist we have'. She has been married twice and has had three children.

Daphne du Maurier

Second daughter of the famous actor and theatre manager-producer, Sir Gerald du Maurier, she has earned an international reputation with such novels as *Rebecca, Jamaica Inn, Frenchman's Creek, My Cousin Rachel*, most of them set in Cornwall, where she has lived at Menabilly near Fowey for more than a quarter of a century. Apart from novels she has written several fascinating non-fiction works, notably a biography of *Bramwell Brontë* and *The Du Mauriers* and *Gerald*, studies of members of her family, and is also author of many short stories, two of which—*The Birds* and *Don't Look Now*—were adapted into highly successful films. Widow of the late Lt General Sir Frederick Browning, she has two daughters, a son and five grandchildren.

Edna O'Brien

Undoubtedly one of our most outstanding short story writers, Edna O'Brien is the author of several volumes of stories, but also equally well known for such novels as *The Girl With Green Eyes*, *The Country Girls*, *Girls in their Married Bliss*, *August is a Wicked Month*, etc. Another of her novels, *Zee and Co*, was filmed with Elizabeth Taylor in the leading role. Born in the West of Ireland she now lives in London with her two sons.

Penelope Mortimer

Born in North Wales and studied at London University—after writing film scripts she turned to novels, and achieved wide recognition with *The Pumpkin Eater*, which was later filmed—among other successful novels have been *My Friend Says Its Bulletproof* and *The Home*. Writing on her work the critic Francis King commented, 'No woman novelist has written of woman in her roles of prisoner, slave and victim more eloquently or more bitterly than Penelope Mortimer.'

Muriel Spark

Regarded as one of the most important writers to have emerged in England since the last war, she originally made her name with short stories—several volumes being published, including *The Go Away Bird* and *Voices at Play*. Now, of course, she is even better known for such novels as *The Ballad of Peckham Rye*, *Memento Mori*,

The Comforters and *The Prime of Miss Jean Brodie*, which later achieved fame both as a play and a film. For some years now she has lived in Rome.

Ruth Fainlight

Although born in New York she has lived mostly in England (married to Alan Sillitoe). She has published four collections of poems, *Cages*, *To See the Matter Clearly*, *The Region's Violence* and *Another Full Moon*, also a collection of short stories, *Daylife and Nightlife*. Three of her stories were included in *Penguin Modern Stories, No. 9*, and she has also had work published by many small private presses.

Susan Hill

Born in Scarborough in 1942 and educated at King's College, London, she was literary critic of a Midlands newspaper, the *Coventry Evening Telegraph*, for five years and still reviews extensively. One of her first novels, *Gentlemen and Ladies*, was runner-up for the John Llewellyn Rhys Prize, while *I'm King of the Castle* won the Somerset Maugham Award for 1971. Since then she has won increasing critical acclaim for both novels and collections of short stories such as *The Albatross*. She is married and lives at Stratford on Avon.

A. L. Barker

Born in 1918, she has published four novels and six books of short stories and novellas, as well as many magazine stories. Winner of the first of the Somerset Maugham Awards in 1947, for a collection of short stories, *Innocents*, and received the Cheltenham Festival of Literature Award in 1962. A Fellow of the Royal Society of Literature, she works in an editorial capacity and writes in her spare time.

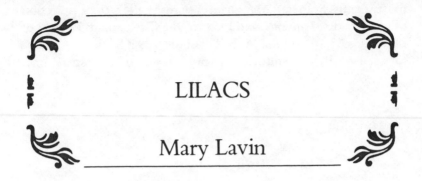

LILACS

Mary Lavin

'That dunghill isn't doing anybody any harm and it's not going out of where it is as long as I'm in this house!' said Phelim Molloy.

'But if it could only be put somewhere else,' said his wife Ros, 'and not right under the window of the room where we eat our bit of food!'

'Didn't you tell me, yourself, a minute ago, you could smell it from the other end of the town? If that's the case I don't see what's going to be the good in moving it from one side of the yard to the other.'

'What I don't see,' said his daughter Kate, 'is the need for us dealing in dung at all.'

'There you are!' said Phelim. 'There you are! I knew all along that was what you had in the back of your mind; both of you, and the one inside too!'—he beckoned backwards with his head towards the door behind him. 'You wanted to be rid of it altogether, not just to shift it from one place to another. Why on earth can't women speak out what they mean? That's a thing always puzzles me.'

'Leave Stacy out of it, Phelim,' said Ros; 'Stacy has one of her headaches.'

'And what gave it to her I'd like to know?' said Phelim. 'I'm supposed to think it was the smell of the dung gave it to her, but I know more than to be taken in by women's nonsensical notions.'

'Don't talk so loud, Phelim,' said Ros; 'she might be asleep.'

'It's a great wonder any of you can sleep a wink at all any night with the smell of that poor harmless heap of dung, out there, that's bringing in good money week after week.'

He turned to his daughter.

'It paid for your education at a fine boarding school.'

He turned to Ros.

'And it paid for Stacy's notions about the violin and the piano, both of which is rotting within there in the room; and not a squeak of a tune ever I heard out of the one or other of them since the day they came into the house!'

'He won't give in,' said Ros to her daughter. 'We may as well keep our breath.'

'You may as well,' said Phelim. 'That's a true thing anyway.' He went over to the yard door. When he opened the door the faint odour of stale manure that hung already about the kitchen was thickened by a hot odour of new manure from the yard. Kate followed her father to the door and banged it shut after him.

As the steel taps on Phelim's shoes rang on the cobbles the two women stood at the window looking out at him. He took up a big yard-brush made of twigs tied to a stick with leather thongs, and he started to brush up dry clots of manure that had fallen from the carts as they travelled from the gate to the dung trough. The dung trough itself was filled to the top, and moisture from the manure was running in yellow streaks down the sides. The manure was brown and it was stuck all over with bright stripes of yellow straw.

'You'll have to keep at him, Mother,' said Kate.

'There's not much use,' said Ros.

'Something will have to be done. That's all about it!' said Kate. 'Only last night at the concert in the Town Hall, just after the lights went down, I heard the new people, that took the bakehouse across the street, telling someone that they couldn't open a window since they came to the town with the terrible smell that was coming from somewhere; I could have died with shame, Mother. I didn't hear what answer they got, but when the lights went up for the interval I saw they were sitting beside Mamie Murtagh, and you know what that one would be likely to say! My whole pleasure in the evening was spoiled, I can assure you.'

'You take things too much to heart, Kate,' said Ros. 'There's Stacy inside there, and if it wasn't for the smell of it I don't believe she'd mind us having it at all. She says to me sometimes, "Wouldn't it be lovely, Mother, if there was a smell of lilacs every time we opened the door?"'

'Stacy makes me tired,' said Kate, 'with her talk about lilacs and lilacs! What does she ever do to try and improve things?'

'She's very timid,' said Ros.

'That's all the more reason,' said Kate, 'my father would listen to her if she'd only speak to him.'

'Stacy would never have the heart to cross anyone.'

'Stacy's a fool.'

'It's the smell that gives her the headaches all the same,' said Ros. 'Ever since she came home from boarding school she's been getting her headaches every Wednesday regular the very minute the first cartload comes in across the yard.'

'Isn't that what I'm saying!' said Kate impatiently, taking down a brown raincoat from a peg behind the door. 'I'm going out for a walk and I won't be back till that smell has died down a bit. You can tell him that too, if he's looking for me.'

When Kate went out Ros took down a copper tea-caddy from the dresser and threw a few grains of tea into a brown earthen tea-pot. Then she poured a long stream of boiling water into the teapot from the great sooty kettle that hung over the flames. She poured out a cup of the tea and put sugar and milk in it, and a spoon. She didn't bother with a saucer, and she took the cup over to the window and set it on the sill to cool while she watched Phelim sweeping in the yard.

In her heart there seemed to be a dark clot of malignance towards him because of the way he thwarted them over the dunghill. But as she looked out at him he put his hand to his back every once in a while, and Ros felt the black clots thinning away. Before the tea was cool enough to swallow, her blood was running bright and free in her veins again and she was thinking of the days when he used to call her by the old name.

She couldn't rightly remember when it was she first started cal-ling herself Ros, or whether it was Phelim started it. Or it might have been someone outside the family altogether. But it was a good name no matter where it came from, a very suitable name for an old woman. It would be only foolishness to go on calling her Rose after she was faded and all dried up. She looked at her hands. They were thin as claws. She went over to the yard door.

'There's tea in the teapot, Phelim,' she called out, and she left the door open. She went into the room where the two girls slept.

'Will I take you in a nice cup of nice hot tea, Stacy?' she said, leaning over the big bed.

'Is it settled?' said Stacy, sitting up.

'No,' said Ros, pulling across the curtain, 'it's to stay where it is.'

'I hope he isn't upset?' said Stacy.

'No. He's sweeping the yard,' said Ros, 'and there's a hot cup of tea in the teapot for him if he likes to take it. You're a good girl, Stacy. How's your poor head?'

'I wouldn't want to upset him,' said Stacy. 'My head is a bit better. I think I'll get up.'

It was, so, to Stacy that Ros turned on the night Phelim was taken bad with the bright pain low in the small of his back. When he died in the early hours of the morning, Ros kept regretting that she had crossed him over the dunghill.

'You have no call to regret anything, Mother,' said Stacy. 'You were ever and always calling him in out of the yard for cups of tea, morning, noon, and night. I often heard you, days I'd have one of my headaches. You've no call at all for regret.'

'Why wouldn't I call him in to a cup of tea on a cold day?' said Ros. 'There's no thanks for that. He was the best man that ever lived.'

'You did all you could for him, Mother,' said Kate, 'and there's no need to be moaning and carrying on like that!'

'Let us not say anything,' said Ros. 'It was you was the one was always at me to talk to him about the dunghill. I wish I never crossed him.'

'That was the only thing you ever crossed him over, Mother,' said Stacy, 'and the smell was really very hard to put up with.'

Phelim was laid out in the parlour beyond the kitchen. He was coffined before the night, but the lid was left off the coffin. Ros and the girls stayed up all night in the room. The neighbours stayed in the house, but they sat in the kitchen where they threw sods of turf on the fire when they were needed, and threw handfuls of tea leaves into the teapot now and again, and brought tea in to the Molloys.

Kate and Stacy sat one each side of their mother and mourned the man they were looking at, lying dead in a sheaf of undertaker linen crimp. They mourned him as they knew him for the last ten years, a heavy man with a red face who was seldom seen out of his big red rubber boots.

Ros mourned the Phelim of the red rubber boots, but she mourned many another Phelim. She mourned him back beyond the time his face used to flush up when he went out in the air. She mourned him the time he never put a hat on when he was going out in the yard. She mourned him when his hair was thick, although it was greying at the sides. She mourned him when he wore a big moustache sticking out stiff on each side. But most of all she mourned him for the early time when he had no hair on his face at all, and when his cheeks were always glossy from being out in the weather. That was the time he had to soap down his curls. That was the time he led her in a piece off the road when they were coming from Mass one Sunday.

'Rose,' he said. 'I've been thinking. There's a pile of money to be made out of manure. I've been thinking that if I got a cart and collected a bit here and a bit there for a few pence I might be able to sell it in big loads for a lot more than I paid for it.'

'Is that so?' she said. She remembered every word they said that day.

'And do you know what I've been thinking too?' he said. 'I've been thinking that if I put by what I saved I might have enough by this time next year to take a lease of the little cottage on the Mill Road.'

'The one with the church window in the gable end?' she said.

'And the two fine sheds,' he said.

'The one with the ivy all down one side?' she said, but she knew well the one he meant.

'That's the very one,' said Phelim. 'How would you like to live there? With me, I mean?'

'Manure has a terrible dirty smell,' she said.

'You could plant flowers, maybe.'

'I'd have to plant ones with a strong perfume,' she said, 'rockets and mignonette.'

'Any ones you like. You'd have nothing else to do all day.'

She remembered well how innocent he was then, for all that he was twenty, and thinking to make a man of himself by taking a wife. His face was white like a girl's, with patches of pink on his cheeks. He was handsome. There were prettier girls by far than her who would have given their eyes to be led in a piece off the road, just for a bit of talk and gassing from Phelim Molloy—let alone a real proposal.

'Will you, Rose?' said Phelim. 'There's a pile of money in manure, even if the people around these parts don't set any store by it.'

The colour was blotching over his cheeks the way the wind blotched a river. He was nervous. He was putting his foot up on the bar of the gate where they were standing, and the next minute he was taking it down again. She didn't like the smell of manure, then, any more than after, but she liked Phelim.

'It's dirty stuff,' she said. And that was her last protest.

'I don't know so much about that,' said Phelim. 'There's a lot in the way you think about things. Do you know, Rose, sometimes when I'm driving along the road I look down at the dung that's dried into the road and I think to myself that you couldn't ask much prettier than it, the way it flashes by under the horses' feet in pale gold rings.' Poor Phelim! There weren't many men would think of things like that.

'All right, so,' she said. 'I will.'

'You will?' said Phelim. 'You will?'

The sun spilled down just then and the dog-roses swayed back and forwards in the hedge.

'Kiss me so,' he said.

'Not here!' she said. The people were passing on the road and looking down at them. She got as pink as the pink dog-roses.

'Why not?' said Phelim. 'If you're going to marry me you must face up to everything. You must do as I say always. You must never be ashamed of anything.'

She hung her head, but he put his hand under her chin.

'If you don't kiss me right now, Rose Magarry, I'll have nothing more to do with you.'

The way the candles wavered round the corpse was just the way the dog-roses wavered in the wind that day.

Ros shed tears for the little dog-roses. She shed tears for the blushes she had in her cheeks. She shed tears for the soft kissing lips of young Phelim. She shed tears for the sunny splashes of gold dung on the roads. And her tears were quiet and steady, like the crying of the small thin rains in windless weather.

When the cold white morning came at last the neighbours got up and stamped their feet on the flags outside the door. They went home to wash and get themselves ready for the funeral.

When the funeral was over Ros came back to the lonely house between her two daughters. Kate looked well in black. It made her thinner and her high colour looked to advantage. Stacy looked the same as ever. The chairs and tables were all pushed against the wall since they took the coffin out. One or two women stayed behind, and there was hot tea and cold meat. There was a smell of guttered-out candles and a heavy smell of lilies.

Stacy drew in a deep breath.

'Oh, Kate!' she said. 'Smell!'

Kate gave her a harsh look.

'Don't remind her,' she said, 'or she'll be moaning again.'

But Ros was already looking out in the yard and the tears were streaming from her eyes again down the easy runnels of her dried and wrinkled face.

'Oh, Phelim,' she said. 'Why did I ever cross you? Wasn't I the bad old woman to cross you over a little heap of dirt and yellow straw?'

Kate bit her lip.

'Don't take any notice of her,' she said to the women. She turned to Stacy. 'Take in our hats and coats,' she said, 'and put a sheet over them.' She turned back to the women. 'Black is terrible for taking the dust,' she said, 'and terrible to clean.' But all the time she was speaking she was darting glances at Ros.

Ros was moaning louder.

'You're only tormenting yourself, Mother,' said Kate. 'He was a good man, one of the best, but he was an obstinate man over that dunghill, so you've no call to be upsetting yourself on the head of that!'

'It was out of the dung he made his first few shillings.'

'How long ago was that?' said Kate. 'And was that any reason for persecuting us all for the last five years with the smell of it coming up under the window, you might say?'

'I think we'll be going, Kate,' said the women.

'We're much obliged to you for your kindness in our trouble,' said Ros and Kate together.

The women went out quietly.

'Are they gone?' said Stacy, coming out of the inside room, looking out the window at the women going down the road.

'Is it the dunghill you were talking about?' she said. 'Because tomorrow is Wednesday!'

'I know that,' said Ros.

'The smell isn't so bad today, is it?' said Stacy. 'Or was it the smell of the flowers drove it out?'

'I wish to goodness you'd look at it in a more serious light, Stacy,' said Kate. 'It's not alone the smell of it, but the way people look at us when they hear what we deal in.'

'It's nothing to be ashamed of,' said Ros. 'It was honest dealing, and that's more than most in this town can say!'

'What do you know about the way people talk, Mother?' said Kate. 'If you were away at boarding school, like Stacy and me, you'd know, then, what it felt like to have to admit your father was making his money out of horse dung.'

'I don't see what great call was on you to tell them!' said Ros.

'Listen to that!' said Kate. 'It's easily seen you were never at boarding school, Mother.'

Stacy had nearly forgotten the boarding school, but she remembered a bit about it then.

'We used to say our father dealt in fertiliser,' she said. 'But

17

someone looked it up in a dictionary and found out it was only a fancy name for manure.'

'Your father would have laughed at that,' said Ros.

'It's not so funny at all,' said Kate.

'Your father had a wonderful sense of humour,' said Ros.

'He was as obstinate as a rock, that's one thing,' said Kate.

'When we knew that was the case,' said Ros, 'why did we cross him? We might have known he wouldn't give in. I wish I never crossed him.'

The old woman folded her knotted hands and sat down by the fire in the antique attitude of grieving womankind.

Kate could talk to Stacy when they were in the far corner of the kitchen getting down the cups and saucers from the dresser.

'I never thought she was so old-looking.'

'She looked terribly old at the graveside,' said Stacy. 'Make her take her tea by the fire.'

'Will you drink down a nice cup of tea, here by the fire, Mother?' said Stacy, going over to the old woman.

Ros took the cup out of the saucer and put the spoon into it. 'Leave that back,' she said, pushing away the saucer. She took the cup over to the window sill.

'It only smells bad on hot days,' she said, looking out.

'But summer is ahead of us!' said Kate, spinning round sharply and looking at the old woman.

'It is and it isn't,' said Ros. 'In the January of the year it's as true to say you have put the summer behind you as it is to say it is ahead of you.'

'Mother?'

Kate came over and, pushing aside the geranium on the window ledge, she leaned her arm there and stared back into her mother's face.

'Mother,' she said. 'You're not by any chance thinking of keeping on the dunghill?'

'I'm thinking of one thing only,' said Ros. 'I'm thinking of him and he young, with no hair on his lip, one day—and the next day, you might say, him lying within on the table and the women washing him for his burial.'

'I wish you'd give over tormenting yourself, Mother.'

'I'm not tormenting myself at all,' said Ros. 'I like thinking about him.'

'He lived to a good age,' said Kate.

'I suppose you'll be saying that about me one of these days,' said Ros, 'and it no time ago since I was sitting up straight behind the horse's tail, on my father's buggy, with my white blouse on me and my gold chain dangling and my hair halfway down my back. The road used to be flashing by under the clittering horse-hooves, and the gold dung dried into bright gold rings.'

'Stacy,' said Kate, that night when they were in bed, 'I don't like to see her going back over the old days like she was all day. It's a bad sign. I hope we won't be laying her alongside Father one of these days.'

'Oh, Kate,' said Stacy, 'don't remind me of poor Father. All the time she was talking about crossing him over the dung I was thinking of the hard things I was saying against him the last time my head was splitting and he was leading in the clattering carts over the cobblestones and the dirty smell of the dung rising up on every wind.'

'You've no call to torment yourself, Stacy,' said Kate.

'That's what you said to Mother.'

'It's true what I say, no matter which of you I say it to. There was no need in having the dunghill at all. It was nothing but obstinacy. Start to say your beads now and you'll be asleep before you've said the first decade. And don't be twitching the clothes off me. Move over.'

It seemed to Stacy that she had only begun the second decade of her beads, when her closed eyes began to ache with a hard white light shining down on them without pity. She couldn't sleep with that hard light on her eyes. She couldn't open her eyes either, because the light pressed down so weightily on her lids. Perhaps, as Kate had said, it was morning and she had fallen asleep? Stacy forced her lids open. The window square was blinding white with hard venomous daylight. The soft night had gone. There was another day before them, but Father was out in the green

19

churchyard where the long grass was always wet even in yellow sunlight.

Stacy lay cold. Her eyes were wide and scopeless and her feet were touching against the chilled iron rail at the foot of the bed. She looked around the whitewashed room and she looked out of the low window, that was shaped like the window of a church, at the cold crinkled edges of the corrugated sheds. Stacy longed for it to be summer, though summer was a long way off. She longed for the warm winds to be daffing through the trees and the dallops of grass to be dry enough for flopping down on, right where you were in the middle of a field. And she longed for it to be the time when the tight hard beads of the lilacs looped out into the soft pear shapes of blossom, in other people's gardens.

And then, as soft as the scent of lilac steals through early summer air, the thought came slowly into Stacy's mind that poor dear Father, sleeping in the long grave-grasses, might not mind them having lilacs now where the dunghill used to be. For it seemed already to Stacy that the dunghill was gone now that poor Father himself was gone. She curled up in the blankets and closed her eyes again, and so it was a long time before she knew for certain that there was a sound of knocking on the big yard-gate and a sound of a horse shaking his brass trappings and pawing the cobbles with his forefoot. She raised her head a little off the pillow. There was the sound of a wooden gatewing flapping back against the wall. There was a rattle of horse-hooves and steel-bound cart-wheels going over the cobbles. 'Kate! Kate!' she shouted, and she shook Kate till she wakened with a flush of frightened red to her cheeks. 'Kate,' she said, 'I thought I heard Father leading in a load of manure across the yard!'

Kate's flush deepened.

'Stacy, if you don't control yourself, your nerves will get the better of you completely. Where will you be then?' But as Kate spoke they heard the dray board of a cart being loosened in the yard and chains fell down on the cobbles with a ringing sound.

Kate sprang out of bed, throwing back the clothes right over the brass footrail, and left Stacy shivering where she lay, with the freezing air making snaps at her legs and her arms and her white neck. Kate stared out of the window.

'I knew this would happen,' she said, 'I could have told you!' Stacy got out of bed slowly and came over across the cold floor in her bare feet. She pressed her face against the icy glass. She began to cry in a thin wavering way like a child. Her nose was running, too; like a child's.

In the yard Ros was leading in a second cart of manure, and talking in a high voice to the driver of the empty cart that was waiting its turn to pass out. She was dressed in her everyday clothes that weren't black, but brown; the dark primitive colour of the earth and the earth's decaying refuse. The cart she led was piled high with rude brown manure, stuck all over with bright stripes of yellow straw, and giving off a hot steam. The steam rose up unevenly like thumby fingers of a clumsy hand and it reached for the faces of the staring women that were indistinct behind the fog their breaths put on the glass.

'Get dressed!' said Kate. 'We'll go down together.'

Ros was warming her hands by the fire when they went into the kitchen. There was a strong odour of manure. Kate said nothing, but she went over and banged the yard door shut. Stacy said nothing. Stacy stood. Ros looked up.

'Well?' said Ros.

'Well?' said Kate, after her, and she said it louder than Ros had said it.

The two women faced each other across the deal table. Stacy sat down on the chair that Ros had just left, and she began to cry in her thin wavy voice.

'Shut up, Stacy!' said Kate.

'Say what you have to say, Kate,' said Ros, and in the minds of all three of them there was the black thought that bitter words could lash out endlessly, now that there was no longer a man in the house to come in across the yard with a heavy boot and stand in the doorway slapping his hands together and telling them to give up their nonsense and lay the table for the meal.

'Say what you have to say,' said Ros.

'You know what we have to say,' said Kate.

'Well, don't say it, so,' said Ros, 'if that's all it is.' She went towards the door.

'Mother!' Stacy went after her and caught the corner of her mother's old skirt. 'You were always saying it would be nice if it was once out of there.'

'Isn't that my only regret, Stacy?' said Ros. 'That was the only thing I crossed him over.'

'But you were right, Mother.'

'Was I?' said Ros, but not in the voice of one asking a question. 'Sometimes an old woman talks about things she knows nothing about. Your father always said it wasn't right to be ashamed of anything that was honest. Another time he said money was money, no matter where it came from. That was a true thing to say. He was always saying true things. Did you hear the priest yesterday when we were coming away from the grave? "God help all poor widows!" he said.'

'What has that got to do with what we're talking about?' said Kate.

'A lot,' said Ros. 'Does it never occur to the two of you that it mightn't be so easy for three women, and no man, to keep a house going and fires lighting and food on the table; to say nothing at all about dresses and finery?'

'I suppose that last is meant for me?' said Kate.

'That's just like what Father himself would say,' said Stacy, but no one heard her. Kate had suddenly moved over near her mother and was leaning with her back against the white rim of the table. When she spoke it was more kindly.

'Did you find out how his affairs were fixed, Mother?' she said.

'I did,' said Ros, and she looked at her daughter with cold eyes. 'I did,' she said again, and that was all she said as she went out the door.

The smell that came in the door made Stacy put her arm over her face and bury her nose in the crook of her elbow. But Kate drew herself up and her fine firm bosom swelled. She breathed in a strong breath.

'Pah!' she said. 'How I hate it!'

'Think if it was a smell of lilacs!' said Stacy, 'Lovely lilacs.'

22

'I wish you'd stop crying,' said Kate. 'You can't blame her, after all, for not wanting to go against him and he dead. It's different for us.'

Stacy's face came slowly out of the crook of her arm. She had a strange wondering look.

'Maybe when you and I are all alone, Kate?' she said, and then as she realised what she was saying she put her arm up quickly over her face in fright. 'Not that I meant any harm,' she said. 'Poor Mother! poor Mother!'

Kate looked at her with contempt.

'You should learn to control your tongue, Stacy. And in any case, I wish you wouldn't be always talking as if we were never going to get married.'

'I sometimes think we never will,' said Stacy.

Kate shook out the tablecloth with a sharp flap in the warm air.

'Maybe you won't,' she said. 'I don't believe you will, as a matter of fact. But I will.' She threw the tablecloth across the back of a chair and looked into the small shaving mirror belonging to their father that still hung on the wall.

In the small mirror Kate could see only her eyes and nose, unless she stood far back from it. And when she did that, as well as seeing herself, she could see the window, and through the window she could see the yard and anyone in it. And so, after she had seen that she looked just as she thought she would look, she stepped back a little from the glass and began to follow the moving reflections of her mother that she saw in it. There seemed a greater significance in seeing her mother in this unreal way than there would have been in seeing her by looking directly out the window. The actions of Ros as she gathered up the fallen fragments of dung seemed to be symbolic of a great malevolent energy directed against her daughters.

'I didn't need to be so upset last night going to bed,' she said to Stacy bitterly. 'There's no fear of her going after my poor father. She's as hardy as a tree!'

But Ros Molloy wasn't cut out to be a widow. If Phelim had been taken from her before the dog-roses had faded on their first summer together she could hardly have moaned him more than she did, an old woman, cold and shivering, tossing in her big brass bed all alone.

The girls eased her work for her at every turn of the hand, but on Wednesday mornings they let her get up alone to open the gates at six o'clock and let in the carts of manure. They didn't sleep however.

As often as not Stacy got up, on to the cold floor in her bare feet, and stood at the window looking out. She crossed her arms over her breast to keep in what warmth she had taken from the blankets, and she told Kate what was going on outside.

'Did she look up at the window?' Kate asked one morning.

'No,' Stacy said.

'Get back into bed so, and don't give her the satisfaction of knowing you're watching her.'

'Kate.'

'What?'

'You don't think I ought to slip down and see if the kettle is boiling for when she comes in, do you, Kate?'

'You know what I think,' said Kate. 'Will you get back into bed and not be standing there freezing!'

'She has only her thin coat on,' said Stacy.

Kate leaned up on one elbow, carefully humping up the clothes with her, pegged to her shoulder.

'By all the pulling and rattling that I hear, she's doing enough to keep up her circulation, without her having any clothes at all on her.'

'She shouldn't be lifting things the way she is,' said Stacy.

'And whose fault is it if she is?' said Kate, slumping back into the hollows of the bed. 'Get back here into bed, you, and stop watching out at her doing things there's no need in her doing at all. That's just what she wants; to have someone watching out at her.'

'She's not looking this way at all, Kate.'

'Oh, isn't she? Let me tell you, that woman has eyes in the back of her head!'

'Oh, Kate,' said Stacy, and she ran over to the bed and threw herself in across Kate, sobbing. Kate lay still for a minute listening to her, and then she leaned up on her other elbow and humped the clothes up over the shoulder. Stacy slept between her and the wall. 'What in the name of God ails you now?' she asked.

'Don't you remember, Kate? That's what she used to say to us when we were small. She used to stand up straight and stiff, with her gold chain on her, and say that we had better not do anything wrong behind her back because she had eyes in the back of her head.'

Kate flopped back again.

'We all have to get old,' she said.

'I know,' said Stacy, 'but all the same you'd hate to see the gold chain dangling down below her waist, like I did the other day, when she took it out of her black box and put it on her.'

Kate sat up again.

'She's not wearing it, is she?'

'She put it back in the box.'

Kate flopped back once more. Her face was flushed from the sudden jerks she gave in the cold morning air.

'I should hope she put it back,' she said, 'that chain is worth a lot of money since the price of gold went up.'

Stacy lay still with her eyes closed. There was something wrong, but she didn't know just what it was. All she wanted was to get the dunghill taken away out of the yard and a few lilacs put there instead. But it seemed as if there were more than that bothering Kate. She wondered what it could be? She had always thought herself and Kate were the same, that they had the same way of looking at things, but lately Kate seemed to be changed.

Kate was getting old. Stacy took no account of age, but Kate was getting old. And Kate took account of everything. Stacy might have been getting old too, if she was taking account of things, but she wasn't. It seemed no length ago to Stacy since they came home from the convent. She couldn't tell you what year it was. She was never definite about anything. Her head was filled with nonsense, Kate said.

'What do you think about when you're lying inside there with a headache?' Kate asked her once.

'Things,' Stacy said.

She would only be thinking of things; this thing and that thing;

things of no account; silly things. Like the times she lay in bed and thought of a big lilac tree sprouting up through the boards of the floor, bending the big bright nails, sending splinters of wood flying till they hit off the window-panes. The tree always had big pointed bunches of lilac blossom all over it; more blossoms than leaves. That just showed, Stacy thought, what nonsense it was. You never saw more blossoms than leaves. But the blossoms weighed down towards her where she lay shivering, and they touched her face.

It was nonsense like that that went dawdling through her mind ne morning, when the knocking at the gate outside kept up for o long that she began to think her mother must have slept it out.

'Do you think she slept it out, Kate?'

'I hope she did,' said Kate. 'It might teach her a lesson.'

'Maybe I ought to slip down and let them in?'

'Stay where you are.'

But Stacy had to get up.

'I'll just look in her door,' she said.

Stacy went out and left the door open.

'Hurry back and shut the door,' said Kate, calling after her.

But Stacy didn't hurry. Stacy didn't come back either.

'Stacy! Stacy!' Kate called out.

She lifted her head off her pillow to listen.

'Stacy? Is there anything wrong?'

Kate sat up in the cold.

'Stacy! Can't you answer a person?'

Kate got out on the floor.

She found Stacy lying in a heap at her mother's bedside, and she hardly needed to look to know that Ros was dead. She as good as knew—she said afterwards—that Stacy would pass out the minute there was something unpleasant.

No wonder Stacy had no lines on her face. No wonder she looked a child, in spite of her years. Stacy got out of a lot of worry, very neatly, by just flopping off in a faint. Poor Ros was washed, and her eyes shut and her habit put on her, before Stacy came round to her senses again.

'It looks as if you're making a habit of this,' said Kate, when

Stacy fainted again, in the cemetery this time, and didn't have to listen, as Kate did, to the sound of the sods clodding down on the coffin.

'But I did hear them, Kate,' Stacy protested. 'I did. I heard them distinctly. But I was a bit confused in my mind still at the time, and I thought it was the sound of the horse-hooves clodding along the road.'

'What horse-hooves? Are you going mad?'

'You remember, Kate. Surely you remember. The ones Mother was always telling us about. Her hair hung down her back and her gold chain dangled, and while she was watching the road flashing by under the clittering horse-hooves she used to think how pretty the gold dung was, dried into bright discs.'

'That reminds me!' said Kate. 'Tomorrow is Wednesday.'

Although Stacy's face was wet with the moisture of her thin scalding tears, she smiled and clasped her hands together.

'Oh Kate!' she said; and then, in broad daylight, standing in the middle of the floor in her new serge mourning dress that scraped the back of her neck all the time, she saw a heavy lilac tree nod at her with its lovely pale blooms bobbing.

'Which of us will get up?' Kate was saying, and watching Stacy while she was saying it.

'Get up?'

'To let them in.'

'To let who in?'

'Who do you think? The men with the manure of course.' Kate spoke casually, but when she looked at Stacy she stamped her foot on the floor.

'Don't look so stupid, Stacy. There isn't any time now to let them know. We can't leave them hammering at the gate after coming miles, maybe. Someone will have to go down and open the gate for them.'

When Stacy heard the first rap on the gate she hated to think of Kate's having to get up.

'I'll get up, Kate,' she said. 'Stay where you are.'

But she got no answer. Kate was walking out across the yard at the time, dressed and ready, and she had the gate thrown back against the wall before the men had time to raise their hands for a second rap.

Stacy dressed as quickly as she could, to have the kettle on as a surprise for Kate. It was the least she might do.

But when Stacy went down the fire was blazing up the chimney and there was a trace of tea in a cup on the table. Poor Kate, thought Stacy, she must have been awake half the night in case she'd let the time slip. Wasn't she great! Stacy felt very stupid. She was no good at all. Kate was great. Here was their great moment. Here was the time for getting rid of a nuisance, and if it was up to her to tell the men not to bring any more cartloads she honestly believed she'd be putting it off for weeks and be afraid to do it in the end, maybe. But Kate was great. Kate made no bones about it. Kate didn't say a word about how she was going to do it, or what she was going to say. She just slipped out of bed and made a cup of tea and went out in the yard and took command of everything. Kate was great.

'What did you say?' asked Stacy, when Kate came in.

'How do you mean?' said Kate and looked at her irritably. 'What on earth gave you such a high colour at this hour of the morning? I never saw you with so much colour in your face before?'

But the colour was fading out already.

'Didn't you tell them not to bring any more?' she asked.

Kate looked as if she were going to say something, and then she changed her mind. Then she changed her mind again, or else she thought of something different to say.

'I didn't like to give them the hard word,' she said.

Stacy flushed again.

'I see what you mean,' she said: 'we'll ease off quietly?'

'Yes,' said Kate. 'Yes, we could do that. Or I was thinking of another plan.'

Stacy knelt up on a hard deal chair and gripped the back of it. There was something very exciting in hearing Kate talk and plan. It gave Stacy a feeling that they had a great responsibility and authority and that they were standing on their own feet.

'You mightn't like the idea,' said Kate, 'at first.'

'Oh, I'm sure I'll love it,' said Stacy.

'It's this then,' said Kate. 'I was thinking last night that instead of doing away with the dunghill we should take in twice as much manure for a while till we made twice as much money, and then we could get out of this little one-story house altogether.'

Stacy was looking out the window.

'Well?' said Kate.

Stacy laid her face against the glass.

'Oh for goodness' sake stop crying,' said Kate; 'I was only making a suggestion.' She began to clatter the cups on the dresser. She looked back at Stacy. 'I thought, you see, that after a bit we might move over to Rowe House. It's been idle a long time. I don't think they'd want very much for it, and it's two-story, what's more, with a front entrance and steps going up to the hall door.'

Stacy dried her face in the crook of her arm and began to put back the cups that Kate had taken down from the dresser, because the table was already set. Her face had the strained and terrible look that people with weak natures have when they force their spirits beyond their bounds.

'I'll never leave this house,' she said; 'never as long as I live.'

'Stay in it, so!' said Kate. 'And rot in it for all I care. But I'm getting out of it the first chance I get! And that dunghill isn't stirring from where it is until I have a fine fat dowry out of it.'

She went into the bedroom and banged the door, and Stacy sat down looking at the closed door. Then she looked out the window. Then she got up and ran her hand down over the buttons of her bodice. They were all closed properly. She took the tea-caddy and began to put two careful spoonfuls of tea into the teapot. When the tea was some minutes made, she went over to the closed door. Once again she ran her hand down the buttons of her bodice; and then she called Kate.

'Your tea is getting cold,' she said, and while she waited for an answer her heart beat out its fear upon her hollow chest.

But Kate was in a fine good humour when she came out, with her arms piled up with dresses and hats and cardboard boxes covered with rose-scattered wallpaper. She left the things down on the window sill and pulled her chair in to the table.

'Is this loaf bread or turnover?' she said. 'It tastes very good. Sit down yourself, Stacy,' and after a mouthful of the hot tea she nodded her head at the things on the window sill.

'There's no point in having a room idle, is there?' she said. 'I may as well move into Mother's room.'

There was no more mention of the dunghill. Kate attended to it. Stacy didn't have her headaches as bad as she used to have them. Not giving in to them was the best cure yet. Kate was right. There was only a throbbing. It wasn't bad.

Stacy and Kate got on great. At least there was no fighting. But the house was as uneasy as a house where two women live alone. At night you felt it most. So Stacy was glad at the back of everything when Con O'Toole began dropping in, although she didn't like him and she thought the smell of stale tobacco that was all over the house next day was worse than the smell of the dung.

'Do you like the smell of his pipe, Kate?' said Stacy one day.

'I never noticed,' said Kate.

'I think it's worse than the smell of the dung!' said Stacy with a gust of bravery.

'I thought we agreed on saying "fertiliser" instead of that word you just used,' said Kate, stopping up in the dusting.

'That was when we were at boarding school!' said Stacy, going on with the dusting.

'I beg your pardon,' said Kate, 'it was when we were mixing with the right kind of people. I wish you wouldn't be so forgetful.'

But next morning Kate came into the parlour when Stacy was nearly finished with the dusting. She threw out her firm chest and drew in a deep breath.

'Pah!' she said. 'It *is* disgusting. I'll make him give up using it as soon as we take up residence at Rowe House. But don't say anything about it to him. He mightn't take it well. Of course I can say anything I like to him. He'll take anything from me. But it's better to wait till after we're married and not come on him with everything all at once.'

That was the first Stacy heard about Kate's getting married, but of course if she had only thought about it she'd have seen the way the wind was blowing. But she took no account of anything.

After the first mention of the matter, however, Kate could

hardly find time to talk about anything else, right up to the fine blowsy morning that she was hoisted up on the car by Con, in her new peacock blue outfit, and her mother's gold chain dangling. Stacy was almost squeezed out of the doorway by the crowd of well-wishers waving them off. They all came back into the house. Such a mess! Chairs pulled about! Crumbs on the cushions! Confetti! Wine spilled all over the carpet! And the lovely iced cake all cut into! Such a time as there would be cleaning it all up! And Stacy thought that when she'd be putting things back in their places would be a good time to make a few changes. That chair with the red plush would be better on the other side of the piano. And she'd draw the sofa out a bit from the wall.

'Will you be lonely, Miss Stacy?' said someone.

'You should get someone in, to keep you company, Miss Stacy,' said someone else.

'At night anyway,' they all said.

They were very kind. Stacy loved hearing them all making plans for her. It was so good-natured. But this was the first time she'd ever got a chance to make a few plans for herself, and she wished they'd hurry up and go.

They didn't stay so very long. They were soon all gone, except Jasper Kane. Jasper liked Stacy, apart from his being the family solicitor, and knowing her father so well.

'Might I inquire, Miss Stacy, what is the first thing you're planning to do, now that you are your own mistress?'

Stacy went over to the window.

'I'm going to plant a few lilac trees, Mr Kane,' she said, because she felt she could trust him. Her father always did.

'Oh!' said Jasper, and he looked out the window, too. 'Where?' he said.

'There!' said Stacy, pointing out of the back window. 'There where the dunghill is now.' She drew a brave breath. 'I'm getting rid of the dunghill, you see,' she said.

Jasper stayed looking out of the window at the dunghill. Then he looked at Stacy. He was an old man.

'But what will you live on, Miss Stacy?' he said.

A ROMANTIC HERO

Olivia Manning

Harold was up at dawn. The first light, coming through thin curtains that would not meet, had awakened him, but he would have
wakened in any case. Indeed, he had scarcely slept. As he dressed,
with noiseless cunning, he felt stiff and chilly and knew he was
catching one of his colds, but he was too excited to give it much
thought.

The night before he had had to find his way by candlelight up
the steep stair of the cottage where he was staying. The room had
smelt musty. He suspected the bed might be damp, but he had to
accept it. How like Angela not to give a thought to such a thing
when arranging a room for him. Strong as a donkey herself, she
treated his fear of damp as a superstition.

The three bedrooms of the cottage, one for the labourer, his wife
and baby, one for Angela and one for Harold, were fitted into a
space so small, the whole of it would not make a reasonable room.
Angela had pointed out that a whisper in one room could be heard
in all of them, so Harold must not visit her bed. Much Harold cared.
His only idea had been to get off to Seaham without her and he
could be sure of doing that only if he left before she woke.

He made his way down the stairs holding his breath. When he
found himself outside the cottage, he felt like a volatile gas released
from a bottle. With the downland turf pneumatic beneath his feet,
the dew glinting in the tender sunlight, he could have sung aloud
from sheer happiness. He remembered that when they were squab-
bling yesterday, Angela had said he only sang when he was angry.

Well, he wanted to sing now, and he was not angry. Far from it. His sense of triumph over Angela proved to him she had had her day. It was all over with Angela—and for him life was taking on meaning and joy.

By some quirk of nature, Harold, a tall man with a thin, constricted look, was impelled to prefer first the company of one sex, then of the other. Although nearly thirty-five years of age, he still saw himself as a young man, one for whom life had yet to burst into the flame of its beginning. And the beginning was now. He could put everything else behind him.

For the last few months he had spent most of his time with Angela. Angela, with a responsible secretarial job in the City, had been a pleasant enough companion at first, and after repeated failure to find satisfaction elsewhere, he had even begun to think of marrying her. Heaven help him if he had! What a risk he had run! What a pass loneliness could bring a man to!

And he had been saved, only yesterday, by a remarkable thing—the most remarkable thing that had ever happened to him. A wonderful thing; a thing that had restored his faith in himself and his future, and confirmed his belief that there awaited him, that there always had awaited him, a felicity so rare that only the exceptional few ever got a glimpse of it.

Angela was spending the first fortnight of her summer holiday walking on the South Downs. Harold had agreed to join her for the weekend. When he boarded the train, he found himself alone, on a non-stop run to Worthing, with the most perfect young man imaginable. Very young, fair, athletic and ... beautiful. Yes, beautiful; with the sort of eyes that Harold described to himself as 'my sort of eyes'. Never before had Providence done such a thing for Harold.

For the first fifteen minutes he was sick with dread of some wretched bore coming down the corridor and joining them, but no one came. As he began to relax, he wanted to speak—to reach out, to make contact, to get things started without further delay. He desired so few people that one he found so eminently desirable seemed to belong to him as by a right. But experience had taught him caution. A too impetuous approach might cause misunderstanding and spoil things before they started. He held himself in check, but he could not keep himself from looking at the young man.

Conscious of Harold's stare, the young man raised his newspaper so only his blond curls were visible above it. Harold noted the tight, shabby jeans that covered long lean legs, the old sandals that revealed the long lean, sunburnt feet, the shirt of Madras cotton with several buttons missing. It seemed to Harold a picture of casual hard-upness, but not of poverty. It was, he decided, exactly right.

Then, suddenly, the young man lowered the paper, stared back with amused blue eyes, and *smiled*.

Harold flushed painfully. He was furious with himself but at the same time his excitement was such it almost choked him. He dared not do anything. He looked out of the window and pretended interest in the London suburbs, then in the fields and cows. He was in a stupor and it was only when he recognised the first curves of the downland that he realised how time was rushing past. If nothing happened, it would soon be too late for anything to happen. He felt panic. He searched his mind for a remark that would be an invitation but not an intrusion. He must say something that without being in any way eccentric or outrageous, would mark him as the unusual, cultivated, interesting person he was—the sort of person that must appeal to a young man like this. He turned his head but before he could speak, the young man leant forward and offered him the newspaper. In his confusion, Harold accepted it, then realised he would have to do something with it. He retired behind it. The offer might be an approach, but what a waste of time! He leafed through the pages as quickly as the situation allowed then, handing the paper back, he spoke his thanks in his high, precise voice, adding after a suitable interval: 'Lovely day.'

'Yes, splendid,' the young man agreed in what Harold was relieved to hear was 'an educated voice'. Voices did not count for much these days. Some people even admired a touch of 'regional accent', but Harold had grown up over a small grocery shop in Bradford and he frankly loathed what he called 'all that kitchen-sink stuff'. He had struggled out of it and now wanted no part of it. He often described his own voice as 'educated' and had been irritated recently when Angela had said that an elocutionist's voice was 'educated' in a sense quite different from that in which he used the word.

'Do you smoke?' The young man offered a squashed pack of cigarettes.

Harold shook his head: 'No, thank you. I have to preserve my voice.'

'Singer?'

'No. Elocutionist.'

The young man lit a cigarette then, lounging in his corner, blowing out smoke and narrowing his eyes against it, he smiled again.

Well! This was seduction if ever Harold had seen it. His frisson of response was such that he felt faint. He had never before had directed upon him such a significant and alluring smile. He glowed with gratitude. This wonderful young man was actually making the running. Had, indeed, made it from the first. He had offered Harold the paper, he had enquired if he were a singer, he had offered a cigarette ...

Seeing himself as the pursued, Harold felt more comfortable but not a whit less excited. Here at last was the answer to all his demands on life. He smiled. At once the young man smiled again. Now Harold had no doubt about it. The situation was his.

Harold was so assured now that as the houses of Worthing appeared, he took the situation in hand: 'Would you care for a cup of tea?'

'Might as well. I've half an hour to wait for the Seaham bus.'

They exchanged names. The young man was called David. They walked down the platform together. It was only as they reached the barrier that Harold remembered calamity: Angela was waiting on the other side. How awful she looked! And she would give David a wrong impression of Harold's interests. As for Angela— Harold saw her bright, bespectacled eyes grow brighter as she saw David and noted David's good looks. Her curiosity was roused. Harold willed her to go away, anywhere, on any excuse, but of course she did not go away. As though she read his thoughts,

Angela grinned at Harold, then flicked a glance at David and back again to Harold. The silly little fool, what was she trying to convey? Introduced to her, David averted his gaze and Harold could not blame him. He must have seen, as Harold himself now saw only too clearly, that she was dumpy, badly dressed and lower middle class.

Harold was on edge until he managed, behind Angela's back, to catch hold of David's hand and give it a squeeze. David looked surprised but Harold felt sure he understood.

They went to the café beside the bus stop. Mercifully, Angela was keeping her mouth shut. She was observing them; no doubt gleefully, imagining that Harold was in for another disappointment. So long as she remained quiet, she could observe to her heart's content.

The café was hot, crowded and redolent of sweat and stale Indian tea. In precise, prim tones, Harold explained to the waitress that he wanted 'China', but either she did not know what he was talking about or pretended not to know.

David had become taciturn and Harold was certain that the presence of Angela had ruined their intimacy. He said he was 'a great walker' and asked David how far Seaham was from the village where he and Angela had their rooms. Here Angela had to chip in with the information that it was all of six miles. Did David walk much? Harold enquired. No, David preferred games and swimming. He went so far as to state that whenever he could, he spent his weekends at a Seaham bungalow.

'You stay there alone?' asked Harold.

'Usually. I'm cramming for the Oxford entrance. I hope to go up this autumn.'

'Lucky you!' For all his good will, Harold could not keep the hiss of envy out of his voice. There had never been any question of his going up to Oxford. His parents had spoiled him, they had given him every material comfort they could afford, but they would not waste money on higher education. They would not even let him try for a grant to one of the neighbouring Redbricks. They had sent him out at sixteen to serve his time in a gentleman's outfitters and he had trained as an elocutionist after working hours.

He had never forgiven them. It had taken him ten years to struggle out of his class. His father had left him three thousand pounds and, bitterly, he had seen it as the price of his youth.

David looked out of the window. His bus was about due. As he did not suggest their meeting again, Harold was forced to say: 'I was thinking of strolling over to Seaham tomorrow.'

'Some stroll!' giggled Angela.

Harold ignored her, determined not to let her ruin his last chance of arranging something with David. Desperately, he said: 'Would you like me to call on you?'

'If you like,' but David gave no information.

By questioning him, Harold learnt that the bungalow was called 'St Chad's' and was by the sea.

'Anyone'll point it out,' David said as he rose and swung a rucksack up on to his shoulder. He said 'Cheerio', giving Harold a glimpse of his seductive, significant smile, and was gone. From their first introduction, he had not looked at or spoken to Angela, a fact that Harold found satisfactory. He gazed intently from the window to watch David's light, easy jump on to the Seaham bus, and he did not return to the realities about him until the bus had driven away.

Angela said: 'What's going on? And under my very nose, what's more!'

Harold, emulating David's aloofness, smiled to himself and said: 'Never you mind.' He was determined not to tell her a thing, not a thing, and he maintained his silence as their own bus took them to Findon and they walked up to the cottage where Angela was staying. But he could not keep it up. During their afternoon walk, she made him tell her everything and by the time he had finished, she was no longer laughing at him.

'I hope you're not making a mistake,' she said.

'I'm quite sure I'm not.'

'You've been mistaken before.'

'Perhaps I have, but this was different. A special sort of understanding existing between us from the start. I felt it at once. As soon as he smiled at me, I knew. I just knew.'

'I must say, he didn't seem very forthcoming in the café.'

'That's because you were there. You don't look your best in that yellow dress. Yellow's a colour that calls for a very good skin.'

'What a waspish creature you are, Harold!—or would be if you had more energy.'

Harold felt more flattered than not by being called waspish. His face in the glass looked to him pathetic rather than dangerous, a deprived face, as though he had as a child been underfed instead of stuffed with pastries, sweet biscuits, ice-creams and all the chocolates that lost their colour when on display in the grocery-shop window. 'Cosseted and spoilt,' he thought, 'spoilt and cosseted', as though some crime had been perpetrated against him. If his mother had not kept him wrapped up in cotton-wool, he would have learnt to resist the coughs and colds that now made his life a misery. Thinking of this, he began to sing to himself in protest and Angela said: 'You always do that when you're annoyed.'

'Do what?'

'Sing to yourself.'

He was suddenly furious and he cried at her: 'You don't understand anything.'

'Poor Harold!' she sadly said.

He stopped in his tracks, turned on her and said: 'These days you are always going out of your way to annoy me. I wonder why?'

'*I* annoy *you*!' she gave an exaggerated gasp that disgusted him. Though she was getting on for thirty, she still had the silliness of the female adolescent. And God, how silly young women were! It was then that he realised that the feminine had become repulsive to him. It seemed to have happened in a moment, in the twinkling of an eye, but no doubt the change in him had been coming during these recent weeks of disagreement with Angela. It was almost impossible for him to understand how he had tolerated her for so long. Angela and he had met one wet Sunday afternoon in the Streatham public library. They had both put up their hands to take down the same copy of Maugham's *Writer's Notebook* and Harold had said impressively: 'I see we have similar tastes,' and Angela had giggled. She had then asked him what he thought of Maugham and had listened respectfully while he spoke his admiration and his reasons for it. They had walked together out of the library and after standing about talking for some time in the rain, had ended up in a teashop in Streatham Hill. He had been rather annoyed when Angela ordered a buck rarebit and relieved when she insisted on paying for it. Here was a girl whom it would be safe to see again. He found her to be no fool and not bad in bed, but what appealed to him and held him for so long was the abject humility that underlay her rather perky manner. He discovered soon enough that all the confidence had been kicked out of her by a bitch of a mother—a woman of cheap good looks, judging from the photograph that Angela kept beside her bed—who convinced Angela that she was too ugly ever to find herself a man. Angela was not ugly; just homely. She had a high-coloured bun of a face and glasses that she took off whenever possible, leaving a red rim on the bridge of her nose. She used no make-up. 'What good would it do on a face like mine?' Gradually her admiration for Harold had deteriorated, and even her sympathy had faded. When she was not treating him as a joke, she was impatient of him and was capable at times of something not far from malice.

He felt that he had borne rather a lot from Angela: he thought of her giggle, her lack of looks and her refusal to attempt any sort of elegance. She said 'What does it matter? Nobody looks at me,' but when she was with him, people looked at the pair of them and her dowdiness was a reflection upon him. He had tried to be tolerant. Angela was his friend—for terrible moments, it seemed she was his only friend. For terrible moments he had had to be grateful to her; had had to think of marrying her. Now he was released from all obligation to her.

As she gave her vulgar, exaggerated gasp, he said: 'You know what you are—you're just an exhibitionist schoolgirl. You annoy people in order to get attention.'

That had stung her. She said: 'Indeed! Then let me tell you what I think about you. You're always saying you're an idealist—and what's the ideal? Someone who'll think you're wonderful, and who admires your voice and your piano-playing and what you call your intellect; and puts up with your self-centred conceit

39

because they imagine you're sensitive and perceptive. Well, you may be sensitive where your own feelings are concerned, but you aren't even aware that other people have any.'

He shrugged this off: 'You don't understand. You've got no depths. You've never been clever enough—or wise enough, I ought to say—to understand how unhappy I've been. You aren't capable of understanding.'

'Everyone's unhappy.'

'Rubbish.'

'Yes, they are. Even if they don't parade their sorrows, they have them. People are full of anxiety; they don't know what hangs over them. It's not just the bomb—it's that life is so broken up and pointless. No one believes in anything, yet they want to believe. Oh, I don't know what it is, but it's the same for everyone. Your trouble is you're out of date. You want to be some sort of romantic hero lifted by your sufferings and your sensitive soul above the common run. Well, that's all over now. You've got to stop going round looking for a free gift of perfect love, and try and understand how other people feel.'

He had listened to all this very patiently in order to show her how mistaken she was. He answered seriously: 'Whatever you say, individual relationships are the most important thing in life.'

'I don't deny it. But they're not given you on a plate. You have to earn them. It's no good thinking that every pretty boy you see is going to be the great love of your life. It's jolly unlikely, apart from anything else.'

He looked at her, the poor, plain, charmless girl, and smiled: 'You know your trouble?' he said. 'You're jealous.'

'You think so? Well, it doesn't matter. The truth is, I'd be jolly glad if you did find someone who adored you. I feel sorry for you. You're so miserably lonely.'

'Don't worry about me, my dear,' he answered lightly, for he really felt now that he would never be lonely again.

As he walked towards Seaham, he could see the blue line of the sea, but it was further away than it looked. Angela had said the distance was six miles but Harold thought it must be eight or nine. He was not, as he had claimed, 'a great walker'. He occasionally took himself on solitary reflective walks to Mitcham Common or Wimbledon or Richmond, but not much further, and there was always somewhere to stop for a cup of tea on the way. Harold would have been thankful for a cup of tea now as, sweating, exhausted and aware of his developing cold, he descended on Seaham which was not, as he had hoped, an unspoilt fishing village, but a collection of seedy bungalows and bath-huts. 'St Chad's' was one of the worst: a converted army hut. The front door stood ajar. Harold entered.

He had pictured himself arriving in time for breakfast—a late breakfast, for David would not get up very early. He might even find him still in bed and . . . but except for a couple of deck-chairs, a kitchen table, a cupboard, a sink, a camp-bed and a wireless set, the hut was empty. Harold tried to accept disappointment cheerfully. This interior was a part of David.

And David himself was not far away. He was lying on the beach, naked except for a sky-blue bathing slip, his shoulders propped against some rusty iron object left behind by the army. He had a text-book open beside him but was occupied in lazily throwing stones for a dog. As Harold's feet crunched in the shingle, he glanced round and said: 'Hallo. I'd forgotten about you.'

Even though he took this to be a coy untruth, Harold was stunned by the cruelty of such a greeting. He came to a stop and might have walked away had not David smiled and said: 'Sit down.'

Harold sat down, awkwardly, on the uncomfortable stones. Some minutes passed before he recovered his confidence and could look at David and see that he was even more handsome undressed than dressed. One direct glance at the beautifully smooth, muscled, sunburnt abdomen and chest, then David turned his gaze on the sea. He was near tears, caught between his hurt and his desire to stay until it was alleviated. For surely, if he did stay, David would make up for his brutality.

'Aren't you going to strip off?' David asked.

Harold, in an acute tone of distant refinement, said: 'I fear I have no bathing costume.'

'I've another slip on the line. Go and get it.'

'I'd rather not.'

'Oh, for Heaven's sake! You look too ridiculous here on the beach in that city gent's outfit.'

Harold forced a laugh: 'I'd look more ridiculous without it.'

'You couldn't.' David turned his back on Harold and called the dog to him. When it came, he caught it, rolled it over and pretended to wrestle with it. In the uproar that resulted, conversation was at a stop. Harold sat uneasily for a few minutes, then got to his feet and went back to the bungalow. The slip on the line was red. He took it inside the hut, undressed and put it on. He knew he was too thin and hated exposing himself. When he came out, he shivered not only from the fresh wind but from self-dislike In the brilliant outdoor light, he felt like a shell-fish that had lost its shell. His skin was hideously white. When he appeared, walking painfully on the stones, David gave a howl of laughter then collapsed, his head buried in his arms, his whole body shaking.

Harold reproved him: 'I'm not at all well. I'm developing one of my colds.'

'Oh dear, oh dear!' David lay helplessly sobbing with laughter. When he at last managed to swallow his laughter back, he said: 'Why don't you run round a bit! It'll warm you up.'

In desolate obedience, Harold tried to run round in circles as he had seen athletes run on the screen, but the stones were agony and soon the dog, attracted by his activity, was bouncing about him, whoofing and snapping at his ankles. He found this intolerable and lost his temper in spite of himself: 'Get off, you brute,' he shouted.

It was evident that David could scarcely keep his laughter under. He called the dog and when it went to him, he cuffed it affectionately about the ears: 'I'll keep him busy,' he said and he began throwing stones again, but somehow Harold was always in the line of fire. The stones whanged round his feet and the dog, tearing after them, tripped him and sent him flying. He rose, rubbing a grazed elbow.

'Sorry!' David's shoulders were shaking again.

Very funny! Harold sat down. When the dog settled beside him, he pushed it irritably away.

'Don't you like animals?' asked David.

'They're all right in their proper place.'

'Isn't the beach a proper place? They seem right to me wherever they are.'

'Unlike human beings, you mean?'

'Well, human beings can look a bit silly at times. Aren't you going to bathe?'

'I don't think so. It's chilly. I've got a cold.'

'Then I'd get dressed if I were you. You look too awful like that.'

Harold, his eyes blurred by tears, stared out to sea for some minutes, then jumped up and returned to the bungalow and his clothing. David arrived while he was lacing up his shoes.

'How about something to eat?' David cheerfully asked.

'No, thank you. I'm going straight back.'

'Don't be an ass.' David turned on the wireless set and, without waiting to hear what noise would come from it, went to the cupboard and brought out bread, cheese, corned-beef and a teapot: 'Here!' he threw a bundle of knives and forks on the table, 'put these straight.' He lit a spirit-stove and filled the kettle.

Harold was hungry and the thought of food cheered him. He saw the hospitality as a peace offering and decided he would feel better when he had had something to eat. He would stay, but not without protest. He said in suffering tones: 'You are so different from what I imagined: so different.'

'Sorry, but it's scarcely my fault.'

Harold adjusted the wireless and found a Beethoven symphony. He stood listening, his expression becoming entranced, until David said: 'Oke. All ready.'

While they were eating, Harold did his best to cross the barrier between them.

'So you'll be up at Oxford in the autumn! I sometimes go there for weekends.'

David made no response. Harold asked: 'What do you intend to study?'

'Mathematics.'

'Good Lord!'

When the meal was over, David lit a cigarette and started clearing the table. Harold watched, making no move, while David poured water into a pan and stacked in the dishes. Throwing a damp, dirty towel towards Harold, David said: 'Let's get it over.'

Harold rose unwillingly. He hated household chores, especially dish-washing. Dish-washing was the job his mother had imposed on him at home and he had always felt it an inferior activity. With a distasteful smile on his lips he took up the towel and said: 'I'm not in the habit of washing dishes, but I don't mind obliging you,' and as he spoke, he slid an arm around David's neck. David dodged away. Without turning or pausing in his work, he calmly said: 'Pull yourself together.'

Harold stood as though he had been slapped in the face, then threw the towel aside and walked out of the bungalow. He paused in the garden, his hands in his pockets, and sang to himself.

'He's a little flirt,' he thought, 'I'll call his bluff,' but he was not certain he could call David's bluff. He went to the wooden paling round the garden and leaning over it, pressed his hands against his eyes.

David came out to hang the towel on the line. He had put on his shirt and jeans. He said: 'At four o'clock I have to go to tea with friends.'

'Don't worry, I'm just leaving.'

'No need. How about a walk along the shore?'

Harold, looking at him, met the smile again and was more disturbed than before. They went together to the water's edge and along the sand strip.

'You don't like men that way?' Harold asked after a long silence.

'I find I prefer women on the whole.'

'Do you mind my being attracted to you?'

'I suppose you can't help it,' David kept bending to pick up stones and skim them across the sea, 'I'd hoped it might be possible to have a friendship without that.'

Stung to an impolitic tartness, Harold asked: 'I can't say that was the impression you gave me.'

'No? Sorry for that. I'd better be getting back. They asked me to come early.' He glanced sideways at Harold and with his provoking smile said: 'Very pretty girl where I'm going.'

'Is there?' Harold was filled with resentment. The smile now seemed unforgivable. His cold was becoming worse. The undressing had done him no good. His hands in his pockets, his eyes on the ground, he began to feel really ill.

David stopped at the gate of one of the larger brick bungalows and held out a hand: 'This is where I leave you.' Harold, ignoring the hand, brushed past him without a word. He walked with a sense of purpose until he reached the brow of the downs, then his pace slowed, weariness came down on him. For the moment he felt only anger. Misery would come later. As he trudged along it seemed to him David had encouraged him simply to make a fool of him, then, bored, had simply dismissed him. But why should he get away with it? Why should Harold let himself be dismissed like that? He was not a fool or a weakling. He came to a stop, then, obstinately resolved, he turned in his tracks and walked back to 'St Chad's'. The door still stood ajar. He went in and, wrapping himself up in a blanket from the bed, sat down beside the wireless set and found some music. The music soothed him, then a sensuous tenderness and longing began to grow in him. He became aware of mysterious desires in himself and mysterious powers. He felt he had genius of a sort, though what sort he could not tell. Intoxicated by the sense of his own personality, he was certain that when David returned everything would be different. The hours passed. He lay entranced, waiting, filled with a delicious anticipation.

The room was completely dark when David returned. He switched on the light as he entered then saw Harold and stared at him blankly. Harold gave a weak titter.

'I couldn't go all that way back. I really didn't feel well enough.'

'What's the matter with you?'

'It's this cold. It's worse. My temperature's up. I must have got a touch of chill down on the beach.'

'You'd better get into bed. I'll make you a hot drink.'

Harold took off his coat and trousers and lay on the bed in his shirt. He doubled the blanket over him. It was miserably thin. 'I'm highly susceptible to colds,' he said. Beneath him the canvas was hard and comfortless: 'I ought to have more covers.'

David took a woollen scarf from the cupboard and threw it to Harold. Wrapping it round his neck, Harold, with morose pleasure, smelt its scent of sweat and sand. He sat up in the bed, grinning wretchedly, and watched David heat in a pan some water, sugar and the end of a bottle of wine. He handed the drink to Harold by stretching from the bottom of the bed.

In silence they ate another meal of corned-beef and cheese. When it was finished and David was washing dishes again, Harold burst out: 'Why do you dislike me?'

'I don't dislike you—particularly.'

'You can't pretend that you like me: yet, at the station, you let me squeeze your hand: and you smiled at me on the train.'

'Doesn't everyone smile?'

'But not like that. You know there are smiles and smiles. You deliberately misled me.'

David went outside to hang the towel on the line.

Harold watched for him to reappear in the doorway, then accused him: 'If you didn't like me, you should have shown it straight away.'

'I suppose I made a mistake.'

'What do you mean—a mistake?' Harold sat upright in his eagerness to discuss himself. 'What is wrong with me?'

David laughed uncomfortably: 'How should I know?'

'Yesterday you were friendly. Today, straight away, you were cruel and cold. I felt you hated me. Why? For what reason? What did I do wrong? What made you change? Did you think I looked ridiculous?'

'Perhaps. A bit.'

'So that was it!' Having been given the answer he expected and dreaded, Harold sank back on to the bed with quivering lips. He said: 'I've found no one to understand me ... ' there was a pause before he could control himself sufficiently to add: ' ... or accept me.'

'Sorry about that.' David lit a candle. Switching off the light that hung naked, dim and fly-blown from the centre of the ceiling, he undressed in the obscurity of the candle's light. Watching him, Harold wondered what he would do when he was ready for bed.

To keep contact, any sort of contact, Harold asked: 'What's wrong with me?'

'How do I know? You're a bit difficult, I should say.'

'How? How am I difficult? In what way?'

'I'd call you artificial. You're not like other fellows.'

This statement of his difference filled Harold with a bleak satisfaction.

As David, in socks, pyjamas and overcoat, settled himself in one deck-chair and put his feet up on the other, Harold gave an anguished cry of disappointment. David ignored it. He blew out the candle and prepared for sleep. Harold protested out of the darkness: 'I quarrelled with my girl-friend for your sake.'

No reply came from David.

'She understands me. Why can't you understand me? She appreciates me. Why can't you? Tell me what prevents you? Tell me ... tell me ... '

Silence.

'I'm only down for the weekend. I've got to go back tomorrow. I've got classes in the afternoon. Poor Angela won't see anything of me. I've left her alone all day. She'll be terribly upset. She may even decide to finish with me, and then I'll have no one. I'll have no one ... no one.'

David gave a slight snore.

Tears slid from Harold's eyes and fell to the grimy pillow. He wondered if he had spoken the truth when he said Angela understood him? Did anyone understand him? Could they understand him? At the thought of his difference, he was comforted as though he were in some way ennobled by his separation from the rest of the human race, and he at last fell asleep.

He awakened again at first light and again got himself up and dressed silently, this time in order to escape without waking David. As he walked once more on the pneumatic turf of the downs and through the gleaming dew, his spirits rose, for he was returning to Angela. Whether she understood him or not, it seemed to him then that her feminine warmth and sympathy were the most desirable things in the world.

MICE AND BIRDS AND BOY

Elizabeth Taylor

'Was this when you were pretty?' William asked, holding the photograph in both hands and raising his eyes to the old lady's with a look of near certainty.

'I was thought to be beautiful,' she said; and she wondered: How long ago was that? Who had been the last person to comment upon her beauty, and how many years ago? She thought that it might have been her husband, from loyalty or from still seeing what was no longer there. He had been dead for over twenty years and her beauty had not, by any means, been the burden of his dying words.

The photograph had faded to a pale coffee-colour, but William could distinguish a cloud of fair hair, a rounded face with lace to the chin, and the drooping, sad expression so many beautiful women have. Poor Mrs May, he thought.

The photographs were all jumbled up in a carved sandalwood box lined with dusty felt. There was a large one, mounted on stiff cardboard, of the big house where Mrs May had lived as a child. It had been pulled down between the wars and in its grounds was built a housing estate, a row of small shops by the bus stop and a children's playground, with swings and slides. William could look out of the narrow window of the old gardener's lodge where Mrs May lived now and watch the shrieking toddlers climbing the frames, swinging on the swings. He never went to the playground himself now that he was six.

'It was all fields,' Mrs May would often say, following his glance.

'All fields and parkland. I used to ride my pony over it. It was a different world. We had two grooms and seven indoor servants and four gardeners. Yet we were just ordinary people. Everybody had such things in those days.'

'Did every child have a pony?' William asked.

'All *country* children had one,' she said firmly.

His curiosity endeared him to her. It was so long since anyone had asked her a question and been interested in the answer. His curiosity had been the beginning of their friendship. Going out into her overgrown little garden one afternoon, she had found him leaning against the rickety fence staring at her house, which was round in shape and had attracted his attention. It was made of dark flint and had narrow, arched windows and an arched door studded with big square-headed nails. A high twisted chimney-stack rose from the centre of the roof. Surrounded by the looped and tangled growth of the garden—rusty, black-leaved briers and crooked apple trees—the place reminded the boy of a menacing-looking illustration by Arthur Rackham in a book he had at home. Then the door had opened and the witch herself had come out, leaning on a stick. She had untidy white hair and a face cross-hatched with wrinkles; but her eyes weren't witch-like, not black and beady and evil, but large and milky blue and kind, though crows had trodden about them.

'How can your house be round inside?' William asked, in his high, clear voice. She looked about her and then saw his red jersey through the fence and, above it, his bright face with its straight fringe of hair. 'How can rooms be round?' he asked. He came up to the broken gate and stood there.

Beyond a row of old elm trees which hid the lodge from the main road, a double-decker bus went by, taking the women from the estate to Market Swanford for their afternoon's shopping. When it had gone, William turned back to the old lady and said: 'Or are they like this shape?' He made a wedge with his hands.

'You had better come and see,' she said. He opened the gate at once and went in. 'She might pop me into the oven,' he thought.

One room was half a circle, the other two were quarters. All three were dark and crammed with furniture. A mouse streaked across the kitchen floor. The sink was stacked with dirty china, the table littered with odds and ends of food in torn paper wrappings.

'Do you live here alone?' he asked.

'Except for the mice; but I should prefer to be alone.'

'You are more like a hermit than a witch.'

'And would rather be,' she said.

He examined a dish of stewed fruit which had a greenish-grey mantling of mould.

'Pooh! It smells like beer,' he said.

'I meant to throw it away, but it seemed such a criminal waste when the natives are starving everywhere.'

In the sitting-room, with frail and shaking hands, she offered him a chocolate box; there was one chocolate left in it. It was stale and had a bloom on it, and might be poisoned, he thought; but he took it politely and turned it about in his mouth. It was very hard and tasted musty. 'Curiosity killed the cat,' his mother would say, when his body was discovered.

Mrs May began then to tell him about the fields and park and her pony. He felt drowsy and wondered if the poison were taking effect. She had such a beautiful voice—wavering, floating—that he could not believe in his heart that she would do him any harm. The room was airless and he sat in a little spoon-shaped velvet chair and stared up at her, listening to a little of her story, here and there. Living alone, except for the mice, she had no one to blame her when she spilt egg and tea down her front, he supposed; and she had taken full advantage of her freedom. She was really very dirty, he decided dispassionately. But smelt nice. She had the cosy smell that he liked so much about his guinea-pigs—a warm, stuffy, old smell.

'I'd better go,' he said suddenly. 'I might come back again tomorrow.'

She seemed to understand at once, but like all grown-up people was compelled to prolong the leave-taking a little. He answered her questions briefly, anxious to be off once he had made up his mind to go.

'There,' he said, pointing up the hill. 'My house is there.' The gilt weather-vane, veering round, glittered in the sun above the slate roofs.

'Our old stables,' Mrs May said quite excitedly. 'Oh, the memories.'

He shut the gate and sauntered off, between piles of bricks and tiles on the site where more houses were being built. Trees had been left standing here and there, looking strange upon the scarred, untidy landscape. William walked round the foundations of a little house, stood in the middle of a rectangle and tried to imagine a family sitting at a table in the middle of it, but it seemed far too small. The walls were only three bricks high. He walked round them, one foot before the other, his arms lifted to keep his balance. Some workmen shouted at him. They were tiling the roof of a nearby house. He took no notice, made a completed round of the walls and then walked off across the rough grass, where Mrs May had ridden her pony when she was a little girl.

'Do you *hear* me?' his mother said again, her voice shrill, with anxiety and vexation. She even took William's shoulder and shook him. 'You are *not* to talk to strangers.'

His sister, Jennifer, who was ballet-mad, practised an arabesque, and watched the scene without interest, her mind on her own schemes.

William looked gravely at his mother, rubbing his shoulder.

'Do you understand?'

He nodded.

'That's right, remember what your mother told you,' his father said, for the sake of peace.

The next morning, William took a piece of cheese from the larder and a pen-knife and went to the building-site. His mother was having an Italian lesson. Some of the workmen were sitting against a wall in the sun, drinking tea and eating bread and cheese, and William sat down amongst them, settling himself comfortably with his back against the wall. He cut pieces of cheese against his thumb as the others did and popped them neatly into his mouth. They drew him into solemn conversation, winking at one another above his head. He answered them politely, but knew that they were making fun of him. One wag, going too far, grimacing too obviously, asked: 'And what is your considered opinion of the present emergency?'

'I don't know,' William replied, and he got up and walked away—more in sorrow than in anger, he tried to convey.

He lingered for a while, watching a bulldozer going over the uneven ground, opening wounds in the fields where Mrs May had ridden her pony; then he wandered on towards the main road. Mrs May came out to her front doorstep and dropped an apronful of crumbs on to the path. Thrushes and starlings descended about her.

'So you're back again,' she called. 'I am shortly off to the shops. It will be nice to have a boy go with me.' She went inside, untying her apron.

He tried to swing on the gate, but it was lopsided. When she came out after a long time, she was wearing a torn raincoat, although it was quite hot already. It had no buttons and hung open. Her dirty jersey was held to her flat chest with rows of jet beads.

William noted that they were much stared at as they passed the bus queue and, in the butcher's shop, Mrs May was the subject of the same knowing looks and gravely-kept straight faces that he himself had suffered from the builders. He felt, uncomfortably, that this behaviour was something that children came to expect, but that an older person should neither expect nor tolerate. He could not find words to explain his keen uneasiness on Mrs May's account.

He watched the butcher unhook a drab piece of liver, slap it on the counter and cut off a slice.

'When I think of the saddles of mutton, the sucking pigs ... ' said Mrs May vaguely, counting out coppers.

'Yes, I expect so,' said the butcher's wife, with a straight face turned towards her husband.

Outside the shop, Mrs May continued the list. 'And ribs of beef, green goose at Michaelmas,' she chattered on to herself, going past the dairy, the grocer's, the draper's, with quick, herringbone steps. William caught glimpses of themselves reflected in the shop windows, against a pyramid of syrup tins, then a bolt of sprigged cotton.

'And what are *you* going to tell *me*?' Mrs May suddenly asked. 'I can't do all the entertaining, you know. Are you quite warm up there in the stables? Have you beds and chairs and all you need?'

'We have even more beds than we need.'

'Well, don't ask me to imagine it, because I can't. Shall we turn back? I'll buy an egg at the dairy and I might get some stale bread for the birds. "My only friends," I say to them, as they come to greet me.'

'You have the mice as well.'

'I can't make friends with mice. The mice get on my nerves, as a matter of fact.'

'You could get a cat,' he suggested.

'And seem more like a witch than ever?'

There appeared to be no stale bread at the baker's. At sight of Mrs May, the woman behind the counter seemed to shutter her face; stood waiting with lowered eyes for them to go.

When they reached Mrs May's broken gate—with only the slice of meat and the egg—William would not go in. He ran home as fast as he could over the uneven ground, his heart banging, his throat aching.

When he reached it, the house was quiet and a strange, spicy smell he could not identify came from the kitchen. His mother, as well as her Italian lessons, had taken up Japanese cooking. His sister, returning from ballet class, with her shoes hanging from her neck by their ribbons, found him lying on the floor pushing a toy car back and forth. Her suspicions were roused; for he was pretending to be playing, she was convinced, with an almost cross-eyed effort at concentration. He began to hum unconcernedly. Jennifer's nose wrinkled. 'It smells as if we're going to have that horrid soup with stalks in it.'

'I like it,' he murmured.

'You would. What have you been doing, anyway?'

Still wearing her coat, she practised a few pliés.

Never waste a moment, he thought.

'Nothing.'

But she was not interested in him; had been once—long ago,

it seemed to her, when his birth she hoped would brighten up the house. The novelty of him had soon worn off.

'The death duties,' Mrs May explained. Because of them, she could not light a fire until the really chilly days and sometimes had only an egg to eat all day. These death duties William thought of as moral obligations upon which both her father and husband had insisted on discharging while dying—some charitable undertakings, plainly not approved of by Mrs May. He was only puzzled by the varying effect of this upon her day-to-day life; sometimes she was miserably conscious of her poverty, but at other times she bought peppermint creams for herself and William and digestive biscuits for the birds.

Every time she opened or shut the garden gate, she explained how she would have had it mended if it were not for the death duties. *The* death duties made them sound a normal sort of procedure, a fairly usual change of heart brought about perhaps by the approach of death and clearly happening not only in Mrs May's family.

The days were beginning to grow chilly, too chilly to be without a fire. The leaves on the great chestnut trees about the building site turned yellow and fell. William went back to school and called on Mrs May only on Saturday mornings. He did not miss her. His life was suddenly very full and some weeks he did not go at all and she fretted for him, watching from a window like a love-sick girl, postponing her visit to the shops. She missed not only him, but her glimpses—from his conversation—of the strange life going on up in the old stables. His descriptions—in answer to her questions—and what she read into them formed a bewildering picture. She imagined the family sitting round the bench in the old harness room, drinking a thin soup with blades of grass in it—the brisk mother, the gentle, dreamy father and an objectionable little girl who kept getting down from the frugal meal to practise pas-de-chats across the old, broken brick floor. She had built the scene from his phrases—'My mother will be cross if I'm late' (more polite, he thought, than, 'My mother will be cross if she knows I came to see you'), and 'My father wouldn't mind.' His sister, it seemed, complained about the soup; apart from this, she only talked of Margot Fonteyn. But confusions came into it—in William's helping to clean silver for a dinner-party and having been sent to bed early for spilling ink on a carpet. Silver and carpets were hard to imagine as part of the old stables.

She had forgotten what a family was like, and had never had much chance of learning—only child and childless wife. William was too young to be a satisfactory informant. He was haphazardly selective, interested too much in his own separate affairs, unobservant and forgetful of the adult world; yet she managed to piece something together and it had slowly grown—a continuous story, without direction or catharsis—but could no longer grow if he were not to visit her.

Holding the curtains, her frail hands shook. When he did come, he was enticed to return. On those mornings now, there were always sweets. But her questions tired him, as they tire and antagonise all children, who begin to feel uneasily in the wrong role. He had by now satisfied his curiosity about her and was content to let what he did not understand—the death duties, for instance—lie at peace.

'You shall have this when I'm gone,' she began to say, closing the lid of the sandalwood box in which she kept the old photographs. Also promised was her father's sword and scabbard, in which William was more interested, and a stuffed parrot called Bertha—once a childhood pet and still talked to as if no change had taken place.

One morning, she saw him playing on the building-site and went out to the gate and called to him, lured him into the garden and then the house with witch-like tactics, sat him down on the spoon-shaped chair and gave him a bag of sweets.

'And how is your mother?' she enquired. She had a feeling that she detested the woman. William nodded absentmindedly, poking about in the sweet bag. His hair was like gold silk, she thought.

'People have always lost patience with me,' she said, feeling his attention wandering from her. 'I only had my beauty.'

She was going on to describe how her husband's attention had also wandered, then thought it perhaps an unsuitable subject to discuss with a child. She had never discussed it with anyone else. Such a vague marriage, and her memories of it were vague, too—seemed farther away than her childhood.

A mouse gnawed with a delicate sound in the wainscot and William turned his gaze towards it, waiting for the minutes to pass until the time when he could rise politely from the dusty chair and say goodbye.

If only he would tell me! Mrs May thought in despair. Tell me what there was for breakfast, for instance, and who said what and who went where, so that I could have something to think about in the evening.

'Oh, well, the winter will come if it means to,' she said aloud. Rain had swept in a gust upon the window, as if cast upon the little panes in spite. 'Nothing we can do can stop it. Only dig in and make ourselves comfortable—roast chestnuts on my little coal shovel,' William glanced from the wainscot to the empty grate, but Mrs May seemed not to see its emptiness. 'Once, when I had a *nice* governess, we roasted some over the school-room fire. But the next governess would never let me do anything that pleased me. "Want must be your master," she said. She had many low phrases of that kind.' 'Yes, want must be your master,' she said again, and sighed.

The visit was running down and her visitor simply sitting there until he could go. Courageously, when he had refused another peppermint cream and showed that he did not want to see again the photograph of her home, she released him, she even urged him to go, speeding him on his way, and watched him from the open door, her hands clasped close to her flat chest. He was like a most beloved caged bird that she had set at liberty. She felt regret and yet a sense of triumph, seeing him go.

She returned to the room and looked dully at the stuffed parrot, feeling a little like crying, but she had been brought up not to do so. 'Yes, want must be your master, Bertha,' she said, in a soft but serene voice.

'I can't see harm in it,' William's father told his wife. Jennifer had seen William leaving Mrs May's and hurried to tell her mother,

56

who began complaining the moment her husband returned for lunch.

'She's stark, staring mad and the place is filthy, everybody says so.'

'Children sometimes see what we can't.'

'I don't know what you mean by that. I forbade him to go there and he repeatedly disobeyed me. You should speak to him.'

So his father spoke to William—rather off-handedly, over his shoulder, while hanging his coat up in the hall, as William passed through.

To be reprimanded for what he had not wanted to do, for what he looked on as a duty, did not vex William. It was the kind of thing that happened to him a great deal and he let it go, rather than tie himself up in explanations.

'You did hear what I said?' his father asked.

'Yes, I heard.'

'Your mother has her reasons. You can leave it at that.'

It happened that he obeyed his parents. His father one day passing Mrs May's garden came on her feeding her birds there. He raised his hat and saw, as she glanced up, her ruined face, bewildered eyes, and was stirred by pity as he walked on.

As the nights grew colder, Mrs May was forced to light a fire and she wandered about the building site collecting sawn-off pieces of batten and wood-shavings. She met William there once, playing with another boy. He returned her greeting, answered her questions unwillingly, knowing that his companion had ducked his head, trying to hide a smile. When she had wandered on at last, there were more questions from his friend. 'Oh, she's only an old witch I know,' he replied.

The truth was that he could hardly remember how once he had liked to go to see her. Then he had tired of her stories about her childhood, grew bored with her photographs, became embarrassed by her and realised, in an adult way, that the little house was filthy. One afternoon, on his way home from school, he had seen her coming out of the butcher's shop ahead of him and had slackened his pace, almost walked backwards not to overtake her.

She was alone again, except for the birds in the daytime, the mice at night. The deep winter came and the birds grew fewer and the mice increased. The cold weather birds, double their summer size, hopped dottily about the crisp, rimed grass, jabbing their beaks into frozen puddles, bewildered as refugees. Out she hurried, first thing in the mornings, to break the ice and scatter crumbs. She found a dead thrush and grieved over it. 'Oh, Bertha, one of ours,' she mourned.

Deep snow came and she was quite cut off—the garden was full of strange shapes, as if heaped with pillows and bolsters, and the birds made their dagger tracks across the drifts. She could not open her door.

Seeing the untrodden path, William's father, passing by, went to borrow a spade from the nearest house and cleared the snow from the gateway to the door. He saw her watching from a window and, when at last she could, she opened the door to thank him.

'I'm afraid I don't know who you are,' she began.

'I live in the old stables up on the hill.'

'Then I know your little boy. He used to visit me. It was very kind of you to come to my rescue.'

William's father returned the spade and then walked home, feeling sad and ashamed. 'Oh, dear, that house,' he said to his wife. 'It is quite filthy—what I glimpsed of it. You were perfectly right. Someone ought to do something to help her.'

'She should help herself. She must have plenty of money—all this building land.'

'I think she misses William.'

'It was just a passing thing,' said his wife, who was a great one herself for passing things. 'He simply lost interest.'

'Lost innocence, perhaps. The truth is, I suppose, that children grow up and begin to lose their simple vision.'

'The truth is,' she said tartly, 'that if people don't wash themselves they go unloved.' Her voice was cold and disdainful. She had summed up many other lives than Mrs May's and knew the tone to use.

The thaw began, then froze in buds upon the red twigs of the dogwood in Mrs May's untidy hedge. The hardening snow was pitted with drips from the branches.

Mrs May was afraid to venture on her frozen path beyond her doorway, and threw her remaining bits of bread from there. There was no one to run an errand for her. The cold drove her inside, but she kept going to the window to see if the ice were melting. Instead, the sky darkened. Both sky and earth were iron.

'It's my old bones,' she said to Bertha. 'I'm afraid for my old bones.'

Then she saw William running and sliding on the ice, his red scarf flying, his cheeks bright. He fell, and scrambled up, laughing.

'It's falling I'm afraid of,' Mrs May whispered to the window pane. 'My old bones are too brittle.'

She went to the front door and opened it. Standing shivering on the step, she called to William. He seemed not to hear and she tried to raise her voice. He took a run and, with his arms flung above his head, slithered across a patch of ice. He shouted to someone out of sight and dashed forward.

Mrs May shut the door again. 'Someone will come,' she told Bertha briskly. She straightened her father's sword suspended above the fireplace and bustled about, trying to tidy the room ready for an unknown visitor. 'There's no knowing what might happen. Anyone might call,' she murmured.

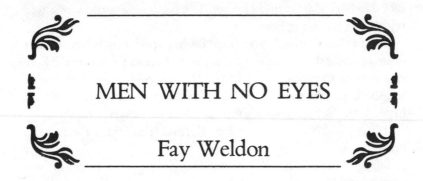

MEN WITH NO EYES

Fay Weldon

Edgar, Minette, Minnie and Mona.

In the evenings three of them sit down to play Monopoly. Edgar, Minette and Minnie. Mona, being only five, sleeps upstairs, alone, in the little back bedroom, where roses, growing up over the porch and along under the thatch, thrust dark companionable heads through the open lattice window. Edgar and Minnie, father and daughter, face each other across the table. Both, he in his prime, she in early adolescence, are already bronzed from the holiday sun, blue eyes bright and eager in lean faces, dull red hair bleached to brightness by the best summer the Kent coast has seen, they say, since 1951—a merciful God allowing, it seems, the glimmer of His smile to shine again on poor humiliated England. Minette, Edgar's wife, sits at the kitchen end of the table. The ladderback chair nearest the porch remains empty. Edgar says it is uncomfortable. Minnie keeps the bank. Minette doles out the property cards.

Thus, every evening this holiday, they have arranged themselves around the table, and taken up their allotted tasks. They do it almost wordlessly, for Edgar does not care for babble. Who does? Besides, Mona might wake, think she was missing something, and insist on joining in.

How like a happy family we are, thinks Minette, pleased, shaking the dice. Minette's own face is pink and shiny from the sun and her nose is peeling. Edgar thinks hats on a beach are affected (an affront, as it were, to nature's generosity) so Minette is content to pay the annual penalty summer holidays impose on her fair complexion and fine mousy hair. Her mouth is swollen from the sun, and her red arms and legs are stiff and bumpy with midge bites. Mona is her mother's daughter and has inherited her difficulty with the sun, and even had a slight touch of sunstroke on the evening of the second day, which Edgar, probably rightly, put down to the fact that Minette had slapped Mona on the cheek, in the back of the car, on the journey down.

'Cheeks afire,' he said, observing his flushed and feverish child. 'You really shouldn't vent your neuroses on your children, Minette.'

And of course Minette shouldn't. Edgar was right. Poor little Mona. It was entirely forgivable for Mona, a child of five, to become fractious and unbiddable in the back of a car, cooped up as she was on a five-hour journey; and entirely unforgivable of the adult Minette, sitting next to her, to be feeling so cross, distraught, nervous and unmaternal that she reacted by slapping. Minette should have, could have diverted: could have sung, could have played Here is the Church, this little pig, something, anything, rather than slapped. Cheeks afire! As well they might be. Mona's with upset at her mother's cruel behaviour: Minette's, surely, with shame and sorrow.

Edgar felt the journey was better taken without stops, and that in any case no coffee available on a motorway was worth stopping for. It would be instant, not real. Why hadn't Minette brought a thermos, he enquired, when she ventured to suggest they stopped. Because we don't *own* a thermos, she wanted to cry, her in her impossible mood, because you say they're monstrously overpriced, because you say I always break the screw; in any case it's not the coffeee I want, it's for you to stop, to recognise our existence, our needs—but she stopped herself in time. That way quarrels lie, and the rare quarrels of Edgar and Minette, breaking out, shatter the neighbourhood, not to mention the children. Well done, Minette.

'Just as well we didn't go to Italy,' said Edgar, on the night of Mona's fever, measuring out, to calm the mother-damaged, fevered cheek, the exact dosage of Junior Aspirin recommended on the back of the packet (and though Minette's doctor once instructed her to quadruple the stated dose, if she wanted it to be effective, Minette knows better than to say so), dissolving it in water, and feeding it to Mona by the spoonful though Minette knows Mona much prefers to suck them—'if this is what half an hour's English sun does to her.'

Edgar, Minette, Minnie and Mona. Off to Italy, camping, every year for the last six years, even when Mona was a baby. Milan, Venice, Florence, Pisa. Oh what pleasure, riches, glory, of country-side and town. This year, Minette had renewed the passports and replaced the sleeping bags, brought the Melamine plates and mugs up to quota, checked the Gaz cylinders, and waited for Edgar to reveal the date, usually towards the end of July, when he would put his ethnographical gallery in the hands of an assistant and they would pack themselves and the tent into the car, happy families, and set off, as if spontaneously, into the unknown; but this year the end of July went and the first week of August, and still Edgar did not speak, and Minette's employers were betraying a kind of incredulous restlessness at Minette's apparent lack of decision, and only then, on 6 August, after a studied absent-mindedness lasting from 31 July to 5 August, did Edgar say 'Of course we can't afford to go abroad. Business is rock-bottom. I hope you haven't been wasting any money on unnecessary equipment?'

'No, of course not,' says Minette. Minette tells many lies: it is one of the qualities which Edgar least likes in her. Minette thinks she is safe in this one. Edgar will not actually count the Melamine plates; nor is he likely to discern the difference between one old lumpy navy-blue sleeping bag and another unlumpy new one. 'We do have the money set aside,' she says cautiously, hopefully.

'Don't be absurd,' he says. 'We can't afford to drive the car round the corner, let alone to Venice. It'll only have sunk another couple of inches since last year, beneath the weight of crap as much as of tourists. It's too depressing. Everything's too depressing.' Oh Venice, goodbye Venice, city of wealth and abandon, and human weakness, glorious beneath sulphurous skies. Goodbye Venice, says Minette in her heart, I loved you well. 'So we shan't be having a holiday this year?' she enquires. Tears are smarting in her eyes. She doesn't believe him. She is tired, strained, work has been

62

exhausting. She is an advertising copywriter. He is teasing, surely. He often is. In the morning he will say something different.

'You go on holiday if you want,' he says in the morning. 'I can't. I can't afford a holiday this year. You seem to have lost all sense of reality, Minette. It's that ridiculous place you work in.' And of course he is right. Times are hard. Inflation makes profits and salaries seem ridiculous. Edgar, Minette, Minnie and Mona must adapt with the times. An advertising agency is not noted for the propagation of truth. Those who work in agencies live fantasy lives as to their importance in the scheme of things and their place in a society which in truth despises them. Minette is lucky that some-one of his integrity and taste puts up with her. No holiday this year. She will pay the money set aside into a building society, though the annual interest is less than the annual inflation rate. She is resigned.

But the next day, Edgar comes home, having booked a holiday cottage in Kent. A miracle. Friends of his own it, and have had a cancellation. Purest chance. It is the kind of good fortune Edgar always has. If Edgar is one minute late for a train, the train leaves two minutes late.

Now, on the Friday, here they are, Edgar, Minette, Minnie and Mona, installed in this amazing rural paradise of a Kentish hamlet, stone-built, thatched cottage, swifts flying low across the triangular green, the heavy smell of farmyard mixing with the scent of the absurd red roses round the door and the night-stocks in the cottage garden, tired and happy after a day on the beach, with the sun shining and the English channel blue and gentle, washing upon smooth pebbles.

Mona sleeps, stirs. The night is hot and thundery, ominous. Infla-tion makes the Monopoly money not so fantastic as it used to be. Minette remarks on it to Edgar.

'Speak for yourself,' he says. Minette recently got a rise, promo-tion. Edgar is self-employed, of the newly impoverished classes.

They throw to see who goes first. Minette throws a two and three. Minnie, her father's daughter, throws a five and a six. Minnie is twelve, a kindly, graceful child, watchful of her mother, adoring her father, whom she resembles.

Edgar throws a double six. Edgar chooses his token—the iron— and goes first.

Edgar, Minette, Minnie and Mona.

Edgar always wins the toss. Edgar always chooses the iron. (He is as good at housekeeping and cooking as Minette, if not better.) Edgar always wins the game. Minnie always comes second. Minette always comes last. Mona always sleeps. Of such stuff are holidays made.

Monopoly, in truth, bores Minette. She plays for Minnie's sake, to be companionable, and for Edgar's, because it is expected. Edgar likes winning. Who doesn't?

Edgar throws a double, lands on Pentonville Road, and buys it for £60. Minette hands over the card; Minnie received his money. Edgar throws again, lands on and buys Northumberland Avenue. Minnie throws, lands on Euston Road, next to her father, and buys it for £100. Minette lands on Income Tax, pays £200 into the bank, and giggles, partly from nervousness, partly at the ridiculous nature of fate.

'You do certainly have a knack, Minette,' says Edgar, unsmiling. 'But I don't know if it's anything to laugh about.'

Minette stops smiling. The game continues in silence. Minette lands in jail. Upstairs Mona, restless, murmurs and mutters in her sleep. In the distance Minette can hear the crackle of thunder. The windows are open, and the curtains not drawn, in order that Edgar can feel close to the night and nature, and make the most of his holiday. The window squares of blank blackness, set into the white walls, as on some child's painting, frighten Minette. What's outside? Inside, it seems to her, their words echo. The rattle of the dice is loud, loaded with some kind of meaning she'd rather not think about. Is someone else listening, observing?

Edgar, Minette, Minnie, Mona. What else?

Mona cries out. Minette gets up. 'I'll go to her,' she says.

'She's perfectly all right,' says Edgar. 'Don't fuss.'

'She might be frightened,' says Minette.

'What of?' enquires Edgar dangerously. 'What is there to be frightened of?' He is irritated by Minette's many fears, especially on holiday, and made angry by the notion that there is anything threatening in nature. Loving silence and isolation himself, he is impatient with those city-dwellers who fear it. Minette and Mona, his feeling is, are city-dwellers by nature, whereas Edgar and Minnie have the souls, the patience, the maturity of the country-dweller, although obliged to live in the town.

'It's rather hot. She's in a strange place,' Minette persists.

'She's in a lovely place,' says Edgar, flatly. 'Of course, she may be having bad dreams.'

Mona is silent again, and Minette is relieved. If Mona is having bad dreams, it is of course Minette's fault, first for having slapped Mona on the cheek, and then, more basically, for having borne a child with such a town-dweller's nature that she suffers from sun-burn and sunstroke.

'Mona by name,' says Minette, 'moaner by nature.'

'Takes after her mother,' says Edgar. 'Minette, you forgot to pay £50 last time you landed in jail, so you'll have to stay there until you throw a double.'

'Can't I pay this time round?'

'No you can't,' says Edgar.

They've lost the rule book. All losses in the house are Minette's responsibility, so it is only justice that Edgar's ruling as to the nature of the game shall be accepted. Minette stays in jail.

Mona by name, moaner by nature. It was Edgar named his chil-dren, not Minette. Childbirth upset her judgement, made her impossible, or so Edgar said, and she was willing to believe it, struggling to suckle her young under Edgar's alternately indifferent and chiding eye, sore from stitches, trying to decide on a name, and unable to make up her mind, for any name Minette liked, Edgar didn't. For convenience' sake, while searching for a compromise, she referred to her first-born as Mini—such a tiny, beautiful baby— and when Edgar came back unexpectedly with the birth certificate, there was the name Minnie and Minette gasped with horror, and all Edgar said was, 'But I thought that was what *You* wanted, it's what *You* called her, the State won't wait for ever for *You* to make up your mind; I had to spend all morning in that place and I ought to be in the gallery: I'm exhausted. Aren't you grateful for any-thing? You've got to get that baby to sleep right through the night somehow before I go mad.' Well, what could she say? Or do? Minnie she was. Minnie Mouse. But in a way it suited her, or at any rate she transcended it, a beautiful loving child, her father's darling, mother's too.

Minette uses Minnie as good Catholics use the saints—as an intercessionary power.

Minnie, see what your father wants for breakfast. Minnie, ask your father if we're going out today.

Edgar, Minette, Minnie and Mona.

When Mona was born Minette felt stronger and happier. Edgar, for some reason, was easy and loving. (Minette lost her job: it had been difficult, looking after the six-year-old Minnie, being pregnant again by accident—well, forgetting her pill—still with the house, the shopping and the cleaning to do, and working at the same time: not to mention the washing. They had no washing machine, Edgar feeling, no doubt rightly, that domestic machinery was noisy, expensive, and not really, in the end, labour saving. Something had to give, and it was Minette's work that did, just in time to save her sanity. The gallery was doing well, and of course Minette's earnings had been increasing Edgar's tax. Or so he believed. She tried to explain that they were taxed separately, but he did not seem to hear, let alone believe.) In any case, sitting up in childbed with her hand in Edgar's, happy for once, relaxed, unemployed—and he was quite right, the work did overstrain her, and what was the point—such meaningless, anti-social work amongst such facile, trendy non-people—joking about the new baby's name, she said, listen to her, moaning. Perhaps we'd better call her Moaner. Moaner by name, moaner by nature. Imprudent Minette. And a week later, there he was, with the birth certificate all made out. Mona.

'Good God, woman,' he cried. 'Are you mad? *You* said you wanted Mona. I took *you* at your word. I was doing what *you* wanted.'

'I didn't say that.' She was crying, weak from childbirth, turmoil, the sudden withdrawal of his kindness, his patience.

'Do you want me to produce witnesses?' He was exasperated. She became pregnant again, a year later. She had an abortion. She

66

couldn't cope, Edgar implied that she couldn't, although he never quite said so, so that the burden of the decision was hers and hers alone. But he was right, of course. She couldn't cope. She arranged everything, went to the nursing home by mini-cab, by herself, and came out by mini-cab the next day. Edgar paid half.

Edgar, Minette, Minnie and Mona. Quite enough to be getting on with.

Minette started going to a psychotherapist once a week. Edgar said she had to; she was impossible without. She burned the dinner once or twice—'how hostile you are,' said Edgar, and after that cooked all meals himself, without reference to anyone's tastes, habits, or convenience. Still, he did know best. Minette, Minnie and Mona adapted themselves splendidly. He was an admirable cook, once you got used to garlic with everything, from eggs to fish.

Presently Minette went back to work. Well, Edgar could hardly be expected to pay for the psychotherapist, and, in any case, electricity and gas bills having doubled even in a household almost without domestic appliances—there was no doubt her earnings came in useful. Presently Minette was paying all the household bills—and had promotion. She became a group head with twenty people beneath her. She dealt with clients, executives, creative people, secretaries, assistants, with ease and confidence. Compared to Edgar and home, anyone, anything was easy. But that was only to be expected. Edgar was real life. Advertising agencies—and Edgar was right about this—are make believe. Shut your eyes, snap your fingers, and presto, there one is, large as life. (That is, if you have the right, superficial, rubbishy attitude to make it happen.) And of course, its employees and contacts can be easily manipulated and modified, as dolls can be, in a doll's house. Edgar was not surprised at Minette's success. It was only to be expected. And she never remembered to turn off the lights, and turned up the central heating much too high, being irritatingly sensitive to cold.

Even tonight, this hot sultry night, with the temperature still lingering in the eighties and lightning crackling round the edges of the sky, she shivers.

'You can't be cold,' he enquires. He is buying a property from

Minnie. He owns both Get Out of Jail cards, and has had a bank error in his favour of £200. Minnie is doing nicely, on equal bargaining terms with her father. Minette's in jail again.

'It's just so dark out there,' she murmurs.

'Of course it is,' he said. 'It's the country. You miss the town, don't you?' It is an accusation, not a statement.

The cottage is on a hillside: marsh above and below, interrupting the natural path from the summit to the valley. The windows are open front and back as if to offer least interruption, throwing the house and its inhabitants open to the path of whatever forces flow from the top to the bottom of hills. Or so Minette suspects. How can she say so? She, the town-dweller, the obfuscate, standing between Edgar and the light of his expectations, his sensitivity to the natural life-forces which flow between the earth and him.

Edgar has green fingers, no doubt about it. See his tomatoes in the window-box of his Bond Street gallery? What a triumph!

'Couldn't we have the windows closed?' she asks.

'What for?' he enquires. 'Do *you* want the windows closed, Minnie?'

Minnie shrugs, too intent on missing her father's hotel on Northumberland Avenue to care one way or the other. Minnie has a fierce competitive spirit. Edgar, denying his own, marvels at it.

'Why do you want to shut out the night?' Edgar demands.

'I don't,' Minette protests. But she does. Yes she does. Mona stirs and whimpers upstairs: Minette wants to go to her, close her windows, stop the dark rose heads nodding, whispering distress, but how can she? It is Minette's turn to throw the dice. Her hand trembles. Another five. Chance. You win £10, second prize in beauty contest.

'Not with your nose in that condition,' says Edgar, and laughs. Minnie and Minette laugh as well. 'And your cheeks the colour of poor Mona's. Still one is happy to know there is a natural justice.'

Edgar, Minette, Minnie and Mona.

A crack of thunder splits the air; one second, two seconds, three seconds—and there's the lightning, double forked, streaking down to the oak-blurred ridge of hills in front of the house.

'I love storms,' says Edgar. 'It's coming this way.'

'I'll just go and shut Mona's window,' says Minette.

'She's perfectly all right,' says Edgar. 'Stop fussing and for God's sake stay out of jail. You're casting a gloom, Minette. There's no fun in playing if one's the only one with hotels.' As of course Edgar is, though Minnie's scattering houses up and down the board.

Minette lands on Community. A £20 speeding fine or take a Chance. She takes a Chance. Pay £150 in school fees.

The air remains dry and still. Thunder and lightning, though monstrously active, remain at their distance, the other side of the hills. The front door creaks silently open, of its own volition. Not a whisper of wind—only the baked parched air.

'Ooh,' squeaks Minnie, agreeably frightened.

Minette is dry-mouthed with terror, staring at the black beyond the door.

'A visitor,' cries Edgar. 'Come in, come in,' and he mimes a welcome to the invisible guest, getting to his feet, hospitably pulling back the empty ladderback chair at the end of the table. The house is open, after all, to whoever, whatever, chooses to call, on the way from the top of the hill to the bottom.

Minette's mouth is open: her eyes appalled. Edgar sees, scorns, sneers.

'Don't, Daddy,' says Minnie. 'It's spooky,' but Edgar is not to be stopped.

'Come in,' he repeats. 'Make yourself at home. Don't stumble like that. Just because you've got no eyes.'

Minette is on her feet. Monopoly money, taken up by the first sudden gust of storm wind, flies about the room. Minnie pursues it, half-laughing, half-panicking.

Minette tugs her husband's inflexible arm.

'Stop,' she beseeches. 'Don't tease. Don't.' No eyes! Oh, Edgar, Minette, Minnie and Mona, what blindness is there amongst you now? What threat to your existence? An immense peal of thunder crackles, it seems, directly overhead: lightning, both sheet and fork, dims the electric light and achieves a strobe-lighting effect of cosmic vulgarity, blinding and bouncing round the white walls, and now, upon the wind, rain, large-dropped, blows in through open doors and windows.

'Shut them,' shrieks Minette. 'I told you. Quickly! Minnie, come and help——'

'Don't fuss. What does it matter? A little rain. Surely you're not frightened of storms?' enquires Edgar, standing just where he is, not moving, not helping, like some great tree standing up to a torrent. For once Minette ignores him and with Minnie, gets door and windows shut. The rain changes its nature, becomes drenching and blinding; their faces and clothes are wet with it. Minnie runs up to Mona's room, to make that waterproof. Still Edgar stands, smiling, staring out of the window at the amazing splitting sky. Only then, as he smiles, does Minette realise what she has done. She has shut the thing, the person with no eyes, in with her family. Even if it wants to go, would of its own accord drift down on its way towards the valley, it can't.

Minette runs to open the back door. Edgar follows, slow and curious.

'Why do you open the back door,' he enquires, 'having insisted on shutting everything else? You're very strange, Minette.'

Wet, darkness, noise, fear make her brave.

'You're the one who's strange. A man with no eyes!' she declares, sharp and brisk as she sometimes is at her office, chiding inefficiency, achieving sense and justice. 'Fancy asking in a man with no eyes. What sort of countryman would do a thing like that? You know nothing about anything, people, country, nature. Nothing.'

I know more than he does, she thinks, in this mad excess of arrogance. I may work in an advertising agency, I may prefer central heating to carrying coals, and a frozen pizza to a fresh mackerel, but I grant the world its dignity. I am aware of what I don't know, what I don't understand, and that's more than you can do. My body moves with the tides, bleeds with the moon, burns in the sun: I, Minette, I am a poor passing fragment of humanity: I obey laws I only dimly understand, but I am aware that the penalty of defying them is at best disaster, at worst death.

Thing with no eyes. Yes. The Taniwha. The Taniwha will get you if you don't look out! The sightless blundering monster of the bush, catching little children who stumble into him, devouring brains, bones, eyes and all. On that wild Australasian shore which my husband does not recognise as country, being composed of sand, shore and palmy forest, rather than of patchworked fields and thatch, lurked a blind and eyeless thing, that's where the Taniwha lives. The Taniwha will get you if you don't watch out! Little Minette, Mona's age, shrieked it at her infant enemies, on her father's instruction. That'll frighten them, he said, full of admonition, care, as ever. They'll stop teasing, leave you alone. Minette's father, tall as a tree, legs like poles. Little Minette's arms clasped round them to the end, wrenched finally apart, to set him free to abandon her, leave her to the Taniwha. The Taniwha will get you if you don't watch out. Wish it on others, what happens to you? Serve you right, with knobs on.

'You know nothing about anything,' she repeats now. 'What country person, after dark, sits with the windows open and invites in invisible strangers? Especially blindness.'

Well, Edgar is angry. Of course he is. He stares at her bleakly. Then Edgar steps out of the back door into the rain, now fitful rather than torrential, and flings himself upon his back on the grass, face turned to the tumultuous heavens, arms outspread, drinking in noise, rain, wind, nature, at one with the convulsing universe.

Minnie joins her mother at the door.

'What's he doing?' she asks, nervous.

'Being at one with nature,' observes Minette, cool and casual for Minnie's benefit. 'He'll get very wet, I'm afraid.'

Rain turns to hail, spattering against the house like machine-gun bullets. Edgar dives for the safety of the house, stands in the kitchen drying his hair with the dish towel, silent, angrier than ever.

'Can't we go on with Monopoly?' beseeches Minnie from the doorway. 'Can't we, Mum? The money's only got a little damp. I've got it all back.'

'Not until your father puts that chair back as it was.'

'What chair, Minette?' enquires Edgar, so extremely annoyed with his wife that he is actually talking to her direct. The rest of the holiday is lost, she knows it.

'The ladderback chair. You asked in something from the night to sit on it,' cries Minette, over the noise of nature, hung now for a sheep as well as a lamb, 'now put it back where it was.'

71

Telling Edgar what to do? Impudence.

'You are mad,' he says seriously. 'Why am I doomed to marry mad women?' Edgar's first wife Hetty went into a mental home after a year of marriage and never re-emerged. She was a very trying woman, according to Edgar.

Mad? What's mad in a mad world? Madder than the dice, sending Minette to jail, back and back again, sending Edgar racing round the board, collecting money, property, power: pacing Minnie in between the two of them, but always nearer her father than her mother? Minnie, hot on Edgar's heels, learning habits to last a lifetime?

All the same, oddly, Edgar goes to the ladderback chair, left pulled back for its unseen guest, and puts it in its original position, square against the table.

'Stop being so spooky,' cries Minnie, 'both of you.'

Minette wants to say 'and now tell it to go away——' but her mouth won't say the words. It would make it too much there. Acknowledgement is dangerous; it gives body to the insubstantial.

Edgar turns to Minette. Edgar smiles, as a sane person, humouring, smiles at an insane one. And he takes Minette's raincoat from the peg, wet as he already is, and races off through the wind to see if the car windows have been properly closed.

Minette is proud of her Bonnie Cashin raincoat. It cost £120, though she told Edgar it was £15.50, reduced from £23. It has never actually been in the rain before and she fears for its safety. She can't ask Edgar not to wear it. He would look at her in blank unfriendliness and say 'but I thought it was a raincoat. You described it as a raincoat. If it's a raincoat why can't you use it in the rain? Or were you lying to me? It isn't a raincoat after all?'

Honestly, she'd rather the coat shrunk than went through all that. Silly garment to have bought in the first place: Edgar was quite right. Well, would have been had he known—and she had, he was right again, been lying. Minette sometimes wonders why she tells so many lies. Her head is dizzy.

The chair at the top of the table seems empty. The man with no eyes is out of the house: Edgar, coat over head, can be seen

72

through the rain haze, stumbling past the front hedge towards the car. Will lightning strike him? Will he fall dead? No.

If the car windows are open, whose fault? Hers, Minnie's?

'I wish you'd see that Mona shut the car door after her.' Her fault, as Mona's mother. 'And why haven't you woken her? This is a wonderful storm.'

And up he goes to be a better mother to Mona than Minette will ever be, waking his reluctant, sleep-heavy younger daughter to watch the storm, taking her on his knee, explaining the nature and function of electrical discharge the while: now ignoring Minette's presence entirely. When annoyed with her, which is much of the time, for so many of Minette's attitudes and pretentions irritate Edgar deeply, he chooses to pretend she doesn't exist.

Edgar, Minette, Minnie and Mona, united, watching a storm from a holiday cottage. Happy families.

The storm passes: soon it is like gunfire, flashing and banging on the other side of the hills. The lights go out. A power-line down, somewhere. No one shrieks, not even Mona: it merely, suddenly, becomes dark. But oh how dark the country is.

'Well,' says Edgar presently, 'where are the matches? Candles?'

Where, indeed. Minette gropes, useless, trembling, up and down her silent haunted home. How foolish of Minette, knowing there was a storm coming, knowing (surely!) that country storms meant country power cuts, not to have located them earlier. Edgar finds them; he knew where they were all the time.

They go to bed. Edgar and Minette pass on the stairs. He is silent. He is not talking to her. She talks to him.

'Well,' she says, 'you're lucky. All he did was make the lights go out. The man with no eyes.'

He does not bother to reply. What can be said to a mad woman that's in any way meaningful?

All night Edgar sleeps on the far edge of the double bed, away from her, forbidding even in his sleep. So away from her, he will sleep for the next four or even five days. Minette lies awake for an hour or so, and finally drifts off into a stunned and unrefreshing sleep.

In the morning she is brisk and smiling for the sake of the children, her voice fluty with false cheer, like some Kensington lady in Harrod's food store. Sweeping the floor, before breakfast, she avoids the end of the table, and the ladderback chair. The man with no eyes has gone, but something lingers.

Edgar makes breakfast. He is formal with her in front of the children, silent when they are on their own, deaf to Minette's pleasantries. Presently she falls silent too. He adorns a plate of scrambled eggs with buttercups and adjures the children to eat them. Minette has some vague recollection of reading that buttercups are poisonous: she murmurs something of the sort and Edgar winces, visibly. She says no more.

No harm comes to the children, of course. She must have misremembered. Edgar plans omelette, a buttercup salad and nettle soup for lunch. That will be fun, he says. Live off the land, like we're all going to have to, soon.

Minette and Mona giggle and laugh and shriek, clutching nettles. If you squeeze they don't sting. Minette, giggling and laughing to keep her children company, has a pain in her heart. They love their father. He loves them.

After lunch—omelette with lovely rich fresh farm eggs, though actually the white falls flat and limp in the bowl and Minette knows they are at least ten days old, but also knows better than to say so, buttercup salad, and stewed nettles, much like spinach—Edgar tells the children that the afternoon is to be spent at an iron age settlement, on Cumber Hill. Mona weeps a little, fearing a hilltop alive with iron men, but Minnie explains there will be nothing there—just a few lumps and bumps in the springy turf, burial mounds and old excavations, and a view all round, and perhaps a flint or two to be found.

'Then why are we going?' asks Mona, but no one answers. 'Will there be walking? Will there be cows? I've got a blister.'

'Mona by name, moaner by nature,' remarks Edgar. But which comes first, Minette wonders. Absently, she gives Minnie and Mona packet biscuits. Edgar protests. Artificial sugar, manufactured crap, ruining teeth, digestion, morale. What kind of mother is she?

'But they're hungry,' she wants to say and doesn't, knowing the reply by heart. How can they be? They've just had lunch.

In the car first Mona is sick, then Minnie. They are both easily sick, and neatly, out of the car window. Edgar does not stop. He says 'you shouldn't have given them those biscuits. I knew this would happen,' but he does slow down.

Edgar, Minette, Minnie and Mona. Biscuits, buttercups and boiled nettles. Something's got to give.

Cumber Hill, skirted by car, is wild and lovely: a smooth turfed hilltop wet from last night's rain, a natural fort, the ground sloping sharply away from the broad summit, where sheep now graze, humped with burial mounds. Here families lived, died, grieved, were happy—fought off invaders, perished: left something of themselves behind, numinous beneath a heavy sky.

Edgar parks the car a quarter of a mile from the footpath which leads through stony farmland to the hill itself, and the tracks which skirt the fortifications. It will be a long walk. Minnie declines to come with them, as is her privilege as her father's daughter. She will sit in the car and wait and listen to the radio. A nature programme about the habits of buzzards, she assures her father.

'We'll be gone a couple of hours,' warns Minette.

'That long? It's only a hill.'

'There'll be lots of interesting things. Flints, perhaps. Even fossils. Are you sure?'

Minnie nods, her eyes blank with some inner determination.

'If she doesn't want to come, Minette,' says Edgar, 'she doesn't. It's her loss.'

It is the first direct remark that Edgar has made to Minette all day. Minette is pleased, smiles, lays her hand on his arm. Edgar ignores her gesture. Did she really think his displeasure would so quickly evaporate? Her lack of perception will merely add to its duration.

Their walking sticks lie in the back of the car—Minette's a gnarled fruit-tree bough, Edgar's a traditional lackthorn (antique, with a carved dog's head for a handle, bought for him by Minette on the occasion of his forty-second birthday, and costing too much, he said by £5, being £20) and Minnie's and Mona's being stout

75

but mongrel lengths of branch from some unnamed and undistinguished tree. Edgar hands Mona her stick, takes up his own and sets off. Minette picks up hers and follows behind. So much for disgrace.

Edgar is brilliant against the muted colours of the hill—a tall, long-legged rust-headed shape, striding in orange holiday trousers and red shirt, leaping from hillock to hillock, rock to rock, black stick slashing against nettle and thistle and gorse. Mona, trotting along beside him, stumpy legged, navy-anoraked, is a stocky, valiant, enthusiastic little creature, perpetually falling over her stick but declining to relinquish it.

Mona presently falls behind and walks with her mother, whom she finds more sympathetic than her father as to nettle-sting and cow-pats. Her hand is dry and firm in Minette's. Minette takes comfort from it. Soon Edgar, relieved of Mona's presence, is so far ahead as to be a dark shape occasionally bobbing into sight over a mound or out from behind a wall or tree.

'I don't see any iron men,' says Mona. 'Only nettles and sheep mess. And cow splats, where I'm walking. Only I don't see any cows either. I expect they're invisible.'

'All the iron men died long ago.'

'Then why have we come here?'

'To think about things.'

'What things?'

'The past, the present, the future,' replies Minette.

The wind gets up, blowing damply in their faces. The sun goes in: the hills lose what colour they had. All is grey, the colour of depression. Winter is coming, thinks Minette. Another season, gone. Clouds, descending, drift across the hills, lie in front of them in misty swathes. Minette can see neither back nor forward. She is frightened: Edgar is nowhere to be seen.

'There might be savage cows in there,' says Mona, 'where we can't see.'

'Wait,' she says to Mona, 'wait,' and means to run ahead to find Edgar, bring him back; but Edgar appears again as if at her will, within earshot, off on a parallel path to theirs, which will take him on yet another circumnavigation of the lower-lying fortifications.

76

'I'll take Mona back to the car,' she calls. He looks astonished. 'Why?'

He does not wait for her answer: he scrambles over a hillock and disappears.

'Because,' she wants to call after him, 'because I am forty, alone and frightened. Because my period started yesterday, and I have a pain. Because my elder child sits alone in a car in mist and rain, and my younger one stands grizzling on a misty hilltop, shivering with fright, afraid of invisible things, and cold. Because if I stay a minute longer I will lose my way and wander here forever. Because battles were fought on this hilltop, families who were happy died and something remains behind, by comparison with which the Taniwha, sightless monster of the far-off jungle, those white and distant shores, is a model of goodwill.'

Minette says nothing: in any case he has gone.

'Let's get back to the car,' she says to Mona.

'Where is it?' enquires Mona, pertinently.

'We'll find it.'

'Isn't Daddy coming?'

'He'll be coming later.'

Something of Minette's urgency communicates itself to Mona: or some increasing fear of the place itself. Mona leads the way back, without faltering, without complaint, between nettles, over rocks, skirting the barbed-wire fence, keeping a safe distance from the cows, at last made flesh, penned up on the other side of the fence.

The past. Minette at Mona's age, leading her weeping mother along a deserted beach to their deserted cottage. Minette's father, prime deserter. Man with no eyes for Minette's distress, her mother's despair. Little Minette with her arms clutched rigidly round her father's legs, finally disentangled by determined adult arms. Whose? She does not know. Her father walking off with someone else, away from the wailing Minette, his daughter, away from the weeping mother, his wife. Later, it was found that one of Minette's fingers was broken. He never came back. Sunday outings, thereafter, just the two of them, Minette and mother, valiantly striving for companionable pleasure, but what use is a three-legged stool with two legs? That's what they were.

The present? Mist, clouds, in front, behind; the wind blowing her misery back in her teeth. Minette and Mona stumble, hold each other up. The clouds part. There's the road: there's the car. Only a few hundred yards. There is Minnie, red hair gleaming, half-asleep, safe.

'England home and safety!' cries Minette, ridiculous, and with this return to normalcy, however baffling, Mona sits down on the ground and refuses to go another step, and has to be entreated, cajoled and bluffed back to the car.

'Where's Daddy?' complains Minnie. It is her children's frequent cry. That and 'Are you all right, Mummy?'

'We got tired and came back,' says Minette.

'I suppose he'll be a long time. He always is.'

Minette looks at her watch. Half-past four. They've been away an hour and a half.

'I should say six o'clock.' Edgar's walks usually last for three hours. Better resign herself to this, than to exist in uneasy expectation.

'What will we do?'

'Listen to the radio. Read. Think. Talk. Wait. It's very nice up here. There's a view.'

'I've been looking at it for three hours,' says Minnie, resigned. 'Oh well.'

'But I'm hungry,' says Mona. 'Can I have an iced lolly?'

'Idiot,' says Minnie to her sister. 'Idiot child.'

There is nothing in sight except the empty road, hills, mist. Minette can't drive. Edgar thinks she would be a danger to herself and others if she learned. If there was a village within walking distance she would take the children off for tea, but there is nothing. She and Minnie consult the maps and discover this sad fact. Mona, fortunately, discovers an ant's nest. Minnie and Minette play I-Spy. Minette, busy, chirpy, stands four square between her children and desolation.

Five o'clock. Edgar reappears, emerging brilliantly out of the mist, from an unexpected direction, smiling satisfaction.

'Wonderful,' he says. 'I can't think why you went back, Minette.'

'Mummy was afraid of the cows,' says Mona.

'Your mother is afraid of everything,' says Edgar. 'I'm afraid she and nature don't get along together.'

They pile back into the car and off they go. Edgar starts to sing. 'One man went to mow.' They all join in. Happy families. A cup of tea, thinks Minette. How I would love a cup of immoral tea, a plate of fattening sandwiches, another of ridiculous iced cakes, in one of the beamed and cosy tea-houses in which the Kentish villages abound. How long since Minette had a cup of tea? How many years? Edgar does not like tea—does not approve of eating between meals. Tea is a drug, he says: it is the rot of the English: it is a laughable substance, a false stimulant, of no nutritive value whatsoever, lining the stomach with tannin. Tea! Minette, do you want a cup of tea? Of course not. Edgar is right. Minette's mother died of stomach cancer, after a million comforting cups. Perhaps they did instead of sex? The singing stops. In the back of the car, Minette keeps silent; presently cries silently, when Mona, exhausted falls asleep. Last night was disturbed.

The future? Like the past, like the present. Little girls who lose their fathers cry all their lives. Hard to blame Edgar for her tears: no doubt she makes Edgar the cause of them. He says so often enough. Mona and Minette shall not lose their father, she is determined on it. Minette will cry now and forever, so that Minnie and Mona can grow up to laugh—though no doubt their laughter, as they look back, will be tinged with pity, at best, and derision, at worst, for a mother who lived as theirs did. Minnie and Mona, saved from understanding.

I am of the lost generation, thinks Minette, one of millions. Interleaving, blotting up the miseries of the past, to leave the future untroubled. I would be happier dead, but being alive, of necessity, might as well make myself useful. She sings softly to the sleeping Mona, chats brightly to Minnie.

Edgar, Minette, Minnie and Mona. Nothing gives.

That night, when Mona is in bed, and Minnie has set up the Monopoly board, Edgar moves as of instinct into the ladderback chair, and Minette plays Monopoly, Happy Families, with the Man with no Eyes.

79

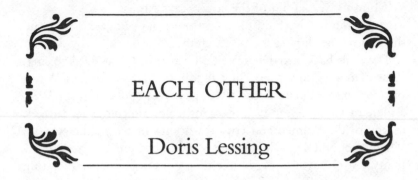

EACH OTHER

Doris Lessing

'I suppose your brother's coming again?'

'He might.'

He kept his back bravely turned while he adjusted tie, collar; and jerked his jaw this way and that to check his shave. Then, with all pretexts used, he remained rigid, his hand on his tie-knot, looking into the mirror past his left cheek at the body of his wife, which was disposed prettily on the bed, weight on its right elbow, its two white forearms engaged in the movements obligatory for filing one's nails. He let his hand drop and demanded: 'What do you mean, he *might*?' She did not answer, but held up a studied hand to inspect five pink arrows. She was a thin, very thin, dark girl of about eighteen. Her pose, her way of inspecting her nails, her pink-striped night-shirt which showed long, thin white legs—all her magazine attitudes, were an attempt to hide an anxiety as deep as his; for her breathing, like his, was loud and shallow.

He was not taken in. The lonely fever in her black eyes, the muscles showing rod-like in the flesh of her upper arm, made him feel how much she wanted him to go; and he thought, sharp because of the sharpness of his need for her: There's something unhealthy about her, yes ... the word caused him guilt. He accepted it, and allowed his mind, which was over-alert, trying to pin down the cause of his misery, to add: Yes, not clean, dirty. But this fresh criticism surprised him, and he remembered her obsessive care of her flesh, hair, nails, and the long hours spent in the bath. *Yes, dirty*, his rising aversion insisted.

Armed by it, he was able to turn, slowly, to look at her direct, instead of through the cold glass. He was a solid, well-set-up, brushed, washed young man who had stood several inches shorter than she at the wedding a month ago but with confidence in the manhood which had mastered her freakish adolescence. He now kept on her the pressure of a blue stare both appealing (of which he was not aware) and aggressive—which he meant as a warning. Meanwhile, he controlled a revulsion which he knew would vanish if she merely lifted her arms towards him.

'What do you mean, he *might*?' he said again.

After some moments of not answering, she said, languid, turning her thin hand this way and that: 'I said, he might.'

This dialogue echoed, for both of them, not only from five minutes before; but from other mornings, when it had been as often as not unspoken. They were on the edge of disaster. But the young husband was late. He looked at his watch, a gesture which said, but unconvincingly, bravado merely: I go out to work while you lie there ... then he about-turned, and went to the door, slowing on his way to it. Stopped. Said: 'Well, in that case I shan't be back to supper.'

'Suit yourself,' she said, languid. She now lay flat on her back, and waved both hands in front of her eyes to dry nail varnish which, however, was three days old.

He said loudly: 'Freda! I mean it. I'm not going to ...' He looked both trapped and defiant; but intended to do everything, obviously, to maintain his self-respect, his masculinity, in the face of—but what? Her slow smile across at him was something (unlike everything else she had done since waking that morning) she was quite unaware of. She surely could not be aware of the sheer brutality of her slow, considering contemptuous smile? For it had invitation in it; and it was this, the unconscious triumph there that caused him to pale, to begin a stammering: 'Fre-Fre-Fred-Freda ...' but give up, and leave the room. Abruptly though quietly, considering the force of his horror.

She lay still, listening to his footsteps go down, and the front door closing. Then, without hurrying, she lifted her long, thin white legs that ended in ten small pink shields over the edge of the bed and stood on them by the window, to watch her husband's well-brushed head jerking away along the pavement. This was a suburb of London, and he had to get to the City, where he was a clerk-with-prospects: and most of the other people down there were on their way to work. She watched him and them, until at the corner he turned, his face lengthened with anxiety. She indolently waved, without smiling. He stared back, as if at a memory of nightmare; so she shrugged and removed herself from the window, and did not see his frantically too-late wave and smile.

She now stood, frowning, in front of the long glass in the new wardrobe: a very tall girl, stooped by her height, all elbows and knees, and even more ridiculous because of the short night-shirt. She stripped this over her head, taking assurance in a side glance from full-swinging breasts and a rounded waist; then slipped on a white négligé that had frills all down it and around the neck, from which her head emerged, poised. She now looked much better, like a model, in fact. She brushed her short, gleaming black hair, stared at length into the deep anxious eyes, and got back into bed.

Soon she tensed, hearing the front door open, softly; and close, softly again. She listened, as the unseen person also listened and watched; for this was a two-roomed flatlet, converted in a semi-detached house. The landlady lived in the flatlet below this one on the ground floor; and the young husband had taken to asking her, casually, every evening, or listening, casually, to easily-given information, about the comings-and-goings in the house and the movements of his wife. But the steps came steadily up towards her, the door opened, very gently, and she looked up, her face bursting into flower as in came a very tall, lank, dark young man. He sat on the bed beside his sister, took her thin hand in his thin hand, kissed it, bit it lovingly, then bent to kiss her on the lips. Their mouths held while two pairs of deep black eyes held each other. Then she shut her eyes, took his lower lip between her teeth, and slid her tongue along it. He began to undress before she let him go; and she asked, without any of the pertness she used for her husband: 'Are you in a hurry this morning?'

'Got to get over to a job in Exeter Street.'

An electrician, he was not tied to desk or office.

He slid naked into bed beside his sister, murmuring: 'Olive Oyl.'

Her long body was pressed against his in a fervour of gratitude for the love-name, for it had never received absolution from her husband as it did from this man; and she returned, in as loving a murmur: 'Pop-eye.' Again the two pairs of eyes stared into each other at an inch or so's distance. His, though deep in bony sockets like hers, were prominent there, the eyeballs rounded under thin, already crinkling, bruised-looking flesh. Hers, however, were delicately outlined by clear white skin, and he kissed the perfected copies of his own ugly eyes, and said, as she pressed towards him: 'Now, now, Olive Oyl, don't be in such a hurry, you'll spoil it.'

'No we won't.'

'*Wait*, I tell you.'

'All right then ...'

The two bodies, deeply breathing, remained still a long while. Her hand, on the small of his back, made a soft, circular pressing motion, bringing him inwards. He had his two hands on her hip-bones, holding her still. But she succeeded, and they joined, and he said again: 'Wait now. Lie still.' They lay absolutely still, eyes closed.

After a while he asked suddenly: 'Well, did he last night?'

'Yes.'

His teeth bared against her forehead and he said: 'I suppose you made him.'

'Why *made* him?'

'You're a pig.'

'All right, then, how about Alice?'

'Oh her! Well, she screamed and said: Stop, Stop.'

'Who's a pig, then?'

She wriggled circularly, and he held her hips still, tenderly murmuring: 'No, no, no, no.'

Stillness again. In the small bright bedroom, with the suburban sunlight outside, new green curtains blew in, flicking the too-large, too-new furniture, while the long white bodies remained still, mouth-to-mouth, eyes closed, united by deep soft breaths.

But his breathing deepened; his nails dug into the bones of

her hips, he slid his mouth free and said: 'How about Charlie then?'

'He made me scream, too,' she murmured, licking his throat, eyes closed. This time it was she who held his loins steady, saying: 'No, no, no, you'll spoil it.'

They lay together, still. A long silence, a long quiet. Then the fluttering curtains roused her, her foot tensed, and she rubbed it delicately up and down his leg. He said, angry, 'Why did you spoil it then, it was just beginning.'

'It's much better afterwards if it's really difficult.' She slid and pressed her internal muscles to make it more difficult, grinning at him in challenge, and he put his hands around her throat in a half-mocking, half-serious pressure to stop her, simultaneously moving in and out of her with exactly the same emulous, taunting but solicitous need she was showing—to see how far they both could go. In a moment they were pulling each other's hair, biting, sinking fingers between thin bones, and then, just before the explosion, they pulled apart, at the same moment, and lay separate, trembling.

'We only just made it,' he said, fond, uxorious, stroking her hair.

'Yes. Careful now, Fred.'

They slid together again.

'Now it will be just perfect,' she said, content, mouth against his throat.

The two bodies, quivering with strain, lay together, jerking involuntarily from time to time. But slowly they quietened. Their breathing, jagged at first, smoothed. They breathed together. They had become one person, abandoned against and in each other, silent and gone.

A long time, a long time, a long ...

A car went past below in the usually silent street, very loud, and the young man opened his eyes and looked into the relaxed gentle face of his sister.

'Freda.'

'Ohhhh!'

'Yes, I've got to go, it must be nearly dinner time.'

'Wait a minute.'

'No, or we'll get excited again, we'll spoil everything.'

They separated gently, but the movements both used, the two hands gently on each other's hips, easing their bodies apart, were more like a fitting together. Separate, they lay still, smiling at each other, touching each other's faces with fingertips, licking each other's eyelids with small cat-licks.

'It gets better and better.'

'Yes.'

'Where did you go this time?'

'You know.'

'Yes.'

'Where did you go?'

'You know. Where you were.'

'Yes. Tell me.'

'Can't.'

'I know. Tell me.'

'With you.'

'Yes.'

'Are we one person then?'

'Yes.'

'Yes.'

Silence again. Again. Again he roused himself.

'Where are you working this afternoon?'

'I told you. It's a baker's shop in Exeter Street.'

'And afterwards?'

'I'm taking Alice to the pictures.'

She bit her lips, punishing them and him, then sunk her nails into his shoulder.

'Well, my darling, I just make her, that's all, I make her come, she wouldn't understand anything better.'

He sat up, began dressing. In a moment he was a tall, sober youth in a dark blue sweater. He slicked down his hair with the young husband's hairbrushes, as if he lived here, while she lay naked, watching.

He turned and smiled, affectionate and possessive, like a husband. There was something in her face, a lost desperation, that made his harden. He crouched beside her, scowling, baring his teeth, gently fitting his thumb on her windpipe, looking straight into her dark eyes. She breathed hoarsely, and coughed. He let his thumb drop.

'What's that for, Fred?'

'You swear you don't do that with Charlie?'

'How could I?'

'What do you mean, you could show him.'

'But why? Why do you think I want to? Fred!'

The two pairs of deep eyes, in bruised flesh, looked lonely with uncertainty into each other.

'How should I know what you want.'

'You're stupid,' she said suddenly, with a small maternal smile.

He dropped his head, with a breath like a groan, on to her breasts, and she stroked his head gently, looking over it at the wall, blinking tears out of her eyes. She said: 'He's not coming to supper tonight, he's angry.'

'Is he?'

'He keeps talking about you. He asked today if you were coming.'

'Why, does he guess?' He jerked his head up off the soft support of her bosom, and stared, his face bitter, into hers. 'Why? You haven't been stupid now, have you?'

'No, but, Fred ... but after you've been with me I suppose I'm different. ...'

'Oh Christ!' He jumped up, desperate, beginning movements of flight, anger, hate, escape—checking each one. 'What do you want then? You want me to make you come then? Well, that's easy enough, isn't it, if that's all you want. All right then, lie down and I'll do it, and I'll make you come till you cry, if that's all ...' He was about to strip off his clothes; but she shot up from the bed, first hastily draping herself in her white frills, out of an instinct to protect what they had. She stood by him, as tall as he, holding his arms down by his sides. 'Fred, Fred, Fred, darling, my sweetheart, don't spoil it, don't spoil it now when ...'

'When what?'

She met his fierce look with courage, saying steadily: 'Well, what do you expect, Fred? He's not stupid, is he? I'm not a ... he makes love to me, well, he is my husband, isn't he? And ... Well what about you and Alice, you do the same, it's normal, isn't it? Perhaps if you and I didn't have Charlie and Alice for coming, we wouldn't be able to do it our way, have you thought of that?'

'Have I thought of that! Well, what do you think?'

'Well, it's normal, isn't it?'

'Normal,' he said, with horror, gazing into her loving face for reassurance against the word. 'Normal, is it? Well, if you're going to use words like that ...' Tears ran down his face, and she kissed them away in a passion of protective love.

'Well, why did you say I must marry him? I didn't want to, you said I should.'

'I didn't think it would spoil us.'

'But it hasn't, has it, Fred? Nothing could be like us. How could it? You know that from Alice, don't you Fred?' Now she was anxiously seeking for his reassurance. They stared at each other, then their eyes closed, and they laid their cheeks together and wept, holding down each other's amorous hands, for fear that what they were might be cheapened by her husband, his girl.

He said, 'What were you beginning to say?'

'When?'

'Just now. You said, don't spoil it now *when*.'

'I get scared.'

'Why?'

'Suppose I get pregnant? Well, one day I must, it's only fair, he wants kids. Suppose he leaves me—he gets in the mood to leave me, like today. Well, he feels something ... it stands to reason. It doesn't matter how much I try with him, you know he feels it ... Fred?'

'What.'

'There isn't any law against it, is there?'

'Against what?'

'I mean, a brother and sister can share a place, no one would say anything.'

He stiffened away from her: 'You're crazy.'

'Why am I? Why, Fred?'

'You're just not thinking, that's all.'

'What are we going to do, then?'

87

He didn't answer, and she sighed, letting her head lie on his shoulder beside his head, so that he felt her open eyes and their wet lashes on his neck.

'We can't do anything but go on like this, you've got to see that.'

'Then I've got to be nice to him, otherwise he's going to leave me, and I don't blame him.'

She wept, silently; and he held her, silent.

'It's so hard—I just wait for when you come, Fred, and I have to pretend all the time.'

They stood silent, their tears drying, their hands linked. Slowly they quieted, in love and in pity, in the same way that they quieted in their long silences when the hungers of the flesh were held by love on the edge of fruition so long that they burned out and up and away into a flame of identity.

At last they kissed, brother-and-sister kisses, gentle and warm.

'You're going to be late, Fred. You'll get the sack.'

'I can always get another job.'

'I can always get another husband. . . .'

'Olive Oyl . . . but you look really good in that white naygleejay.'

'Yes, I'm just the type that's no good naked, I need clothes.'

'That's right—I must go.'

'Coming tomorrow?'

'Yes. About ten?'

'Yes.'

'Keep him happy, then. Ta-ta.'

'Look after yourself—look after yourself, my darling, look after yourself. . . .'

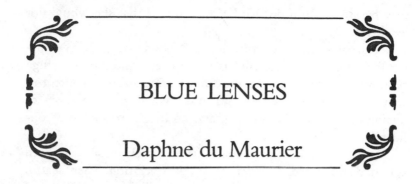

BLUE LENSES

Daphne du Maurier

This was the day for the bandages to be removed and the blue lenses fitted. Marda West put her hand up to her eyes and felt the crêpe binder, and the layer upon layer of cotton-wool beneath. Patience would be rewarded at last. The days had passed into weeks since her operation, and she had lain there suffering no physical discomfort, but only the anonymity of darkness, a negative feeling that the world and the life around was passing her by. During the first few days there had been pain, mercifully allayed by drugs, and then the sharpness of this wore down, dissolved, and she was left with a sense of great fatigue, which they assured her was reaction after shock. As for the operation itself, it had been successful. Here was definite promise. A hundred per cent successful.

'You will see,' the surgeon told her, 'more clearly than ever before.'

'But how can you tell?' she urged, desiring her slender thread of faith to be reinforced.

'Because we examined your eyes when you were under the anaesthetic,' he replied, 'and again since, when we put you under for a second time. We would not lie to you, Mrs West.'

This reassurance came from them two or three times a day, and she had to steel herself to patience as the weeks wore by, so that she referred to the matter perhaps only once every twenty-four hours, and then by way of a trap, to catch them unawares. 'Don't throw the roses out. I should like to see them,' she would say, and the day-nurse would be surprised into the admission. 'They'll be over before you can do that.' Which meant that she would not see this week.

Actual dates were never mentioned. Nobody said, 'On the fourteenth of the month you will have your eyes.' And the subterfuge continued, the pretence that she did not mind and was content to wait. Even Jim, her husband, was now classed in the category of 'them', the staff of the hospital, and no longer treated as a confidante.

Once, long ago, every qualm and apprehension had been admitted and shared. This was before the operation. Then, fearful of pain and blindness, she had clung to him and said, 'What if I never see again, what will happen to me?' picturing herself as helpless and maimed. And Jim, whose anxiety was no less harsh than hers, would answer, 'Whatever comes, we'll go through it together.'

Now, for no known reason except that darkness, perhaps, had made her more sensitive, she was shy to discuss her eyes with him. The touch of his hand was the same as it had ever been, and his kiss, and the warmth of his voice; but always, during these days of waiting, she had the seed of fear that he, like the staff at the hospital, was being too kind. The kindness of those who knew towards the one who must not be told. Therefore, when at last it happened, when at his evening visit the surgeon said, 'Your lenses will be fitted tomorrow,' surprise was greater than joy. She could not say anything, and he had left the room before she could thank him. It was really true. The long agony had ended. She permitted herself only a last feeler, before the day-nurse went off duty—'They'll take some getting used to, and hurt a bit at first?'—her statement of fact put as a careless question. But the voice of the woman who had tended her through so many weary days replied, 'You won't know you've got them, Mrs West.'

Such a calm, comfortable voice, and the way she shifted the pillows and held the glass to the patient's lips, the hand smelling faintly of the Morny French Fern soap with which she washed her, these things gave confidence and implied that she could not lie.

'Tomorrow I shall see you,' said Marda West, and the nurse, with the cheerful laugh that could be heard sometimes down the corridor outside, answered, 'Yes, I'll give you your first shock.'

It was a strange thought how memories of coming into the nursing-home were now blunted. The staff who had received her were dim shadows, the room assigned to her, where she still lay, like a wooden box built only to entrap. Even the surgeon, brisk and efficient during those two rapid consultations when he had recommended an immediate operation, was a voice rather than a presence. He gave his orders and the orders were carried out, and it was difficult to reconcile this bird-of-passage with the person who, those several weeks ago, had asked her to surrender herself to him, who had in fact worked this miracle upon the membranes and the tissues which were her living eyes.

'Aren't you feeling excited?' This was the low, soft voice of her night-nurse, who, more than the rest of them, understood what she had endured. Nurse Brand, by day, exuded a daytime brightness; she was a person of sunlight, of bearing in fresh flowers, of admitting visitors. The weather she described in the world outside appeared to be her own creation. 'A real scorcher,' she would say, flinging open windows, and her patient would sense the cool uniform, the starched cap, which somehow toned down the penetrating heat. Or else she might hear the steady fall of rain and feel the slight chill accompanying it. 'This is going to please the gardeners, but it'll put paid to Matron's day on the river.'

Meals, too, even the dullest of lunches, were made to appear delicacies through her method of introduction. 'A morsel of brill *au beurre*?' she would suggest happily, whetting reluctant appetite, and the boiled fish that followed must be eaten, for all its tastelessness, because otherwise it would seem to let down Nurse Brand, who had recommended it. 'Apple fritters—you can manage two, I'm sure,' and the tongue began to roll the imaginary fritter, crisp as a flake and sugared, which in reality had a languid, leathery substance. And so her cheerful optimism brooked no discontent—it would be offensive to complain, lacking in backbone to admit, 'Let me just lie. I don't want anything.'

The night brought consolation and Nurse Ansel. She did not expect courage. At first, during pain, it had been Nurse Ansel who had administered the drugs. It was she who had smoothed the pillows and held the glass to the parched lips. Then, with the passing weeks, there had been the gentle voice and the quiet encouragement. 'It will soon pass. This waiting is the worst.' At night the patient had only to touch the bell, and in a moment Nurse Ansel was by the bed. 'Can't sleep? I know, it's wretched for you. I'll give you just two and a half grains, and the night won't seem so long.'

How compassionate, that smooth and silken voice. The imagination, making fantasies through enforced rest and idleness, pictured some reality with Nurse Ansel that was not hospital—a holiday abroad, perhaps, for the three of them, and Jim playing golf with an unspecified male companion, leaving her, Marda, to wander with Nurse Ansel. All she did was faultless. She never annoyed. The small shared intimacies of night-time brought a bond between nurse and patient that vanished with the day, and when she went off duty, at five minutes to eight in the morning, she would whisper, 'Until this evening,' the very whisper stimulating anticipation, as though eight o'clock that night would not be clocking-in but an assignation.

Nurse Ansel understood complaint. When Marda West said wearily, 'It's been such a long day,' her answering 'Has it?' implied that for her too the day had dragged, that in some hostel she had tried to sleep and failed, that now only did she hope to come alive.

It was with a special secret sympathy that she would announce the evening visitor. 'Here is someone you want to see, a little earlier than usual,' the tone suggesting that Jim was not the husband of ten years but a troubadour, a lover, someone whose bouquet of flowers had been plucked in an enchanted garden and now brought to a balcony. 'What gorgeous lilies!', the exclamation half a breath and half a sigh, so that Marda West imagined exotic dragon-petalled beauties growing to heaven, and Nurse Ansel, a little priestess, kneeling. Then shyly, the voice would murmur, 'Good evening, Mr West. Mrs West is waiting for you.' She would hear the gentle closing of the door, the tip-toeing out with the lilies and the almost soundless return, the scent of the flowers filling the room.

It must have been during the fifth week that Marda West had tentatively suggested, first to Nurse Ansel and then to her husband, that perhaps when she returned home the night-nurse might go with them for the first week. It would chime with Nurse Ansel's own holiday. Just a week. Just so that Marda West could settle to home again.

'Would you like me to?' Reserve lay in the voice, yet promise too.

'I would. It's going to be so difficult at first.' The patient, not knowing what she meant by difficult, saw herself as helpless still, in spite of the new lenses, and needing the protection and the reassurance that up to the present only Nurse Ansel had given her. 'Jim, what about it?'

His comment was something between surprise and indulgence. Surprise that his wife considered a nurse a person in her own right, and indulgence because it was the whim of a sick woman. At least, that was how it seemed to Marda West, and later, when the evening visit was over and he had gone home, she said to the night-nurse, 'I can't make out whether my husband thought it a good idea or not.'

The answer was quiet yet reassuring. 'Don't worry. Mr West is reconciled.'

But reconciled to what? The change in routine? Three people round the table, conversation, the unusual status of a guest who, devoting herself to her hostess, must be paid? (Though the last would not be mentioned, but glossed over at the end of a week in an envelope.)

'Aren't you feeling excited?' Nurse Ansel, by the pillow, touched the bandages, and it was the warmth in the voice, the certainty that only a few hours now would bring revelation, which stifled at last all lingering doubt of success. The operation had not failed. Tomorrow she would see once more.

'In a way,' said Marda West, 'it's like being born again. I've forgotten how the world looks.'

'Such a wonderful world,' murmured Nurse Ansel, 'and you've been patient for so long.'

The sympathetic hand expressed condemnation of all those who had insisted upon bandages through the waiting weeks. Greater indulgence might have been granted had Nurse Ansel herself been in command and waved a wand.

'It's queer,' said Marda West, 'tomorrow you won't be a voice to me any more. You'll be a person.'

'Aren't I a person now?'

A note of gentle teasing, of pretended reproach, which was all part of the communication between them, so soothing to the patient. This must surely, when sight came back, be foregone.

'Yes, of course, but it's bound to be different.'

'I don't see why.'

Even knowing she was dark and small—for so Nurse Ansel had described herself—Marda West must be prepared for surprise at the first encounter, the tilt of the head, the slant of the eyes, or perhaps some unexpected facial form like too large a mouth, too many teeth.

'Look, feel ...' and not for the first time Nurse Ansel took her patient's hand and passed it over her own face, a little embarrassing, perhaps, because it implied surrender, the patient's hand a captive. Marda West, withdrawing it, said with a laugh, 'It doesn't tell me a thing.'

'Sleep, then. Tomorrow will come too soon.' There came the familiar routine of the bell put within reach, the last-minute drink, the pill, and then the soft, 'Good night, Mrs West. Ring if you want me.'

'Thank you. Good night.'

There was always a slight sense of loss, of loneliness, as the door closed and she went away, and a feeling of jealousy, too, because there were other patients who received these same mercies, and who, in pain, would also ring their bells. When she awoke—and this often happened in the small hours—Marda West would no longer picture Jim at home, lonely on his pillow, but would have an image of Nurse Ansel, seated perhaps by someone's bed, bending to give comfort, and this alone would make her reach for the bell, and press her thumb upon it, and say, when the door opened, 'Were you having a nap?'

'I never sleep on duty.'

She would be seated, then, in the cubby-hole midway along the passage, perhaps drinking tea or entering particulars of charts into a ledger. Or standing beside a patient, as she now stood beside Marda West.

'I can't find my handkerchief.'

'Here it is. Under your pillow all the time.'

A pat on the shoulder (and this in itself was a sort of delicacy), a few moments of talk to prolong companionship, and then she would be gone, to answer other bells and other requests.

'Well, we can't complain of the weather!' Now it was the day itself, and Nurse Brand coming in like the first breeze of morning, a hand on a barometer set fair. 'All ready for the great event?' she asked. 'We must get a move on, and keep your prettiest nightie to greet your husband.'

It was her operation in reverse. This time in the same room, though, and not a stretcher, but only the deft hands of the surgeon with Nurse Brand to help him. First came the disappearance of the crêpe, the lifting of the bandages and lint, the very slight prick of an injection to dull feeling. Then he did something to her eyelids. There was no pain. Whatever he did was cold, like the slipping of ice where the bandages had been, yet soothing too.

'Now, don't be disappointed,' he said. 'You won't know any difference for about half an hour. Everything will seem shadowed. Then it will gradually clear. I want you to lie quietly during that time.'

'I understand. I won't move.'

The longed-for moment must not be too sudden. This made sense. The dark lenses, fitted inside her lids, were temporary for the first few days. Then they would be removed and others fitted.

'How much shall I see?' The question dared at last.

'Everything. But not immediately in colour. Just like wearing sunglasses on a bright day. Rather pleasant.'

His cheerful laugh gave confidence, and when he and Nurse Brand had left the room she lay back again, waiting for the fog to clear and for that summer day to break in upon her vision, however subdued, however softened by the lenses.

Little by little the mist dissolved. The first object was angular, a wardrobe. Then a chair. Then, moving her head, the gradual forming of the window's shape, the vases on the sill, the flowers Jim had brought her. Sounds from the street outside merged with the shapes, and what had seemed sharp before was now in harmony. She thought to herself, 'I wonder if I can cry? I wonder if the lenses will keep back tears,' but, feeling the blessing of sight restored, she felt the tears as well, nothing to be ashamed of—one or two which were easily brushed away.

All was in focus now. Flowers, the wash-basin, the glass with the thermometer in it, her dressing gown. Wonder and relief were so great that they excluded thought.

'They weren't lying to me,' she thought. 'It's happened. It's true.'

The texture of the blanket covering her, so often felt, could now be seen as well. Colour was not important. The dim light caused by the blue lenses enhanced the charm, the softness of all she saw. It seemed to her, rejoicing in form and shape, that colour would never matter. There was time enough for colour. The blue symmetry of vision itself was all-important. To see, to feel, to blend the two together. It was indeed rebirth, the discovery of a world long lost to her.

There seemed to be no hurry now. Gazing about the small room and dwelling upon every aspect of it was richness, something to savour. Hours could be spent just looking at the room and feeling it, travelling through the window and to the window of the houses opposite.

'Even a prisoner,' she decided, 'could find comfort in his cell if he had been blinded first, and had recovered his sight.'

She heard Nurse Brand's voice outside, and turned her head to watch the opening door.

'Well ... are we happy once more?'

Smiling, she saw the figure dressed in uniform come into the room, bearing a tray, her glass of milk upon it. Yet, incongruous, absurd, the head with the uniformed cap was not a woman's head at all. The thing bearing down upon her was a cow ... a cow on a woman's body. The frilled cap was perched upon wide horns.

The eyes were large and gentle, but cow's eyes, the nostrils broad and humid, and the way she stood there, breathing, was the way a cow stood placidly in pasture, taking the day as it came, content, unmoved.

'Feeling a bit strange?'

The laugh was a woman's laugh, a nurse's laugh, Nurse Brand's laugh, and she put the tray down on the cupboard beside the bed. The patient said nothing. She shut her eyes, then opened them again. The cow in the nurse's uniform was with her still.

'Confess now,' said Nurse Brand, 'you wouldn't know you had the lenses in, except for the colour.'

It was important to gain time. The patient stretched out her hand carefully for the glass of milk. She sipped the milk slowly. The mask must be worn on purpose. Perhaps it was some kind of experiment connected with the fitting of the lenses—though how it was supposed to work she could not imagine. And it was surely taking rather a risk to spring such a surprise, and, to people weaker than herself who might have undergone the same operation, downright cruel?

'I see very plainly,' she said at last. 'At least, I think I do.'

Nurse Brand stood watching her, with folded arms. The broad uniformed figure was much as Marda West had imagined it, but that cow's head tilted, the ridiculous frill of the cap perched on the horns ... where did the head join the body, if mask it in fact was?

'You don't sound too sure of yourself,' said Nurse Brand. 'Don't say you're disappointed, after all we've done for you.'

The laugh was cheerful, as usual, but she should be chewing grass, the slow jaws moving from side to side.

'I'm sure of myself,' answered her patient, 'but I'm not so sure of you. Is it a trick?'

'Is what a trick?'

'The way you look ... your ... face?'

Vision was not so dimmed by the blue lenses that she could not distinguish a change of expression. The cow's jaw distinctly dropped.

'Really, Mrs West!' This time the laugh was not so cordial.

Surprise was very evident. 'I'm as the good God made me. I dare say he might have made a better job of it.'

The nurse, the cow, moved from the bedside towards the window and drew the curtains more sharply back, so that the full light filled the room. There was no visible join to the mask: the head blended to the body. Marda West saw how the cow, if she stood at bay, would lower her horns.

'I didn't mean to offend you,' she said, 'but it *is* just a little strange. You see ...'

She was spared explanation because the door opened and the surgeon came into the room. At least, the surgeon's voice was recognisable as he called, 'Hullo! How goes it?', and his figure in the dark coat and the sponge-bag trousers was all that an eminent surgeon's should be, but ... that terrier's head, ears pricked, the inquisitive, searching glance? In a moment surely he would yap, and a tail wag swiftly?

This time the patient laughed. The effect was ludicrous. It must be a joke. It was, it had to be; but why go to such expense and trouble, and what in the end was gained by the deception? She checked her laugh abruptly as she saw the terrier turn to the cow, the two communicate with each other soundlessly. Then the cow shrugged its too ample shoulders.

'Mrs West thinks us a bit of a joke,' she said. But the nurse's voice was not over-pleased.

'I'm all for that,' said the surgeon. 'It would never do if she took a dislike to us, would it?'

Then he came and put his hand out to his patient, and bent close to observe her eyes. She lay very still. He wore no mask either. None, at least, that she could distinguish. The ears were pricked, the sharp nose questing. He was even marked, one ear black, the other white. She could picture him at the entrance to a fox's lair, sniffing, then quick on the scent scuffing down the tunnel, intent upon the job for which he was trained.

'Your name ought to be Jack Russell,' she said aloud.

'I beg your pardon?'

He straightened himself but still stood beside the bed, and the bright eye had a penetrating quality, one ear cocked.

'I mean,' Marda West searched for words, 'the name seems to suit you better than your own.'

She felt confused. Mr Edmund Greaves, with all the letters after him on the plate in Harley Street, what must he think of her?

'I know a James Russell,' he said to her, 'but he's an orthopaedic surgeon and breaks your bones. Do you feel I've done that to you?'

His voice was brisk, but he sounded a little surprised, as Nurse Brand had done. The gratitude which was owed to their skill was not forthcoming.

'No, no, indeed,' said the patient hastily, 'nothing is broken at all, I'm in no pain. I see clearly. Almost too clearly, in fact.'

'That's as it should be,' he said, and the laugh that followed resembled a short sharp bark.

'Well, nurse,' he went on, 'the patient can do everything within reason except remove the lenses. You've warned her, I suppose?'

'I was about to, sir, when you came in.'

Mr Greaves turned his pointed terrier nose to Marda West.

'I'll be in on Thursday,' he said, 'to change the lenses. In the meantime, it's just a question of washing out the eyes with a solution three times a day. They'll do it for you. Don't touch them yourself. And above all don't fiddle with the lenses. A patient did that once and lost his sight. He never recovered it.'

'If you tried that,' the terrier seemed to say, 'you would get what you deserved. Better not make the attempt. My teeth are sharp.'

'I understand,' said the patient slowly. But her chance had gone. She could not now demand an explanation. Instinct warned her that he would not understand. The terrier was saying something to the cow, giving instructions. Such a sharp staccato sentence, and the foolish head nodded in answer. Surely on a hot day the flies would bother her—or would the frilled cap keep insects away?

As they moved to the door the patient made a last attempt.

'Will the permanent lenses,' she asked, 'be the same as these?'

'Exactly the same,' yapped the surgeon, 'except that they won't be tinted. You'll see the natural colour. Until Thursday, then.'

He was gone, and the nurse with him. She could hear the murmur of voices outside the door. What happened now? If it was really some kind of test, did they remove their masks instantly?

It seemed to Marda West of immense importance that she should find this out. The trick was not truly fair: it was a misuse of confidence. She slipped out of bed and went to the door. She could hear the surgeon say, 'One and a half grains. She's a little overwrought. It's the reaction, of course.'

Bravely, she flung open the door. They were standing there in the passage, wearing the masks still. They turned to look at her, and the sharp bright eyes of the terrier, the deep eyes of the cow, both held reproach, as though the patient, by confronting them, had committed a breach of etiquette.

'Do you want anything, Mrs West?' asked Nurse Brand.

Marda West stared beyond them down the corridor. The whole floor was in the deception. A maid, carrying dust-pan and brush, coming from the room next door, had a weasel's head upon her small body, and the nurse advancing from the other side was a little prancing kitten, her cap coquettish on her furry curls, the doctor beside her a proud lion. Even the porter, arriving at that moment in the lift opposite, carried a boar's head between his shoulders. He lifted out luggage, uttering a boar's heavy grunt.

The first sharp prick of fear came to Marda West. How could they have known she would open the door at that minute? How could they have arranged to walk down the corridor wearing masks, the other nurses, and the other doctor, and the maid appear out of the room next door, and the porter come up in the lift? Something of her fear must have shown in her face, for Nurse Brand, the cow, took hold of her and led her back into her room.

'Are you feeling all right, Mrs West?' she asked anxiously.

Marda West climbed slowly into bed. If it was a conspiracy what was it all for? Were the other patients to be deceived as well?

'I'm rather tired,' she said, 'I'd like to sleep.'

'That's right,' said Nurse Brand, 'you got a wee bit excited.'

She was mixing something in the medicine glass, and this time, as Marda West took the glass, her hand trembled. Could a cow see clearly how to mix medicine? Supposing she made a mistake?

'What are you giving me?' she asked.

'A sedative,' answered the cow.

100

Buttercups and daisies. Lush green grass. Imagination was strong enough to taste all three in the mixture. The patient shuddered. She lay down on her pillow and Nurse Brand drew the curtains close.

'Now just relax,' she said, 'and when you wake up you'll feel so much better.' The heavy head stretched forward—in a moment it would surely open its jaws and moo.

The sedative acted swiftly. Already a drowsy sensation filled the patient's limbs.

Soon peaceful darkness came, but she awoke, not to the sanity she had hoped for, but to lunch brought in by the kitten. Nurse Brand was off duty.

'How long must it go on for?' asked Marda West. She had resigned herself to the trick. A dreamless sleep had restored energy and some measure of confidence. If it was somehow necessary to the recovery of her eyes, or even if they did it for some unfathomable reason of their own, it was their business.

'How do you mean, Mrs West?' asked the kitten, smiling. Such a flighty little thing, with its pursed-up mouth, and even as it spoke it put a hand to its cap.

'This test on my eyes,' said the patient, uncovering the boiled chicken on her plate. 'I don't see the point of it. Making yourself such guys. What is the object?'

The kitten, serious, if a kitten could be serious, continued to stare at her. 'I'm sorry, Mrs West,' she said, 'I don't follow you. Did you tell Nurse Brand you couldn't see properly yet?'

'It's not that I can't see,' replied Marda West. 'I see perfectly well. The chair is a chair. The table is a table. I'm about to eat boiled chicken. But why do you look like a kitten, and a tabby kitten at that?'

Perhaps she sounded ungracious. It was hard to keep her voice steady. The nurse—Marda West remembered the voice, it was Nurse Sweeting, and the name suited her—drew back from the trolley-table.

'I'm sorry,' she said, 'if I don't come up to scratch. I've never been called a cat before.'

Scratch was good. The claws were out already. She might purr to the lion in the corridor, but she was not going to purr to Marda West.

'I'm not making it up,' said the patient. 'I see what I see. You are a cat, if you like, and Nurse Brand's a cow.'

This time the insult must sound deliberate. Nurse Sweeting had fine whiskers to her mouth. The whiskers bristled.

'If you please, Mrs West,' she said, 'will you eat your chicken, and ring the bell when you are ready for the next course?'

She stalked from the room. If she had a tail, thought Marda West, it would not be wagging, like Mr Greaves's, but twitching angrily.

No, they could not be wearing masks. The kitten's surprise and resentment had been too genuine. And the staff of the hospital could not possibly put on such an act for one patient, for Marda West alone—the expense would be too great. The fault must lie in the lenses, then. The lenses, by their very nature, by some quality beyond the layman's understanding, must transform the person who was perceived through them.

A sudden thought struck her, and pushing the trolley-table aside she climbed out of bed and went over to the dressing-table. Her own face stared back at her from the looking-glass. The dark lenses concealed the eyes, but the face was at least her own.

'Thank heaven for that,' she said to herself, but it swung her back to thoughts of trickery. That her own face should seem unchanged through the lenses suggested a plot, and that her first idea of masks had been the right one. But why? What did they gain by it? Could there be a conspiracy amongst them to drive her mad? She dismissed the idea at once—it was too fanciful. This was a reputable London nursing-home, and the staff was well known. The surgeon had operated on royalty. Besides, if they wanted to send her mad, or kill her even, it would be simple enough with drugs. Or with anaesthetics. They could have given her too much anaesthetic during the operation, and just let her die. No one would take the roundabout way of dressing up staff and doctors in animals' masks.

She would try one further proof. She stood by the window, the curtain concealing her, and watched for passers-by. For the moment there was no one in the street. It was the lunch-hour, and traffic was slack. Then, at the other end of the street, a taxi crossed, too far away for her to see the driver's head. She waited. The porter came out from the nursing-home and stood on the steps, looking up and down. His boar's head was clearly visible. He did not count, though. He could be part of the plot. A van drew near, but she could not see the driver . . . yes, he slowed as he went by the nursing-home and craned from his seat, and she saw the squat frog's head, the bulging eyes.

Sick at heart, she left the window and climbed back into bed. She had no further appetite and pushed away her plate, the rest of the chicken untasted. She did not ring her bell, and after a while the door opened. It was not the kitten. It was the little maid with the weasel's head.

'Will you have plum tart or ice cream, madam?' she asked.

Marda West, her eyes half-closed, shook her head. The weasel, shyly edging forward to take the tray, said, 'Cheese, then, and coffee to follow?'

The head joined the neck without any fastening. It could not be a mask, unless some designer, some genius, had invented masks that merged with the body, blending fabric to skin.

'Coffee only,' said Marda West.

The weasel vanished. Another knock on the door and the kitten was back again, her back arched, her fluff flying. She plonked the coffee down without a word, and Marda West, irritated—for surely, if anyone was to show annoyance, it should be herself?— said sharply, 'Shall I pour you some milk in the saucer?'

The kitten turned. 'A joke's a joke, Mrs West,' she said, 'and I can take a laugh with anyone. But I can't stick rudeness.'

'Miaow,' said Marda West.

The kitten left the room. No one, not even the weasel, came to remove the coffee. The patient was in disgrace. She did not care. If the staff of the nursing-home thought they could win this battle, they were mistaken. She went to the window again. An elderly cod, leaning on two sticks, was being helped into a waiting car by the boar-headed porter. It could not be a plot. They could not know she was watching them. Marda went to the telephone and asked the exchange to put her through to her husband's office. She remembered a moment afterwards that he would still be at lunch.

Nevertheless, she got the number, and as luck had it he was there.

'Jim ... Jim, darling.'

'Yes?'

The relief to hear the loved familiar voice. She lay back on the bed, the receiver to her ear.

'Darling, when can you get here?'

'Not before this evening, I'm afraid. It's one hell of a day, one thing after another. Well, how did it go? Is everything O.K.?'

'Not exactly.'

'What do you mean? Can't you see? Greaves hasn't bungled it, has he?'

How was she to explain what had happened to her? It sounded so foolish over the telephone.

'Yes, I can see. I can see perfectly. It's just that ... that all the nurses look like animals. And Greaves, too. He's a fox terrier. One of those little Jack Russells they put down the foxes' holes.'

'What on earth are you talking about?'

He was saying something to his secretary at the same time, something about another appointment, and she knew from the tone of his voice that he was very busy, very busy, and she had chosen the worst time to ring him up. 'What do you mean about Jack Russell?' he repeated.

Marda West knew it was no use. She must wait till he came. Then she would try to explain everything, and he would be able to find out for himself what lay behind it.

'Oh, never mind,' she said. 'I'll tell you later.'

'I'm sorry,' he told her, 'but I really am in a tearing hurry. If the lenses don't help you, tell somebody. Tell the nurses, the Matron.'

'Yes,' she said, 'yes.'

Then she rang off. She put down the telephone. She picked up a magazine, one left behind at some time or other by Jim himself, she supposed. She was glad to find that reading did not hurt her eyes. Nor did the blue lenses make any difference, for the photographs of men and women looked normal, as they had always done. Wedding groups, social occasions, débutantes, all were as usual. It was only here, in the nursing-home itself and in the street outside, that they were different.

It was much later in the afternoon that Matron called in to have a word with her. She knew it was Matron because of her clothes. But inevitably now, without surprise, she observed the sheep's head.

'I hope you're quite comfortable, Mrs West?'

A note of gentle inquiry in the voice. A suspicion of a baa?

'Yes, thank you.'

Marda West spoke guardedly. It would not do to ruffle the Matron. Even if the whole affair was some gigantic plot, it would be better not to aggravate her.

'The lenses fit well?'

'Very well.'

'I'm so glad. It was a nasty operation, and you've stood the period of waiting so very well.'

That's it, thought the patient. Butter me up. Part of the game, no doubt.

'Only a few days, Mr Greaves said, and then you will have them altered and the permanent ones fitted.'

'Yes, so he said.'

'It's rather disappointing not to observe colour, isn't it?'

'As things are, it's a relief.'

The retort slipped out before she could check herself. The Matron smoothed her dress. And if you only knew, thought the patient, what you look like, with that tape under your sheep's chin, you would understand what I mean.

'Mrs West ...' The Matron seemed uncomfortable, and turned her sheep's head away from the woman in the bed. 'Mrs West, I hope you won't mind what I'm going to say, but our nurses do a fine job here and we are all very proud of them. They work long hours, as you know, and it is not really very kind to mock them, although I am sure you intended it in fun.'

Baa. ... Baa. ... Bleat away. Marda West tightened her lips.

'Is it because I called Nurse Sweeting a kitten?'

'I don't know what you called her, Mrs West, but she was quite distressed. She came to me in the office nearly crying.'

Spitting, you mean. Spitting and scratching. Those capable little hands are really claws.

'It won't happen again.'

She was determined not to say more. It was not her fault. She had not asked for lenses that deformed, for trickery, for make believe.

'It must come very expensive,' she added, 'to run a nursing-home like this.'

'It is,' said the Matron. Said the sheep. 'It can only be done because of the excellence of the staff, and the cooperation of all our patients.'

The remark was intended to strike home. Even a sheep can turn.

'Matron,' said Marda West, 'don't let's fence with each other. What is the object of it all?'

'The object of what, Mrs West?'

'This tomfoolery, this dressing up.' There, she had said it. To enforce her argument she pointed at the Matron's cap. 'Why pick on that particular disguise? It's not even funny.'

There was silence. The Matron, who had made as if to sit down to continue her chat, changed her mind. She moved slowly to the door.

'We, who were trained at St Hilda's, are proud of our badge,' she said. 'I hope, when you leave us in a few days, Mrs West, that you will look back on us with greater tolerance than you appear to have now.'

She left the room. Marda West picked up the magazine she had thrown down, but the matter was dull. She closed her eyes. She opened them again. She closed them once more. If the chair had become a mushroom and the table a haystack, then the blame could have been put on the lenses. Why was it only people had changed? What was so wrong with people? She kept her eyes shut when her tea was brought her, and when the voice said pleasantly, 'Some flowers for you, Mrs West,' she did not even open them, but waited for the owner of the voice to leave the room. The flowers were carnations. The card was Jim's. And the message on it said, 'Cheer up. We're not as bad as we seem.'

She smiled, and buried her face in the flowers. Nothing false about them. Nothing strange about the scent. Carnations were carnations, fragrant, graceful. Even the nurse on duty who came to put them in water could not irritate her with her pony's head. After all, it was a trim little pony, with a white star on its forehead. It would do well in the ring. 'Thank you,' smiled Marda West.

The curious day dragged on, and she waited restlessly for eight o'clock. She washed and changed her nightgown, and did her hair. She drew her own curtains and switched on the bedside lamp. A strange feeling of nervousness had come upon her. She realized, so strange had been the day, that she had not once thought about Nurse Ansel. Dear, comforting, bewitching Nurse Ansel. Nurse Ansel, who was due to come on duty at eight. Was she also in the conspiracy? If she was, then Marda West would have a showdown. Nurse Ansel would never lie. She would go up to her, and put her hands on her shoulders, and take the mask in her two hands, and say to her, 'There, now take it off. You won't deceive me.' But if it was the lenses, if all the time it was the lenses that were at fault, how was she to explain it?

She was sitting at the dressing-table, putting some cream on her face, and the door must have opened without her being aware; but she heard the well-known voice, the soft beguiling voice, and it said to her, 'I nearly came before. I didn't dare. You would have thought me foolish.' It slid slowly into view, the long snake's head, the twisting neck, the pointed barbed tongue swiftly thrusting and swiftly withdrawn, it came into view over her shoulders, through the looking-glass.

Marda West did not move. Only her hand, mechanically, continued to cream her cheek. The snake was not motionless: it turned and twisted all the time, as though examining the pots of cream, the scent, the powder.

'How does it feel to see yourself again?'

Nurse Ansel's voice emerging from the head seemed all the more grotesque and horrible, and the very fact that as she spoke the darting tongue spoke too paralysed action. Marda West felt sickness rise in her stomach, choking her, and suddenly physical reaction proved too strong. She turned away, but as she did so the steady hands of the nurse gripped her, she suffered herself to be led to her bed, she was lying down, eyes closed, the nausea passing.

'Poor dear, what have they been giving you? Was it the sedative? I saw it on your chart,' and the gentle voice, so soothing and so calm, could only belong to one who understood. The patient did not open her eyes. She did not dare. She lay there on the bed, waiting.

'It's been too much for you,' said the voice. 'They should have kept you quiet, the first day. Did you have visitors?'

'No.'

'Nevertheless, you should have rested. You look really pale. We can't have Mr West seeing you like this. I've half a mind to telephone him to stay away.'

'No ... please, I want to see him. I must see him.'

Fear made her open her eyes, but directly she did so the sickness gripped her again, for the snake's head, longer than before, was twisting out of its nurse's collar, and for the first time she saw the hooded eye, a pin's head, hidden. She put her hand over her mouth to stifle her cry.

A sound came from Nurse Ansel, expressing disquiet.

'Something has turned you very sick,' she said. 'It can't be the sedative. You've often had it before. What was the dinner this evening?'

'Steamed fish. I wasn't hungry.'

'I wonder if it was fresh. I'll see if anyone has complained. Meanwhile, lie still, dear, and don't upset yourself.'

The door quietly opened and closed again, and Marda West, disobeying instructions, slipped from her bed and seized the first weapon that came to hand, her nail-scissors. Then she returned to her bed again, her heart beating fast, the scissors concealed beneath the sheet. Revulsion had been too great. She must defend herself, should the snake approach her. Now she was certain that what was happening was real, was true. Some evil force encompassed the nursing-home and its inhabitants, the Matron, the nurses, the visiting doctors, her surgeon—they were all caught up in it, they were all partners in some gigantic crime, the purpose of which could not be understood. Here, in Upper Watling Street, the malevolent plot was in process of being hatched, and she, Marda West, was one of the pawns; in some way they were to use her as an instrument.

One thing was very certain. She must not let them know that she suspected them. She must try and behave with Nurse Ansel as she had done hitherto. One slip, and she was lost. She must pretend to be better. If she let sickness overcome her, Nurse Ansel might bend over her with that snake's head, that darting tongue.

The door opened and she was back. Marda West clenched her hands under the sheet. Then she forced a smile.

'What a nuisance I am,' she said. 'I felt giddy, but I'm better now.'

The gliding snake held a bottle in her hand. She came over to the wash-basin and, taking the medicine-glass, poured out three drops.

'This should settle it, Mrs West,' she said, and fear gripped the patient once again, for surely the words themselves constituted a threat. 'This should settle it'—settle what? Settle her finish? The liquid had no colour, but that meant nothing. She took the medicine-glass handed to her, and invented a subterfuge.

'Could you find me a clean handkerchief, in the drawer there?'

'Of course.'

The snake turned its head, and as it did so Marda West poured the contents of the glass on to the floor. Then fascinated, repelled, she watched the twisting head peer into the contents of the dressing-table drawer, search for a handkerchief, and bring it back again. Marda West held her breath as it drew near the bed, and this time she noticed that the neck was not the smooth glow-worm neck that it had seemed on first encounter, but had scales upon it, zigzagged. Oddly, the nurse's cap was not ill-fitting. It did not perch incongruously as had the caps of kitten, sheep and cow. She took the handkerchief.

'You embarrass me,' said the voice, 'staring at me so hard. Are you trying to read my thoughts?'

Marda West did not answer. The question might be a trap.

'Tell me,' the voice continued, 'are you disappointed? Do I look as you expected me to look?'

Still a trap. She must be careful. 'I think you do,' she said slowly, 'but it's difficult to tell with the cap. I can't see your hair.'

Nurse Ansel laughed, the low, soft laugh that had been so alluring during the long weeks of blindness. She put up her hands, and in a moment the whole snake's head was revealed, the flat, broad top, the tell-tale adder's V. 'Do you approve?' she asked.

Marda West shrank back against her pillow. Yet once again she forced herself to smile.

'Very pretty,' she said, 'very pretty indeed.'

The cap was replaced, the long neck wriggled, and then, deceived, it took the medicine-glass from the patient's hand and put it back upon the wash-basin. It did not know everything.

'When I go home with you,' said Nurse Ansel, 'I needn't wear uniform—that is, if you don't want me to. You see, you'll be a private patient then, and I your personal nurse for the week I'm with you.'

Marda West felt suddenly cold. In the turmoil of the day she had forgotten the plans. Nurse Ansel was to be with them for a week. It was all arranged. The vital thing was not to show fear. Nothing must seem changed. And then, when Jim arrived, she would tell him everything. If he could not see the snake's head as she did—and indeed, it was possible that he would not, if her hyper-vision was caused by the lenses—he must just understand that for reasons too deep to explain she no longer trusted Nurse Ansel, could not, in fact, bear her to come home. The plan must be altered. She wanted no one to look after her. She only wanted to be home again, with him.

The telephone rang on the bedside-table and Marda West seized it, as she might seize salvation. It was her husband.

'Sorry to be late,' he said. 'I'll jump into a taxi and be with you right away. The lawyer kept me.'

'Lawyer?' she asked.

'Yes, Forbes & Millwall, you remember, about the trust fund.'

She had forgotten. There had been so many financial discussions before the operation. Conflicting advice, as usual. And finally Jim had put the whole business into the hands of the Forbes & Millwall people.

'Oh, yes. Was it satisfactory?'

'I think so. Tell you directly.'

He rang off, and looking up she saw the snake's head watching her. No doubt, thought Marda West, no doubt you would like to know what we were saying to one another.

'You must promise not to get too excited when Mr West comes.' Nurse Ansel stood with her hand upon the door.

'I'm not excited. I just long to see him, that's all.'

'You're looking very flushed.'

'It's warm in here.'

The twisting neck craned upward, then turned to the window. For the first time Marda West had the impression that the snake was not entirely at its ease. It sensed tension. It knew, it could not help but know, that the atmosphere had changed between nurse and patient.

'I'll open the window just a trifle at the top.'

If you were all snake, thought the patient, I could push you through. Or would you coil yourself round my neck and strangle me?

The window was opened, and pausing a moment, hoping perhaps for a word of thanks, the snake hovered at the end of the bed. Then the neck settled in the collar, the tongue darted rapidly in and out, and with a gliding motion Nurse Ansel left the room.

Marda West waited for the sound of the taxi in the street outside. She wondered if she could persuade Jim to stay the night in the nursing-home. If she explained her fear, her terror, surely he would understand. She would know in an instant if he had sensed anything wrong himself. She would ring the bell, make a pretext of asking Nurse Ansel some question, and then, by the expression on his face, by the tone of his voice, she would discover whether he saw what she saw herself.

The taxi came at last. She heard it slow down, and then the door slammed and, blessedly, Jim's voice rang out in the street below. The taxi went away. He would be coming up in the lift. Her heart began to beat fast, and she watched the door. She heard his footstep outside, and then his voice again—he must be saying something to the snake. She would know at once if he had seen the head. He would come into the room either startled, not believing his eyes, or laughing, declaring it a joke, a pantomime. Why did he not hurry? Why must they linger there, talking, their voices hushed?

The door opened, the familiar umbrella and bowler hat the first objects to appear round the corner, then the comforting burly figure, but—God . . . no . . . please God, not Jim too, not Jim, forced into a mask, forced into an organisation of devils, of liars . . . Jim had a vulture's head. She could not mistake it. The brooding eye, the blood-tipped beak, the flabby folds of flesh. As she lay in sick and speechless horror, he stood the umbrella in a corner and put down the bowler hat and the folded overcoat.

'I gather you're not too well,' he said, turning his vulture's head and staring at her, 'feeling a bit sick and out of sorts. I won't stay long. A good night's rest will put you right.'

She was too numb to answer. She lay quite still as he approached the bed and bent to kiss her. The vulture's beak was sharp.

'It's reaction. Nurse Ansel says,' he went on, 'the sudden shock of being able to see again. It works differently with different people. She says it will be much better when we get you home.'

We . . . Nurse Ansel and Jim. The plan still held then.

'I don't know,' she said faintly, 'that I want Nurse Ansel to come home.'

'Not want Nurse Ansel?' He sounded startled. 'But it was you who suggested it. You can't suddenly chop and change.'

There was no time to reply. She had not rung the bell, but Nurse Ansel herself came into the room. 'Cup of coffee, Mr West?' she said. It was the evening routine. Yet tonight it sounded strange, as though it had been arranged outside the door.

'Thanks, Nurse, I'd love some. What's this nonsense about not coming home with us?' The vulture turned to the snake, the snake's head wriggled, and Marda West knew, as she watched them, the snake with darting tongue, the vulture with his head hunched between his man's shoulders, that the plan for Nurse Ansel to come home had not been her own after all; she remembered now that the first suggestion had come from Nurse Ansel herself. It had been Nurse Ansel who had said that Marda West needed care during convalescence. The suggestion had come after Jim had spent the evening laughing and joking and his wife had listened, her eyes bandaged, happy to hear him. Now watching the smooth snake whose adder's V was hidden beneath the nurse's cap, she knew why Nurse Ansel wanted to return with her, and she knew too why Jim had not opposed it, why in fact he had accepted the plan at once, had declared it a good one.

The vulture opened its blood-stained beak. 'Don't say you two have fallen out?'

'Impossible.' The snake twisted its neck, looked sideways at the vulture, and added, 'Mrs West is just a little bit tired tonight. She's had a trying day, haven't you, dear?'

How best to answer? Neither must know. Neither the vulture, nor the snake, nor any of the hooded beasts surrounding her and closing in, must ever guess, must ever know.

'I'm all right,' she said. 'A bit mixed-up. As Nurse Ansel says, I'll be better in the morning.'

The two communicated in silence, sympathy between them. That, she realised now, was the most frightening thing of all. Animals, birds and reptiles had no need to speak. They moved, they looked, they knew what they were about. They would not destroy her, though. She had, for all her bewildered terror, the will to live.

'I won't bother you,' said the vulture, 'with these documents tonight. There's no violent hurry anyway. You can sign them at home.'

'What documents?'

If she kept her eyes averted she need not see the vulture's head. The voice was Jim's, steady and reassuring.

'The trust fund papers Forbes & Millwall gave me. They suggest I should become a co-director of the fund.'

The words struck a chord, a thread of memory belonging to the weeks before her operation. Something to do with her eyes. If the operation was not successful she would have difficulty in signing her name.

'What for?' she asked, her voice unsteady. 'After all, it is my money.'

He laughed. And, turning to the sound, she saw the beak open. It gaped like a trap, and then closed again.

'Of course it is,' he said. 'That's not the point. The point is that I should be able to sign for you, if you should be ill or away.'

Marda West looked at the snake, and the snake, aware, shrank into its collar and slid towards the door. 'Don't stay too long, Mr West,' murmured Nurse Ansel. 'Our patient must have a real rest tonight.'

She glided from the room and Marda West was left alone with her husband. With the vulture.

'I don't propose to go away,' she said, 'or be ill.'

'Probably not. That's neither here nor there. These fellows always want safeguards. Anyway, I won't bore you with it now.'

Could it be that the voice was over-casual? That the hand, stuffing the document into the pocket of the greatcoat, was a claw? This was a possibility, a horror, perhaps to come. The bodies changing too, hands and feet becoming wings, claws, hoofs, paws, with no touch of humanity left to the people about her. The last thing to go would be the human voice. When the human voice went, there would be no hope. The jungle would take over, multitudinous sounds and screams coming from a hundred throats.

'Did you really mean that,' Jim asked, 'about Nurse Ansel?'

Calmly she watched the vulture pare his nails. He carried a file in his pocket. She had never thought about it before—it was part of Jim, like his fountain pen and his pipe. Yet now there was reasoning behind it: a vulture needed sharp claws for tearing its victim.

'I don't know,' she said. 'It seemed to me rather silly to go home with a nurse, now that I can see again.'

He did not answer at once. The head sank deeper between the shoulders. His dark city suit was like the humped feathers of a large brooding bird. 'I think she's a treasure,' he said. 'And you're bound to feel groggy at first. I vote we stick to the plan. After all, if it doesn't work we can always send her away.'

'Perhaps,' said his wife.

She was trying to think if there was anyone left whom she could trust. Her family was scattered. A married brother in South Africa, friends in London, no one with whom she was intimate. Not to this extent. No one to whom she could say that her nurse had turned into a snake, her husband into a vulture. The utter hopeless-

114

ness of her position was like damnation itself. This was her hell. She was quite alone, coldly conscious of the hatred and cruelty about her.

'What will you do this evening?' she asked quietly.

'Have dinner at the club, I suppose,' he answered. 'It's becoming rather monotonous. Only two more days of it, thank goodness. Then you'll be home again.'

Yes, but once at home, once back there, with a vulture and a snake, would she not be more completely at their mercy than she was here?

'Did Greaves say Thursday for certain?' she asked.

'He told me so this morning, when he telephoned. You'll have the other lenses then, the ones that show colour.'

The ones that would show the bodies too. That was the explanation. The blue lenses only showed the heads. They were the first test. Greaves, the surgeon, was in this too, very naturally. He had a high place in the conspiracy—perhaps he had been bribed. Who was it, she tried to remember, who had suggested the operation in the first place? Was it the family doctor, after a chat with Jim? Didn't they both come to her together and say that this was the only chance to save her eyes? The plot must lie deep in the past, extend right back through the months, perhaps the years. But, in heaven's name, for what purpose? She sought wildly in her memory to try to recall a look, or sign, or word which would give her some insight into this dreadful plot, this conspiracy against her person or her sanity.

'You look pretty peaky,' he said suddenly. 'Shall I call Nurse Ansel?'

'No ...' It broke from her, almost a cry.

'I think I'd better go. She said not to stay long.'

He got up from the chair, a heavy, hooded figure, and she closed her eyes as he came to kiss her good night. 'Sleep well, my poor pet, and take it easy.'

In spite of her fear she felt herself clutch at his hand.

'What is it?' he asked.

The well-remembered kiss would have restored her, but not the stab of the vulture's beak, the thrusting blood-stained beak.

When he had gone she began to moan, turning her head upon the pillow.

'What am I to do?' she said. 'What am I to do?'

The door opened again and she put her hand to her mouth. They must not hear her cry. They must not see her cry. She pulled herself together with a tremendous effort.

'How are you feeling, Mrs West?'

The snake stood at the bottom of the bed, and by her side the house physician. She had always liked him, a young pleasant man, and although like the others he had an animal's head it did not frighten her. It was a dog's head, an Aberdeen's, and the brown eyes seemed to quiz her. Long ago, as a child, she had owned an Aberdeen.

'Could I speak to you alone?' she asked.

'Of course. Do you mind, nurse?' He jerked his head at the door, and she had gone. Marda West sat up in bed and clasped her hands.

'You'll think me very foolish,' she began, 'but it's the lenses. I can't get used to them.'

He came over, the trustworthy Aberdeen, head cocked in sympathy.

'I'm sorry about that,' he said. 'They don't hurt you, do they?'

'No,' she said, 'no, I can't feel them. It's just that they make everyone look strange.'

'They're bound to do that, you know. They don't show colour.' His voice was cheerful, friendly. 'It comes as a bit of a shock when you've worn bandages so long,' he said, 'and you mustn't forget you were pulled about quite a bit. The nerves behind the eyes are still very tender.'

'Yes,' she said. His voice, even his head, gave her confidence. 'Have you known people who've had this operation before?'

'Yes, scores of them. In a couple of days you'll be as right as rain.' He patted her on the shoulder. Such a kindly dog. Such a sporting, cheerful dog, like the long-dead Angus. 'I'll tell you another thing,' he continued. 'Your sight may be better after this than it's ever been before. You'll actually see more clearly in every way. One patient told me that it was as though she had been wearing spectacles all her life, and then, because of the operation, she realised she saw all her friends and her family as they really were.'

'As they really were?' She repeated his words after him.

'Exactly. Her sight had always been poor, you see. She had thought her husband's hair was brown, but in reality it was red, bright red. A bit of a shock at first. But she was delighted.'

The Aberdeen moved from the bed, patted the stethoscope on his jacket, and nodded his head. 'Mr Greaves did a wonderful job on you, I can promise you that,' he said. 'He was able to strengthen a nerve he thought had perished. You've never had the use of it before—it wasn't functioning. So who knows, Mrs West, you may have made medical history. Anyway, sleep well and the best of luck. See you in the morning. Good night.' He trotted from the room. She heard him call good night to Nurse Ansel as he went down the corridor.

The comforting words had turned to gall. In one sense they were a relief, because his explanation seemed to suggest there was no plot against her. Instead, like the woman patient before her with the deepened sense of colour, she had been given vision. She used the words he had used himself. Marda West could see people as they really were. And those whom she had loved and trusted most were in truth a vulture and a snake ...

The door opened and Nurse Ansel, with the sedative, entered the room.

'Ready to settle down, Mrs West?' she asked.

'Yes, thank you.'

There might be no conspiracy, but even so all trust, all faith, were over.

'Leave it with a glass of water. I'll take it later.'

She watched the snake put the glass on the bedside table. She watched her tuck in the sheet. Then the twisting neck peered closer and the hooded eyes saw the nail-scissors half-hidden beneath the pillow.

'What have you got there?'

The tongue darted and withdrew. The hand stretched out for the scissors. 'You might have cut yourself. I'll put them away, shall I, for safety's sake?'

117

Her one weapon was pocketed, not replaced on the dressing-table. The very way Nurse Ansel slipped the scissors into her pocket suggested that she knew of Marda West's suspicions. She wanted to leave her defenceless.

'Now, remember to ring your bell if you want anything.'

'I'll remember.'

The voice that had once seemed tender was over-smooth and false. How deceptive are ears, thought Marda West, what traitors to truth. And for the first time she became aware of her own new latent power, the power to tell truth from falsehood, good from evil.

'Good night, Mrs West.'

'Good night.'

Lying awake, her bedside clock ticking, the accustomed traffic sounds coming from the street outside, Marda West decided upon her plan. She waited until eleven o'clock, an hour past the time when she knew that all the patients were settled and asleep. Then she switched out her light. This would deceive the snake, should she come to peep at her through the window-slide in the door. The snake would believe that she slept. Marda West crept out of bed. She took her clothes from the wardrobe and began to dress. She put on her coat and shoes and tied a scarf over her head. When she was ready she went to the door and softly turned the handle. All was quiet in the corridor. She stood there motionless. Then she took one step across the threshold and looked to the left, where the nurse on duty sat. The snake was there. The snake was sitting crouched over a book. The light from the ceiling shone upon her head, and there could be no mistake. There were the trim uniform, the white starched front, the stiff collar, but rising from the collar the twisting neck of the snake, the long, flat, evil head.

Marda West waited. She was prepared to wait for hours. Presently the sound she hoped for came, the bell from a patient. The snake lifted its head from the book and checked the red light on the wall. Then, slipping on her cuffs, she glided down the corridor to the patient's room. She knocked and entered. Directly she had disappeared Marda West left her own room and went to the head of the staircase. There was no sound. She listened carefully, and then crept downstairs. There were four flights, four floors, but the stairway itself was not visible from the cubby-hole where the night nurses sat on duty. Luck was with her.

Down in the main hall the lights were not so bright. She waited at the bottom of the stairway until she was certain of not being observed. She could see the night-porter's back—his head was not visible, for he was bent over his desk—but when it straightened she noticed the broad fish face. She shrugged her shoulders. She had not dared all this way to be frightened by a fish. Boldly she walked through the hall. The fish was staring at her.

'Do you want anything, madam?' he said.

He was as stupid as she expected. She shook her head.

'I'm going out. Good night,' she said, and she walked straight past him, out of the swing-door, and down the steps into the street. She turned swiftly to the left, and, seeing a taxi at the further end, called and raised her hand. The taxi slowed and waited. When she came to the door she saw that the driver had the squat black face of an ape. The ape grinned. Some instinct warned her not to take the taxi.

'I'm sorry,' she said. 'I made a mistake.'

The grin vanished from the face of the ape. 'Make up your mind, lady,' he shouted, and let in his clutch and swerved away.

Marda West continued walking down the street. She turned right and left, and right again, and in the distance she saw the lights of Oxford Street. She began to hurry. The friendly traffic drew her like a magnet, the distant lights, the distant men and women. When she came to Oxford Street she paused, wondering of a sudden where she should go, whom she could ask for refuge. And it came to her once again that there was no one, no one at all; because the couple passing her now, a toad's head on a short black body clutching a panther's arm, could give her no protection, and the policeman standing at the corner was a baboon, the woman talking to him a little prinked-up pig. No one was human, no one was safe, the man a pace or two behind her was like Jim, another vulture. There were vultures on the pavement opposite. Coming towards her, laughing, was a jackal.

She turned and ran. She ran, bumping into them, jackals, hyenas, vultures, dogs. The world was theirs, there was no human left. Seeing her run they turned and looked at her, they pointed, they screamed and yapped, they gave chase, their footsteps followed her. Down Oxford Street she ran, pursued by them, the night all darkness and shadow, the light no longer with her, alone in an animal world.

'Lie quite still, Mrs West, just a small prick, I'm not going to hurt you.'

She recognised the voice of Mr Greaves, the surgeon, and dimly she told herself that they had got hold of her again. She was back at the nursing-home, and it did not matter now—she might as well be there as anywhere else. At least in the nursing-home the animal heads were known.

They had replaced the bandages over her eyes, and for this she was thankful. Such blessed darkness, the evil of the night hidden.

'Now, Mrs West, I think your troubles are over. No pain and no confusion with these lenses. The world's in colour again.'

The bandages were being lightened after all. Layer after layer removed. And suddenly everything was clear, was day, and the face of Mr Greaves smiled down at her. At his side was a rounded, cheerful nurse.

'Where are your masks?' asked the patient.

'We didn't need masks for this little job,' said the surgeon. 'We were only taking out the temporary lenses. That's better, isn't it?'

She let her eyes drift round the room. She was back again all right. This was the shape, there was the wardrobe, the dressing-table, the vases of flowers. All in natural colour, no longer veiled. But they could not fob her off with stories of a dream. The scarf she had put round her head before slipping away in the night lay on the chair.

'Something happened to me, didn't it?' she said. 'I tried to get away.'

The nurse glanced at the surgeon. He nodded his head.

'Yes,' he said, 'you did. And, frankly, I don't blame you. I blame myself. Those lenses I inserted yesterday were pressing upon a tiny nerve, and the pressure threw out your balance. That's all over now.'

His smile was reassuring. And the large warm eyes of Nurse Brand—it must surely be Nurse Brand—gazed down at her in sympathy.

'It was very terrible,' said the patient. 'I can never explain how terrible.'

'Don't try,' said Mr Greaves. 'I can promise you it won't happen again.'

The door opened and the young physician entered. He too was smiling. 'Patient fully restored?' he asked.

'I think so,' said the surgeon. 'What about it, Mrs West?'

Marda West stared gravely at the three of them, Mr Greaves, the house physician and Nurse Brand, and she wondered what palpitating wounded tissue could so transform three individuals into prototypes of an animal kingdom, what cell linking muscle to imagination.

'I thought you were dogs,' she said. 'I thought you were a hunt terrier, Mr Greaves, and that you were an Aberdeen.'

The house physician touched his stethoscope and laughed.

'But I am,' he said, 'it's my native town. Your judgement was not wholly out, Mrs West. I congratulate you.'

Marda West did not join in the laugh.

'That's all right for you,' she said. 'Other people were not so pleasant.' She turned to Nurse Brand. 'I thought you were a cow,' she said, 'a kind cow. But you had sharp horns.'

This time it was Mr Greaves who took up the laugh. 'There you are, nurse,' he said, 'just what I've often told you. Time they put you out to grass and to eat the daisies.'

Nurse Brand took it in good part. She straightened the patient's pillows and her smile was benign. 'We get called some funny things from time to time,' she said. 'That's all part of our job.'

The doctors were moving towards the door, still laughing, and Marda West, sensing the normal atmosphere, the absence of all strain, said, 'Who found me, then? What happened? Who brought me back?'

Mr Greaves glanced back at her from the door. 'You didn't get very far, Mrs West, and a damn good job for you, or you mightn't be here now. The porter followed you.'

'It's all finished with now,' said the house physician, 'and the episode lasted five minutes. You were safely in your bed before any harm was done, and I was here. So that was that. The person who really had the full shock was poor Nurse Ansel when she found you weren't in your bed.'

Nurse Ansel. . . . The revulsion of the night before was not so easily forgotten. 'Don't say our little starlet was an animal too?' smiled the house doctor. Marda West felt herself colour. Lies would have to begin. 'No,' she said quickly, 'no, of course not.'

'Nurse Ansel is here now,' said Nurse Brand. 'She was so upset when she went off duty that she wouldn't go back to the hostel to sleep. Would you care to have a word with her?'

Apprehension seized the patient. What had she said to Nurse Ansel in the panic and fever of the night? Before she could answer the house doctor opened the door and called down the passage.

'Mrs West wants to say good morning to you,' he said. He was smiling all over his face. Mr Greaves waved his hand and was gone, Nurse Brand went after him, and the house doctor, saluting with his stethoscope and making a mock bow, stepped back against the wall to admit Nurse Ansel. Marda West stared, then tremulously began to smile, and held out her hand.

'I'm sorry,' she said, 'you must forgive me.'

How could she have seen Nurse Ansel as a snake! The hazel eyes, the clear olive skin, the dark hair trim under the frilled cap. And that smile, that slow, understanding smile.

'Forgive you, Mrs West?' said Nurse Ansel. 'What have I to forgive you for? You've been through a terrible ordeal.'

Patient and nurse held hands. They smiled at one another. And, oh heaven, thought Marda West, the relief, the thankfulness, the load of doubt and despair that was swept away with the new-found sight and knowledge.

'I still don't understand what happened,' she said, clinging to the nurse. 'Mr Greaves tried to explain. Something about a nerve.'

Nurse Ansel made a face towards the door. 'He doesn't know

himself,' she whispered, 'and he's not going to say either, or he'll find himself in trouble. He fixed those lenses too deep, that's all. Too near a nerve. I wonder it didn't kill you.'

She looked down at her patient. She smiled with her eyes. She was so pretty, so gentle. 'Don't think about it,' she said. 'You're going to be happy from now on. Promise me?'

'I promise,' said Marda West.

The telephone rang, and Nurse Ansel let go her patient's hand and reached for the receiver. 'You know who this is going to be,' she said. 'Your poor husband.' She gave the receiver to Marda West.

'Jim ... Jim, is that you?'

The loved voice sounding so anxious at the other end. 'Are you all right?' he said. 'I've been through to Matron twice, she said she would let me know. What the devil has been happening?'

Marda West smiled and handed the receiver to the nurse.

'You tell him,' she said.

Nurse Ansel held the receiver to her ear. The skin of her hand was olive smooth, the nails gleaming with a soft pink polish.

'Is that you, Mr West?' she said. 'Our patient gave us a fright, didn't she?' She smiled and nodded at the woman in the bed. 'Well, you don't have to worry any more. Mr Greaves changed the lenses. They were pressing on a nerve, and everything is now all right. She can see perfectly. Yes, Mr Greaves said we could come home tomorrow.'

The endearing voice blended to the soft colouring, the hazel eyes. Marda West reached once more for the receiver.

'Jim, I had a hideous night,' she said. 'I'm only just beginning to understand it now. A nerve in the brain ...'

'So I gather,' he said. 'How damnable. Thank God they traced it. That fellow Greaves can't have known his job.'

'It can't happen again,' she said. 'Now the proper lenses are in, it can't happen again.'

'It had better not,' he said, 'or I'll sue him. How are you feeling in yourself?'

'Wonderful,' she said, 'bewildered, but wonderful.'

'Good girl,' he said. 'Don't excite yourself. I'll be along later.'

His voice went. Marda West gave the receiver to Nurse Ansel, who replaced it on the stand.

'Did Mr Greaves really say I could go home tomorrow?' she asked.

'Yes, if you're good.' Nurse Ansel smiled and patted her patient's hand. 'Are you sure you still want me to come with you?' she asked.

'Why, yes,' said Marda West. 'Why, it's all arranged.'

She sat up in bed and the sun came streaming through the window, throwing light on the roses, the lilies, the tall-stemmed iris. The hum of traffic outside was close and friendly. She thought of her garden waiting for her at home, and her own bedroom, her own possessions, the day-to-day routine of home to be taken up again with sight restored, the anxiety and fear of the past months put away for ever.

'The most precious thing in the world,' she said to Nurse Ansel, 'is sight. I know now. I know what I might have lost.'

Nurse Ansel, hands clasped in front of her, nodded her head in sympathy. 'You've got your sight back,' she said, 'that's the miracle. You won't ever lose it now.'

She moved to the door. 'I'll slip back to the hostel and get some rest,' she said. 'Now I know everything is well with you I'll be able to sleep. Is there anything you want before I go?'

'Give me my face-cream and my powder,' said the patient, 'and the lipstick and the brush and comb.'

Nurse Ansel fetched the things from the dressing-table and put them within reach upon the bed. She brought the hand-mirror, too, and the bottle of scent, and with a little smile of intimacy sniffed at the stopper. 'Gorgeous,' she murmured. 'This is what Mr West gave you, isn't it?'

Already, thought Marda West, Nurse Ansel fitted in. She saw herself putting flowers in the small guest-room, choosing the right books, fitting a portable wireless in case Nurse Ansel should be bored in the evenings.

'I'll be with you at eight o'clock.'

The familiar words, said every morning now for so many days and weeks, sounded in her ear like a melody, loved through repetition. At last they were joined to the individual, the person who smiled, the one whose eyes promised friendship and loyalty.

'See you this evening.'

The door closed. Nurse Ansel had gone. The routine of the nursing-home, broken by the fever of the night before, resumed its usual pattern. Instead of darkness, light. Instead of negation, life.

Marda West took the stopper from the scent-bottle and put it behind her ears. The fragrance filtered, becoming part of the warm, bright day. She lifted the hand-mirror and looked into it. Nothing changed in the room, the street noises penetrated from outside, and presently the little maid who had seemed a weasel yesterday came in to dust the room. She said, 'Good morning,' but the patient did not answer. Perhaps she was tired. The maid dusted, and went her way.

Then Marda West took up the mirror and looked into it once more. No, she had not been mistaken. The eyes that stared back at her were doe's eyes, wary before sacrifice, and the timid deer's head was meek, already bowed.

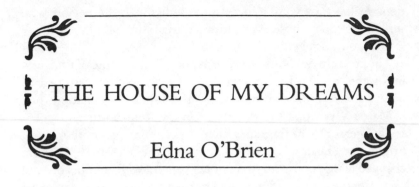

THE HOUSE OF MY DREAMS

Edna O'Brien

She hurried home from the neighbour's house to have a few spare moments to herself. The rooms were stripped, the windows bare, the dust and the disrepair of the ledges totally revealed, everything gone except for the few things she insisted on taking herself—a geranium, a ewer, and a few little china coffee cups that miraculously had escaped being broken. There was a broom against the wall—a soft green twig that scarcely grazed the floor or penetrated to the rubble adhering there. Neighbours were good the day one moved house. No, that was not fair. She had had good neighbours, and a variety of them. She had spent nights with them, got drunk with some of them, slept with one of them, and later regretted it, quarrelled with one of them, and with another had made a definite plan to have a walk in the country, once a week, but excuses always intervened, hers and the woman's.

She went to the children's room and hollered 'Hey round the corner po-po, waiting for Henry Lee.' This was the room where nightly, her children used to squabble over who would have the top bunk, and where she brought cups of hot milk, thick with honey, for the colds and congestions they did not have, and where her elder son used to enjoy looking up at the skylight, listening to the rain go pitter-patter, hoping for the snow to fall, listening (though one cannot hear it) to the sun coming up and lighting the pane of glass, watching the gradual change from dark sheet to transparent sheet, and then to a resemblance of something dipped in a quick wash of bright morning gold. Her son had dreamt that there were pink flamingoes in a glass, a glass that he was drinking from, and that they were there because of a special bacteria in the water. That pink, or rather those multiples of feathered pink, layer upon layer, could compare with no colour that he had ever seen. He feasted on it.

The room was empty except for the marks of casters, the initial J. daubed on the wall, and the various stains. When she repeated 'Hey round the corner, po-po', there was not the slightest hint of an echo. Ah yes! The children had ritually buried a coin under one of the loose floor-boards, and no doubt it was down there, somewhere; in its hole, covered in dust and maybe smeared with cobweb.

The night she had served their father with a custody writ, she had gone all around the house, and lifted off the telephones, and watched them where they lay, somehow like numbed animals, black things or white things, or a red thing, that had gone temporarily dead. In the middle of the night her husband came and slipped the threatening letter in under the hall door (she had nailed down the letter box), and she was there cowering and waiting for it, the letter saying, 'They are mine, they are not yours, you are going to be a nervous corpse if you take this to court, you gain nothing except your gross humiliation, you are bound to lose, I cannot show you any mercy, I am really determined to do everything within the law to get custody of those children, no holds barred.' She had read it and re-read it and wrung her hands and wondered how she could have married such a man.

Another time she had waited in the hall, being too shy to stand at the window and at intervals had pushed the letter box open to peep out into space. She was waiting for a man who did not appear. They happened to have the same birthday and that factor along with his smile, made her think somehow he would come, and listening for the car or the taxis she had found herself in a particular stance, a stance repeated from long ago, waiting behind a window in a flannel nightgown for a man, her father, who anyhow might thrash her to death. It was as if all those past states only begged to be repeated, to be relieved, to go on for ever and ever, amen. Those things like shackles that bound her.

The house had been her fortress. And yet there were snags. The time when a total stranger knocked, a tall thin man, asking if he could have a word with her, stepping inside on to the rubber mat and telling her that he had no intention of leaving her alone. It happened to be late spring, and he was framed by the hawthorn tree and looking at it, and the soft nearly-emergent petals she thought 'If I pretend not to be in the least bit afraid, he will go away.' That was what she did—stared at the tree, giving the impression that someone else was in the house, that she was not petrified, that she was not stranded, not alone. He repeated his intention, then she dismissed him saying, 'We will see about that' and she closed the door very quietly. But back in the house she began to tremble and was too incapacitated even to lift the telephone to call anyone, then when she heard his footsteps go away, she lay down on the floor and wondered why it was that she could not have talked to him, but she knew why it was, because she was petrified of such people. They were usually fanatical, they had a funny stare, and they laughed at things that were no laughing stock. The first such person she had ever come across had been a woman, a tall streelish creature whose mania gave her a wild energy, made her stalk fields, roads, by-roads, lanes, made her rap on people's doors at all hours of day and night, insult them about their jobs, their self-importance, their furniture and everything that they had taken to be enhancing. She could not have appeared casual for fear he might strangle her, or misbehave, treat the floor as a lavatory, or worse, split her head off. She had the glass changed, so that she was enabled to see out but no caller could see in. He came a few times but was told to scarper by a builder, who was in her employment.

It had been a nice lunch, delicate—poached eggs and leaf spinach. When she sat down the neighbour handed her a linen napkin and said 'There you are pet.' They drank wine, they clinked glasses, they recalled Christmases, numerous parties, the Scottish boy whom they both fancied and deceived each other over. At the time it had rankled. She herself had met him on the road one morning, by the merest chance, and he had the temerity to tell her he had been looking for a hardware shop although it was a street solely of private houses. But that was well behind her. The garden would go on blooming. The Virginia creeper would attach itself to everything and finally encumber everything. She had put down three trees, numerous creepers, herbs and wonderful bright shrubs that defied the nourishless London soil. She would recall the garden in times to come, the evenings sitting out on the low wall, looking at the river, or again at the blocks of flats on the opposite side, feeling the vibrations of the distant tube train go right through her stomach and her bowels, admiring the flowers, and sometimes getting down to stake up a rose that had straggled and bowed along the ground. It had been a home. 'No place like home' her parents used to say whenever they went away from their ramshackle farm, to be ill, or to shop for a day, or in the case of her father to go on binges.

She went up to her bedroom. Nothing left of its character but the wallpaper. Beige wallpaper with bosses of red roses, each rose like an embryo bud, and all intricately joined by stems that were as thin as thread, and on the point of ravelling. Not many people had seen her bedroom, but those who had, were still in it like ghosts, spectres, frozen in the positions that they had once unthinkingly occupied. There was a boy, blond, freckled, who had never made love to her, but had harboured some true feelings for her. He used always to arrive with a group but almost always got too drunk to go home, and once though not drunk, felt disinclined to go home and took off his boots by the fire, and held the soles of his feet towards it, asking if by any chance seers read feet, if feet had lines of destiny just like hands. She thought that maybe shyness had deterred him, or maybe distaste. He used to talk in the early morning, the very early morning, touching the stems of the roses with his forefinger, watching the careens of the birds through the window, and the course of the river beyond. People used to envy her that view of the river. Yes it was a shame to leave. At night because of the aspect of the water and its lap, it often seemed as if it were another city altogether, and now just as the trees were beginning to grow she was leaving it all behind. She ought to desecrate it, do some misdeed, such as at school when they got holidays and used to throw compasses and chalk about, used to chant 'Kick up tables, kick up chairs, kick Sister so-and-so down the stairs, no more Latin, no more French, no more sitting on a hard old bench.' But those were the carefree days, or seemed to be.

'I am loathe to leave' she thought, and dragged the broom over the bare wood floor. Dust rose out of nowhere, so she filled a coffee cup with water and spattered it over the floor to keep the motes down. Once, during a very special party she thought that the freckled boy must not be coming, and then just as her hopes were dashed, he arrived with a new girl, a girl not unlike herself, but younger, tougher and more self-assured. The girl had asked for cigars immediately, and strode around the room smoking a cigar, telling all the men that she knew they lusted after her. She was both clever and revolting. At the end of the night there was only the three of them left and they sat in a little huddle. He was right in the throes of a sentence, when all of a sudden he fell fast asleep, the way children do, leaving the two of them to watch over him, which they did like vultures. Together they removed his high boots, his suède jacket, and his outer sweater. When at last the girl fell asleep, she herself went around her own house, stacking glasses, thinking it had been a good party, primarily because he was there. And occasionally, even in those very early days things would suddenly become otherwise, and her heart would enter on a disaster. She would forget a name, even her own name, or a cigarette butt in a glass would be enlarged a hundredfold, and once the violets came out of a brooch and it seemed to her they were exuding either sweat or tears. The cheeky girl rang her employer the moment she wakened, and asked how Kafka, her dog, was. Then she borrowed money and walking away from him with a strut, said 'Isn't he chubby,' his function in her life now completed.

The children used to have parties too, birthday parties, where all the glasses of diluted orange would be lined up on the tray, and the piles of paper hats towered into a cone; and later meringue crumbs would be sent flying about the place and some children would be found crying because they had not gone to the lavatory. It was worst when they left to go away to boarding school—empty rooms, empty beds, and two bicycles just lying there in the shed. They would come home for holidays and there would be the usual bustle again, various garments left on the various steps of the stairs, but it was always as if they were visitors, and gradually the house began to have something of the chilliness of a tomb.

But she met the holy man, and having talked to him at length, and hearing his creed she asked him to join her, to come under her roof. The very first evening, however, she had a premonition, because arriving as he did at the appointed hour, and with his ruck-sack, she saw that he had a black scarf draped over his head, and catching sight of him in the doorway he looked like nothing so much as a harlot—his Asiatic features sharply defined, his eyes like darts and full of expectation. They sat by the fire, she served the casserole, bringing a little table close for him to balance his plate on. He even drank some wine. He told her of his daydream to go by boat down the French canals, throughout the length of a summer. When the time came to retire it seemed to her that he let out some sort of whimper.

Once in her bedroom she locked her door and began to tremble. She had just embarked on another catastrophe. On his way to bed he coughed loudly, and it seemed to her that he lingered on the landing, just outside her door. She was inside, cringing, listening. She seemed to be always listening, cringing, in some bed, or under some bed, or behind some pile of furniture, or behind a door that was weighed down with overcoats and trench-coats. She seemed to be always the culprit, although in truth the other person was the killer.

In the morning the holy man slipped a note under her bedroom door, to say she was to join him the moment she wakened, as they did not want to lose a moment of their precious time together. She greeted him coldly in the kitchen, but already she could see that he was hanging on her words, on her looks, and on her every gesture. After three days it was intolerable. His sighs filled the house, and the rooms that were tolerably cheerful with flowers and pretty objects, these too began to accumulate a sadness. She found herself hiding, anywhere, in the lavatory, in the garden shed, in the park, even though it was bitter cold. He would rush with a towel and slippers whenever she came in and had some mush ready, which he insisted she eat. He called her 'angel' and used this endearment at every possible moment. The neighbours said he would have to go. She knew he would have to go.

The day she told him he said it was his greatest fear realised, that of becoming happy at long last—his wife had died ten years before—only to be robbed of it. He broke down, said how he had dreamed of bringing her up the French canals, of buoying her with cushions so that she could see the countryside, loving her and caring for her and lulling her to sleep.

On the day of his departure he wrote a note, saying that he would stay in his room, his 'hole' as he called it, and not bother her, and not require any food, and leave quietly at four as arranged. At lunchtime she called him to partake of a soup she had made. He was in his saffron robe, all neat and groomed, like a man about to set out on a journey. But he was shivering, and his eyes had a veil over them, a heavy veil of tears. He sat and dragged the spoon through the thick potato soup, and at first she thought that it must be some way of cooling it, but as the time went by she saw that it was merely a ploy to fiddle with it, like a child.

He did not say a word. She clapped her hands and much too raucously, said 'High diddle diddle the cat and the fiddle the cow jumped over the moon. The little dog laughed to see such sport and the dish ran away with the spoon.' He looked at her as if she had gone mad. She said 'Please don't take it so badly.' He said she was the second person he had ever loved, said how his wife had been a European too, sired in a dark wet country, a lover of rain and a lover of music. He loved nothing Asiatic, nothing related to his own land, not even the sunshine or the bright colours or the smells that pervaded the air of Bombay. His destiny was his dead wife, and now her.

Anger overtook her so that she wanted to beat him with the spoon, grind his face into the mush of soup, she wanted to humiliate him. When she was clearing away the dishes, he said again that he would stay in his 'hole' and leave quietly at four. But when the clock struck she waited for his footsteps on the stairs, and then along the hall, but she waited in vain. She prayed to God that he would go.

At five she decided that he must have killed himself, and before going up, she took the precaution to call in the neighbour. Together they climbed the stairs, smoking vigorously, manifesting a display of courage. He was sitting in the middle of the floor with his rucksack on, his head lowered. He appeared to be praying. He said 'Angel' and how he must have lost track of time. Then he said it was too late to go, and that he would postpone his departure until the morrow.

Eventually she had to call the police, and upon leaving he handed her a note which said that he would never get in touch with her, never ever, but telling her where he would be at each and every given hour. He was taking employment as cook, and he wrote his employer's number, stressing that he would be there at all hours, except when he intended to travel by bus, two afternoons a week, to take guitar lessons. Then he gave her the various possible numbers of the guitarist, who had no fixed abode. Next morning another letter was slipped under the door, and so each morning faithfully until he died seven days later. She refused to admit her guilt.

Soon after she decided to have the renovations done—kitchen and living room made into one, a big picture window, to afford a grander view of the river, and a stained glass window in which a medley of colours could interact as they did in the church windows seen long ago. The cubes and the circles and the slithers of light, that had fascinated her in childhood, were still able to repossess her at a moment's flounder. Like the knots, and the waits, and the various sets of chattering teeth. Other things too—shouts, murmurs, screams, an elderly drunk falling down a stair, his corpse later laid out in an off-white monkish habit, on a wrought-iron bed, and she herself being told that he had died of pneumonia, that he had not died of a fall.

So many puzzling things were said, things that contradicted one another. They congratulated you for singing, then told you never to open your gob again as long as you lived. Your tongue was not your friend, it was too thick and unwieldy, it doubled back in your throat, it parched, it longed for lozenges. Yes, rows, and the prefaces to rows, and thumpings and beatings and the rash actions of your sister the flighty one, going out at night, winter night, with blue satin knickers on, which she had stolen, going to a certain gateway, to cavort with a travelling creamery manager, coming in long after midnight, and trying desperately not to be heard, but being heard and accosted fiercely.

For some curious reason creaks are more pronounced in the dark, and her sister was always heard and always badly punished so that there were cries after midnight and don't, don't, don't. Her sister bled on that stair, then soon after her mother, her father, a clergyman and two other important men interrogated her about her private life. Her sister denied everything, just stayed there, glued to the damp area of the stairs. Then the next day, her mother, her sister, and herself walked along a hedged road and every minute her sister was cross-examined, and every minute she denied the accusations and said she was a virgin. They were on their way to another doctor, a doctor who did not know them. When they passed an orchard the little apples were already formed on the trees and they were desperately bright, but hard and inedible. Her sister had been found to have lied—had tried to abort herself, was sent to the Magdalen laundry for the five remaining months and had her bitter confinement there.

But there had been consoling things too—treats. On Sundays a trifle left to set on the other side of the stained glass panel, a trifle in a big pudding bowl, left down on tiles to cool. She would go down the stairs in her nightdress, creep, go through the glass door, squat down on those tiles, and scoop out some of the lovely cold jollop with her hands, and swallow it. It was cakey. Later it would be covered over with a layer of whipped cream then sprinkled with hundreds and thousands which would shine away as they were being swallowed. She never got a walloping for that misdemeanour because in her mother's eyes she was a little mite. On the other hand her father punished her for everything, particularly for sleeping in her mother's bed. When her father got in she tried not to look, not to listen, not to see, not to hear and not to be. She moved over to the wall, smelt the damp of the paper and could even smell the mortar behind the paper. There were mice in that room. They scuttled. Shame, shame, shame. Always for one second, a dreadful swoon used to overwhelm her too. Her bones and every bit of her dissolved. Then she contracted and steadied herself.

After her father went back to his own bed, she and her mother ate the chocolate sweets, little brown buttons. They simply used to melt on the tongue, like Holy Communion. They were so soothing, and so satisfying after the onslaught. Then the worst was over for a week or so, until it happened again.

On one side of the bed was a lattice, and when a finger was put through, it was like a finger being dispatched into space. Fingers alone could do nothing but fingers seamed to knuckles, belonging to palms, to wrists and to arms, could stir cakes or pound potatoes, or shake the living daylights out of someone, out of one's own self. One's lights were in there, residing, not as an illumination but as offal. Lights that were given to dogs, to curs and did not show the way as did a lamp or a lantern.

Saturday mornings were languor time. Her mother brought her tea and fingers of toast. The sun would be streaming through the blind, making shapes and gestures, warming the weeping, historied walls, the dark linoleum would be lit up, the dust rambling all over it, the dust an amusement in itself, while out on the landing the sun beamed through a stained glass window resulting in a different pattern altogether. Happily she munched on those fingers of toast. Even the stone hot water bottle that had gone cold became a source of pleasure, as she pressed on it with her feet, and pushed it right down to the rungs of the brass bed and threatened to eject it. When her father threatened her with the slash hook her nostrils went out like angels' wings, and she sped with the prodigal speed over three marsh fields, to a neighbour's house, to one of the cottagers who was stirring damson jam, while at the same time giving her husband a bath in the aluminium tub. They laughed at her because of the way she shook and asked if perhaps she had seen the banshee.

'No pet, no one can help you, you can only help yourself,' the neighbour had just said. Was that true? Would that always be true?

She went into her empty bathroom. The woodwork was as new and blond as in a showroom, and the bar of almond-shaped soap hanging from the tap asked to be used. She whispered things. She looked at the shower, its beautiful blue trough and the glass-fronted door. They had taken a shower together, she and a new man, a hulky fellow. She hung his shirt over the glass door to serve as a sort of screen. She came and came. He was so good-looking, and so heavy, and so warm, and so urgent, as he pressed upon her that she thought she might burst, like fruit. It was such a pity that he turned out to be crass. 'Let's get married,' he said at once.

She brought him to Paris, and in the hotel room he made himself at home, threw his belongings about, started to swagger, ordered the most expensive champagne, and booked two long-distance telephone calls. Her children were in the adjoining suite. They had not wanted him to come, but remembering the pleasure in the shower, that full knob of flesh inside her, truer, more persuasive than words or deeds, the scalding half happiness, she had let him accompany them, knowing she could not afford it, knowing that he would cadge. The moment he used her toothbrush she knew. She went out to the chemist to buy another, and he said what a pity that she hadn't bought him some after-shave.

She could not sleep with him again. She went down, and reserved another room for him, a cheaper room. They quarrelled disgracefully. He picked up the telephone and asked the telephonist would she like him to come down and fuck her. He said he was 'bad news' but that bad news travelled like wildfire. He moved to the other room but would not leave them alone. He followed them wherever they went and hence the visit was ruined. He rang her saying he was a health officer and had to look at her cunt. He ordered the costliest wines from the cellars and she was certain he would steal furniture or linen. It was a beautiful hotel with circular rooms, and little separated balconies on each landing, affording a view into the well of the hall. The bathroom was like a sitting room, with even a chaise for lying on, and the walls were a lovely warm pink. It was a dry paint, like a powder, and the walls were warm to nestle against. She sat on the chaise and very formally cursed him.

In the maid's room she stood over the wash basin. That was one room she had neglected. The wash basin was an eyesore. Would the new people have it mended, or have it removed? The new owner was a doctor, and there would be a sign chalked up on the pavement saying 'Doctor—in constant use.' The Spanish maid had been a nice girl, but a slut. She used to do old-fashioned things like plait her hair at night, or press her clothes by putting them under the mattress. They used to talk a lot, were chatter-boxes. The first day the maid arrived was in January, and the children were playing snowballs, and had just acquired a new dog. The new dog left little piddles all over the floor, tiny yellow piddles, no bigger than a capsule, and the dinner was specially special because of the new girl, and the children were as bright as cherries, what with the exercise and having been pasted with snowballs, and the excitement of a new dog.

The girl had had a mad father who broke clocks, and a mother who pampered her. She came from a small town in the north of Spain, where there was nothing to do in the evenings, except go for a walk with other girls. The girl ironed her hair to straighten it, and took camomile tisane for her headaches. They exchanged dreams. In the mornings she used to go to the girl's room, sit at the foot of the bed, and take a long time deciding what she should wear that day.

The girl began to dream in English, dreamt of cats, shoals of cats, coming through the window, miaowing, and of herself trying to get the latch closed, trying to push them back. The girl got spoiled, stayed in bed three or four certain days of each month, left banana skins under her pillow, neglected her laundry, and never took the hairs out of her brush or comb. Eventually she had to go. Another parting. So also the little dog, because although house-trained, he developed a nervous disease which made him whine

137

all the time even in sleep, and made him grit his little teeth and grind them, and grind most things.

It was not long after, that something began to go awry. She got the first sniff of it, like a foretaste, and it was a sniff as of blood freshly drawn. Yet it was nothing. Naturally there was a space where the small bay window had been. The builder had hung a strip of sacking there but she was certain something would come through, not simply a burglar, or wind, or rain, but some catastrophe, some unknown, a beast of prey. Whenever she entered that room she felt that something had just vacated it. A wolf she thought. It made people laugh. 'A wolf,' they said, 'the proverbial big bad wolf.' She rummaged through her old books for a copy of *Red Riding Hood*, but could not find it. She could remember it. It was a cloth book with serrated edges. The edges were cut carefully, so that the book did not ravel. She saw the little specks of cloth that had been ripped out, in a heap on the floor, coloured like confetti.

When the big new window was delivered, that hall door had to be taken off its hinges. Six men carried it through, each one bossing the other, telling the other to get a move on, to move on for Christ's sake, to do this, to do that, to watch it, watch it. She saw it break into smithereens a hundred times over, but it wasn't in fact until it was in, and well puttied, that she realised what a risk they had taken. She opened a bottle of whiskey, and they drank, looking out at the river, that happened on that day to have the sheen and consistency of liquid paraffin. It was like a bright skin over the brown water. She imagined spoons of it being donated to loads of constipated tourists who went by on the pleasure boats.

Naturally there was a party to christen the room. Would that have been the time that he brought the insolent girl, who had a dog called Kafka, or was that another time? They were all jumbled together, those parties, those times, like the dishes stacked on the long refectory table, or the bottles of wine, or the damp gold champagne labels, or the beautiful entrées. Perfection and waste.

She placed two men together, whereupon one took offence thinking he was assumed to be a homosexual. She had to bring him out into the garden, and in the moonlight solemnly tell him that she had not been sensitive, that she was a careless, a bad hostess. He was full of umbrage. He said he should not have come. She knew that he would never be invited again. A foreign woman stayed on, and they drank a bit, and picked at the food and drank more, and lay down on the mat by the dying fire. Even the embers were grey. She puffed on it and slowly one coal came to life, then another. Without thinking about it, she began to caress the woman and soon realised that she was well on the way to seducing her.

It was a strange sensation, as if touching gauze, or some substance that was about to vanish into thin air. Like the clocks of dandelions that were and then were not, fugitive dandelions vanishing, running away, everything running away, everything escaping its former state.

The woman asked her to go on, to please go on. She thought of other loves, other touches, and it was as if all these things were getting added together in her, like numbers, being totted up in a vast cash register, poor numbers that would never be able to be separated.

She did go on, and then her own eyes swam in her head, and for no reason she recalled the transparent paper that her mother used to apply to the lower halves of window panes, paper with patterns of butterflies, and the consistency of water, when dampened. They were both wet. Her fingers inside the woman would leave a tell-tale for all time.

They didn't know what to say. The woman spoke about her chap, what a regular maniac he was. Then the woman told her some facts, about her sordid childhood in Cairo, about being a little girl, constantly raped by uncles and cousins, and great uncles, and great-great uncles, and with each similar revelation she would say 'horrible eh, horrible eh.'

The woman had lived through wars, had half starved, had eaten cactus root, had been bruised and beaten by soldiers, and hideous though these events were they had not made her deep, or brave, they had not penetrated to her. She was like any other woman at the tail-end of a party, a little drunk, a little fatigued, soured about her fate.

The little dog bared his eye teeth at them. He knew he was being put down, before it happened, hence bit doors, wainscotting, and the legs of chairs, but avidly in anticipation of his fate. She hadn't told the children until it was over. They cried. Then they forgot. But did they forget? They too had brimming hearts. Children's hearts broke but they did not know that for a long time. One day they discovered it, and then it was as if some part of them had been removed unthinkingly, on a ritual operating table.

Soon after that she caught the illness, or rather it descended on her, an escalating fever. It centred in the throat, the nose and behind the eyes, and everything about her felt raw. The neighbour used to come to see her, bring Bovril in a thermos, and the doctor came twice a day. But when they were gone it used to possess her again, that look of terror. Would her heart be plucked out of her body, would the roof fall in, would a rat come out of its hiding. She often saw one, on the head of the bed, on the bedknob, poised, bristling.

A girl she'd known had had a rat in her bedroom that got killed by a cat, after hours and hours of play, and had witnessed the last screeching tussle, the leaps, then described the remains—a little heart of dry triangular flesh and a string which was the tail. The girl had found a nice bloke and moved with him into his barge. The very day the girl saw him she wrote him a note saying no person, animal, insect, or thing, had sniffed about her sex for almost a year and asked were there any offers. They clicked.

At the height of the fever, small flying creatures assembled and performed a medieval drama. They flew from the ceiling, perched on the various big brass curtain rings, hid in the dusty hollow space above the wardrobe, and hissed at one another; hiss–hiss. They chattered in a rich and barbarous language. She could comprehend it, though she could not speak it. They stripped her, bare. They worked in pairs, sometimes like angels, sometimes like little imps. They too had tails. They worked quickly, everything was quick and preordained.

She lay prostrate. Her nipples were like two aching mouths, unable to beseech. The Leader, half man, half woman, lay upon her and in that unfamiliar, mocking, rocking copulation, all strength seemed to be sucked out of her. Her nipples had nothing left to give. After milk came blood, and after blood, lymph. Her seducer, though light as a proverbial feather had one long black curved whisker, jutting from his left nostril, and there was no part of her body that did not come under the impact of its maddening trail. The others kept up some kind of screeching chorus. She was wrung dry.

She came to on the floor. She saw the pictures, and her oval, silver-backed mirror, as if she had been away on a long long journey and she resaluted them. In the silence there was a heaviness, as of something snoring, and various hairs had got into the glass of orange juice beside the bed.

The next day when the temperature had abated somewhat, she decided to get a grip on herself, to find the use of her legs again, and to walk around. There was even a walking stick that someone had left behind. She opened a door that led into a room, a little vacant room as it happened, but it was no longer empty, she saw numbers of coffins, throughout the room, lifting and flying about, and she heard a saw cutting through wood slowly and obstinately.

'Good God, I am dying,' she thought, as the coffins careened about, and then she closed the door and then opened it again, and the room was as it should be, with a single bed, covered in an orange counterpane, a lamp with a white globe, a buckled dressing table, and a painting that represented a very purring heart.

That was the first time. Not long after, the wash-basin in the maid's room took a little dance, and the enamel was like a meal inside her mouth, crushing her teeth. They said it was bad to be alone. It was.

She lost interest in cooking and housekeeping, wagged her finger at her own self, and pronounced a ridiculous verdict, 'You are slipping, slipping.' Very often she caught sight of a bright sixpence concealed inside a wad of dough, and she thought that if she could get it, and keep it in her purse, it would be a good augury for the future. Yes, she was slipping. Her hardworking mother would not approve. Her mother had been a good cook, superb at puddings, blood puddings, suet puddings, and of course the doyen of all, the inimitable Queen of puddings.

The neighbours suggested she take driving lessons, and she did. On the very second lesson, she headed straight for a pond, escaped only because the instructor grabbed the steering wheel. All she could hear was 'The pond, the pond.' She saw it, with its fine fuzz of green scum, looking exceedingly calm and undangerous. The instructor drove home.

She went to a boy called Pierre, to have streaks and highlighting. Consequently, her hair at night suggested the lights of Aladdin's cave. She should have street-walked. She got a new outfit. She got new boots. They were the colour of hessian and thickly crusted with threaded flowers. In the shop, the male assistant told her that their consultant psychiatrist could tell any woman's character from the footwear she chose. For that she smirked.

There was only one tune in her head, and it was that London Bridge was falling down, falling down. She would sit far back into a chair and try and keep still. But very often it would come, this mutiny, and there was no knowing what blood battles, what carnivals, what mad eyes and bulbous eyeballs would swim before her. Get thee to a nunnery, she said to them in vain. The bills poured in. Nevertheless, she bought unnecessary things, an ivory inlaid occasional table, a rocking chair.

The chair had to stay in the shop window for three days, until a dexterous man came to haul it out. She used to go up to the shop and look at it, observe the word 'Sold' in bold red letters and her name just beneath it. She envisaged sitting on it, going rock a bye baby. She never did, because it had to go back to the shop, still with its corrugated wrapping on it since the cheque had bounced.

She had stopped work supposedly for a month, but by then it was several months. She had been replaced by a younger girl and the column that used to carry her name and her oval-faced likeness each Tuesday morning now had a cute little photograph of a blonde lady, who used the pseudonym of Sappho. Her former editor wrote and said if he could ever do anything for her, he would be only too glad to help. It was both touching and useless.

As time went on she was selling instead of buying. Her dresses,

both chiffon affairs, in beautiful airy designs, were in a shop window not far away, and her fox cape had been snatched up in two
minutes after she had deposited it, in the second-hand market. She
saw the new owner go out in it, strutting, and she wanted to stab
her. The new owner wore red platform shoes and she herself made
a note to procure a pair when her ship came home.

The children guessed but never said. They got little presents for
her—usually nice notebooks and biros—to try and coax her back
to work. From school they wrote insouciant notes—how they were
out of socks, they were almost out of underwear, they wondered
if she'd had the leak fixed. A man whom she'd met in the park,
another nutter, drew her a graph of her waning sexuality, and presented her with a sealed letter. He wrote:

It appears you do not appreciate a mature
person, such as myself, you know many
cultured children, some you worship, and
some you ridicule, but dear friend, you say you
are very occupied, so is The Pope, The United
Nations, The Brotherhood of Workers, The
Black Militants, The White Pacifists; all
playing similar games.
Fellow puppet of nature, from outside,
stationed in my space, time, and tranquillity, I
observe the stardust drifting and pulsating
through the Milky Way. Good-bye. It is not
the end of me.

Then he told her to beware. All because she stood him up one day
on a park bench, where he was going anyhow, for his afternoon
ration of fresh air.

She let the bills come and then dropped them into the boiler.
She was glad she had not converted to oil, otherwise there would
have been no boiler, and no ashes, and no ash pan with its lovely
big surreal clinkers. The house was silent, and yet in those silences
she would hear a little gong, summoning her to something, to
prayer perhaps, and then the voices real and imagined, were like

packing needles, being dispatched in one ear and out the other, through the brawn of her head. Yet no one had died, not even her parents so that there was no excuse for those ridiculous coffins.

Still morning was morning. She would creep down into the garden, quietly, so that she did not even disturb the pigeons out of their roost, and at once she would be possessed of such a nice feeling, a safeness—talking amicably to the sweetness of nature about her. There were still such things, the milky air, the camelias in their trembling back-drop of shining foliage, which she would smell and touch and inhale, and thank for being there. Symbols of another world, a former world, a beautiful world. What world? Where, when and why had she gone wrong?

It was inside that things were worst. If she sat, or lingered too long in any room, it seemed as if the books, the encyclopedias might commence to talk, the pages might fly open, and reveal something dire. At intervals the walls purred. She was several sizes, tiny and shrinking, holding a doll's stomach, messing, making it say 'ma ma, ba ba', she was beating nettles with a stick, she was squatting under the trees, she was a freak being hoisted up on stilts, she was flying, not flying, fixed frozen. She began to lock the door, on one room after another, and she would listen outside these doors, and peer through their keyholes, but not go in. She locked every room in that house, had a camp bed down in the hall, and was ready to fly at the slightest hint of irregularity. In the end she rented a room in a small hotel, and came home only for a change of clothing, or to collect the mail.

'Knock-knock.' He was there. She went out smiling and he helped her with the few things that she was carrying. He hesitated before pulling on the choke. In the back seat were two cardboard boxes, full of empty milk bottles, and the moment they started up, two or three of the bottles rolled off.

'Any regrets?' Yes, plenty of regrets. She was going to a place named after a lake and she and others would be under supervision. He said she would be all right, that there were plenty others in the same boat. Her hackles did not rise.

144

Ah, never did the house look so lovely as just then, the sheltering eaves from which the birds were darting in and out, the multi-coloured brick with its hues of violet and crimson, the paintwork, that with a bit of effort could be renewed. She had thrown it all away, she had let it go. Her lungs burst for a moment, with regret, and she thought of the alternative, of how blissful it would be, to be going in there and starting all over again, with wooden spoons and a kitchen table, and a primus or a stove; a few belongings. Then she checked herself. It was no use wishing. She saw the living death and the demons behind her, she saw the sad world that she had invented for herself, but of the future she saw nothing, not even one little godsend.

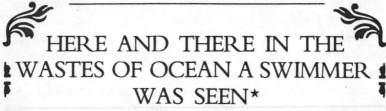

HERE AND THERE IN THE WASTES OF OCEAN A SWIMMER WAS SEEN*

Penelope Mortimer

It was reasonable to assume that every member of the audience knew what I looked like. There was no hope of their mistaking me for an auditor, member of the administration or friend of the deceased. I had, in fact, dressed to reassure them, in clothes they would expect to find on my corpse: my father's marriage suit, which I had hung under the shower and then stuffed into my neighbour's dryer; a shirt I vaguely remembered buying in Buffalo or Syracuse sometime in the '50s, held together with an ignoble and collapsing tie; a pair of shoes I had found under the bed—possibly not mine, bed or shoes. I had practised in front of the mirror that particular face of benign alarm, artless criminality, that they knew from the back cover of my book jackets, choosing this rather than the sullen smudge I presented at prize-givings, unavoidable cocktail parties and demonstrations, and when snapped falling off an inflatable mattress in somebody else's pool. I had not brushed my hair or regulated my beard. They expected their money's worth—a considerable fortune, taking into account real estate and foreign investments. They were going to get it.

I squinted up at the Chairman, knowing that in five minutes or so I would be balanced on that incalculable height; he, having the mind of a judge or ringmaster, stood up there without a fear in his head, hands loosely clasping both sides of the lectern, apparently unaware of the sea of faces far below him. Blood jumped in the soles of my feet. I looked away, pretending to ex-

* *Apparent rari nautes in gurgito vasto* (Virgil, *Aeneid* 1.118).

amine the audience with a narrowed critical gaze, though in fact I could see nothing through the lights and the blue spirals of smoke. I didn't wish to attend to the Chairman's words of praise, his phrases of lethal homage. Homage kills. God talks to no one, and imposes on us his own image of isolation and anger. Although there was paper and a pencil on the table, I didn't write this down.

But in order to calm my feet, I crossed my right leg over my left; and then, after a considered interval, the left over the right. I pulled the paper an inch or so towards me and drew a very small question mark on the top right-hand corner of the top sheet, and embellished it with antennae. I looked up, as though my attention had been caught by something sudden and unusual. Nothing was sudden and nothing, as yet, unusual.

I had not so much decided to tell them the truth tonight, as reached a point where there was, as far as I could see, no alternative. Their familiarity with lies had bred, in myself, an unendurable contempt. The lies that I myself had told them had become an unendurable burden to me. I was largely responsible for the fact that they found the processes of thought, of cogitation, analysis, deduction and judgement so easy. I had fooled them—though many of them were old enough to know better—that their world was a ball turning round the sun, instead of a handful of twigs tied with fraying string, a live being, a thimble, or an object with all the complex shapes and construction of a wheelbarrow. Mind you, my intentions had not been altogether unkind. It is hard to spend much of one's life like an ant, toiling up and down, over and under and across a wheelbarrow. If it were a question of relying on my brain alone (as I had deluded them was possible), I couldn't have coped at all. My brain could only cope with one indisputable fact: it is contained within my skull.

The Chairman droned on. I listened for a moment, in hope (one hopes, in time, for the worst to happen and be done with it) of hearing a coda. The person he was describing bore as little relation to the person I knew as the insipid Virgin of a Woolworth's painting to the little scrubber of Bethelem. The Jewish story was in my mind that evening because I had recently, perhaps at lunchtime, been in Woolworth, where I had seen these fairly large compositions selling for $21.95—the Sermon on the Mount, the Carpenter's Shop, the Annunciation, Gethsemane; it must have been the wrong time of year for the Nativity, or else they were sold out. I had been, and obviously still was, extraordinarily impressed by the manufacturer's complete lack of talent combined with such devotion. I felt almost maniacal devotion, to falsehood. The things had, for me, a terrible grandeur. They were farting at history. With their peacock blues and resonant crimsons, their hot, furry texture, their moppet saviours and implacably genteel saints, they seduced my soul and sent me out of the store weeping. At least, I felt I was weeping; as I did now, on the rostrum, touching with my ears the hot, furry texture of my life and achievements, aggrandised by the Chairman into something recognisable to the audience: an appalling lie.

I stopped listening for a few moments, distracted from grief by wondering why I had gone to Woolworth in the first place. Almost certainly I hadn't acquired any electrical equipment, writing paper, fertiliser or ruled cash books. Had I needed any of these things? What was I missing? Why, today, had I found it necessary to walk three blocks to Woolworth, and come away empty-handed? I was engrossed by these questions, with their suggestion of deprivation. But the Chairman had turned (miraculously stable, it seemed to me) and was looking down, his arm extended, palm upward, in a gesture which might, at any moment, be inviting. I held myself, actually clasped myself in readiness. The Chairman was about to reach his conclusion.

He had made a pretty thorough résumé, it seemed, of all the known information on his subject. He had confined himself to this information, not stating to which sex I belonged, or mentioning the probable—according to the statistics, and the amount of cholesterol I consumed—date of my death. I was also reasonably certain that he hadn't touched on my fear of rodents, detestation of Wagner, love of certain forgotten children, corrosion by boredom, dislike of cereal in any form, tendency to sudden and catastrophic fatigue, nasty habits, unpopular attitudes or obsessional neuroses. Well, why should he? Like a schizophrenic, a giant or a midget, a hermaphrodite or surviving member of an antique tribe, I was

148

an exhibit. The Chairman had drawn attention to my ability to use a typewriter, no more; that, and the fact that I had two heads whose commingled thoughts could be translated, more or less, into words. A minor freak, the possibility that I peed too frequently, became constipated in strange environments, occasionally had my hair cut, fucked more often than I fell in love, wondered about prayer, gave as much pain as I received, smoked three packs of low-tar cigarettes a day in memory of dead parents, was of little interest to them.

He had finished. He turned, he descended, he sat down. After a moment's hesitation (as though I didn't know what I was there for, as though I were waiting for some other daredevil to take my place) I stood up, walked, began to climb. With each step, treading air, I rose higher. There was applause, but I was too intent, too afraid of slipping from an undignified height, to acknowledge it. At last, having taken the final step, I steadied myself on the lectern, but didn't yet look down. I placed some blank sheets of paper with my fingertips, flicked the microphone, poured some warm vodka from the carafe into a plastic glass, cleared my throat. Then I looked down.

Not one face was distinct in the haze, though I fancied I saw a small tent, presumably a hat, pitched in the front row, and a few pairs of spectacles flashed like signals. My mind was completely blank, nothing in it but one or two vast, blurred images, a bed of unidentifiable memory. I watched myself, reflected back from their eyes, standing on this high and perilous place, lost, not knowing how I got there; curious now, rather than frightened; someone who had reached the end of the line, the ultimate simplification of Stop, past any alternative.

'If it's all right with you,' I said (my voice, high and singing, become a wind), 'I'd rather pause for questions during the course of this talk. There may not be time at the end. And you all have buses, trains and so on to catch....' I knew, I was telling them, about buses and trains; I had been to Queens and the Bronx; I was familiar with Woolworth. They seemed placid. So I began.

'I was born on an island.'

In thirty seconds' silence I could hear their thoughts. I was born bang in the middle of Nebraska, where I stayed for ten days, and to which I never returned. I adjusted the microphone. The Chairman was a small man.

'I have slides, but it seems nobody thought to bring a projector. However, if anybody's interested, they can be seen later. You can get the general idea by holding them up to the light.'

Not a ripple. I waited, testing the boards, trying to measure the distance. On impact, I would plunge through and under an uneven mass of flesh. But then I doubted whether there was sufficient flesh compared with the amount of bone, steel, plastic, wood, nail fibre, hairweed, tin, leather; and, of course, blood. I would be smashed to bits, no doubt of it.

'I was born on an island.'

Someone sneezed; possibly hay fever, some debilitating allergy.

'The island was extremely small.' I grasped the lectern, stabilising myself. 'Manhattan, of course, is about thirteen miles long and two miles wide, and is largely composed of pre-Cambrian stone, approximately two billion years old. Those of you who have pocket calculators can, if you wish, discover how many days or hours pre-Cambrian stone has been in existence. One of the oldest forms of stone found on Manhattan is called Brooklyn gneiss. Excuse me—I mean, of course, on Long Island, which is larger than Manhattan, being about a hundred and fifteen miles long and twenty-three miles wide. Manhattan schist is, of course, found on Manhattan. In fact, Manhattan is largely composed of Manhattan schist, with just a small, a very small patch or pocket of serpentine, a group of minerals which is believed to arise in igneous rocks during a late pneumatolytic or hydrothermal stage of their consolidation. The Holiday Inn is built on serpentine. The Plaza, the Algonquin, the Hilton, in fact all other hotels of note, including the Grand Central YMCA, are built on Manhattan schist.'

They waited, sluggish, afraid to commit themselves. My information fell on their faces, and dried there while I spoke. I raised my voice, belligerent.

'I was born on an island. It was extremely small. Smaller than Manhattan and, obviously, much smaller than Long Island. It was smaller than Praslin Island, of which I shall speak later. In fact, being a peak of a sub-oceanic mountain, it was barely large enough to swing a cat. Compared with this island, I assure you, Sark, which is three miles long and one and a half miles wide, is a continent. Rumm, Eigg and Muck are continents, to those who live on them.'

Many of them, I knew, became confused here, believing that I was for some reason talking about rum, egg and muck. So much the better. If I could get them sufficiently confused their flesh might part, a Red Sea, letting me through on dry land.

'Now let me describe to you this extremely small island. It's a pity about the projector. If I'd known, I would have brought my own.'

The Chairman swivelled far below me, hiding his face, I imagined, in distress or shame.

'The previous inhabitants had left a number of houses, or I suppose more accurately dwellings. I'm not sure that *is* more accurate. You may think, and perhaps rightly, that they're the same thing. These dwellings, anyway, were crammed together—crammed, obviously, through lack of space. Later on, my father made a raft and lived on that for a while. However, it leaked. And although he thought up many cunning contrivances to give him shade and shelter, none of them were at all efficient. Also my mother found it too much for her, ferrying the food and laundry back and forth.'

Some of them, I knew, were beginning to hope for my toes to curl over the edge, muscles tighten, arms rise to a steeple above my head. I lolled for a moment, dangerously, rubbing the back of my neck.

'There was one dwelling for my father—who, as I've told you, briefly abandoned it. Another for my mother, who somehow managed to make a garden. And another for me, where I began to live very shortly after I was born. Naturally, during the birth itself I was in my mother's house. As, nine months previously, she must have been in my father's. Or vice versa. Apart from these unavoidable contacts, we kept to ourselves.'

Another sneeze. Holding tight, peering down, bestowing on the sneezer a moment of fantasy, of grace beyond the humdrum realities of life, I murmured 'Bless you.' There were a few sniggers, the usual response to benediction of any kind. Oh my crass lovers, how you will relish my downfall, my falling down. My knees trembled.

'There were other dwellings on the island, but they were empty, and during the time we were there they fell into disuse. Well, they didn't fall into it. They were never used at all. They were intended, I suppose, for other members of the family, brothers and sisters, possibly aunts, uncles or grandparents. Nieces and nephews. Cousins. Second cousins. No, probably not second cousins because there were only about twelve dwellings in all, and we occupied three of them. I daresay they were intended for grandparents, and other children. I never went into them, but sometimes looked through the windows, which were impenetrably dirty because my mother didn't have the time, or possibly the inclination, to clean them. I don't know which, because I never called on my mother, or she on me. She left my food on the windowsill, or inside the porch if it was raining, and woke me up in the mornings by clapping her hands. As though applauding my dreams. Which were probably scanty. Having nothing to feed on.'

I paused, troubled. Alone on islands, what do children dream? I must have fed through the nights on my mother's careful arrangements of orange carrot, purple beetroot, white cauliflower, greenish cabbage piled around varying shades of meat; by beige pastry, blackberries and black currants, brown sugar, golden syrup. But how did she get these things? Were they brought by boat, helicopter? Paid for how? I must not embark on dreams, fantasy, speculation. I must stick to the facts, otherwise I would stumble and plunge clumsily, instead of soaring with grace.

'The island,' I continued, 'was, naturally, surrounded by ocean, which undoubtedly teemed with life of sorts, plant and fish. Of all sorts, I daresay, except animal—though the odd whale may have passed by, without our knowing it. As for vegetation, there were a few bushes. I don't know what kind of bushes they were. Possibly laurel. If we had a projector some of you, perhaps, could identify the bushes. And my mother had her garden. My father and I didn't own anything, least of all the ground under our feet.'

I took a drink. Most of them were waiting now—blobs of faces raised—for me to launch myself. Let them wait. Though I could only move a few inches forward, and couldn't go back, and couldn't step to left or right, and certainly couldn't move upwards (ascending to the high ceiling where, unless there were an opening, I would stick, quivering like a dart), I could at least stay where I was more or less indefinitely, disregarding the submarine creaks of the Chairman. The urge to dive and be done with it had left me, for the time being.

'I suggested that at intervals we would stop for questions. Are there any questions?'

There was a soft, composite sigh. The tent, or hat, heaved a little. They seemed to be turning to each other, some searching their pockets for illicit cigarettes, though I couldn't see the flames of matches or lighters because of the haze and the distance.

At last a man's voice asked, 'Is this intended to be an allegory?'

'I'm sorry?'

'Is what you're telling us . . . allegorical?'

I was profoundly puzzled. 'I don't understand what you mean.'

A long pause, though not a silence. I relaxed, benign, patient.

A woman's voice, possibly a girl's: 'But you were born in Nebraska.'

'A mistake, I assure you.'

The woman or girl was spelling it out, aggrieved: 'Norway, Nebraska.'

'I've never been in Norway. I'm afraid you were misinformed.'

Convince people that they've been misinformed and you can tell them it's noon at midnight, they'll believe you. This is one of the basic rules of politics and of religious proselytising: it is also the only reason for moving from one romantic attachment to another and is, in some circles, known as spellbinding.

'Is it true that you've recently signed a contract for two million dollars?'

'No. If I had, why would I be here?' The contract was, in fact, for a slightly smaller sum; its signature was the last word I would ever write. In any case, I always translated my income directly into other currencies and unmanageable objects, and the question was impertinent.

153

'What is it called? What is the name of the island?'

'Roxburry.'

'Where is it?'

'If we had a projector, I could show you exactly.' I hesitated, taking my hands off the lectern for a moment to make them think that they had got me this time. 'Roxburry is in the Eastern Hemisphere, between fifty-five and fifty-eight degrees North and five and eight degrees West. Look it up on your maps when you get home. Such as it is, it's largely composed of Archean gneiss, which is an even more resistant gneiss than the gneiss we were talking about earlier. Which was, if you remember, Brooklyn gneiss. "Gneiss", by the way, in the original Slavonic, means "rotted" or "decomposed". You might therefore say that our Western civilisation is built on rotten mineral. And you would be right.'

I smiled at them, and possibly they smiled at me.

'Shall I continue?'

Nobody said no. I poured another vodka out of the carafe, took a sip, swallowing slowly. I inched—but hoped almost imperceptibly—forward.

'A garden rooted in Archean gneiss, you may think, might not be a great success. To my mother, however, her garden was a lovesome thing, god wot. Rose plot, fringed pool, ferned grot, the veriest school of peace. And yet the fool contends that God is not. You are, I know, familiar with all nineteenth-century writers, indeed some of you have devoted your lives to them. I doubt, however, whether any of you know if Thomas Brown was referring to his garden in Clifton or his garden in the Isle of Man, or indeed either. But perhaps if anyone does . . .' No. If anyone did, I didn't want to be told. I took a deep breath and bellowed, 'Not God? In gardens? When the eve is cool? Nay, but I have a sign—'tis very sure God walks in mine!'

In the startled silence that followed this presumptuous statement, I clung to the lectern and momentarily closed my eyes. The image alarmed me as much as I hoped it alarmed them. Monumental feet trample the green mountains; gross lambs devastate the pasture; God is a trespasser. It was essential to keep talking until, by some method or other, by island-hopping, constructing frail bridges and unreliable canoes, I reached my destination, my origin.

'My mother thought something along these lines while digging, or more accurately trowelling her gneiss. She wotted God, I believe, though knew little, if anything, of the Isle of Man. This unpredictable place, though one of the British Isles or Islands, has its own legal system and is not, for some reason, subject to the tax laws of the United Kingdom. Whether this was so in Thomas Brown's day, I don't know. The rock on the Isle of Man is generally thought to date from the Upper Cambrian age, and is therefore remotely related to that of Manhattan. It would be difficult, in fact, to find a substance that is not remotely related to all other substances. Impossible. It would be—and I am positive of this—impossible to find a substance that is not remotely related to all other substances. This may be the one cause we have for judicious optimism.'

Shocked, perhaps, by this first familiar, reassuring and completely meaningless phrase, somebody dropped something, a notebook or purse; an umbrella, perhaps, more of a thud than a clatter. I very much wanted to be sitting quietly in a waiting room, a place of farewell, holding someone's hand. The train pulls in, the nurse opens the door, the jailer enters with the priest and says 'It's time.' There is no more to be said. It's over. I tried to clear away the light, as though rubbing mist off a window pane. It was hard to retain my balance.

'I have never been to the Isle of Man,' I told them, hoping that this, at least, they would remember. 'This surprises me, in view of the fact that in the year of my birth, of its population of 60,284 persons, 11,410 were visitors. Statistically, therefore, it would seem likely that, at one time or another, one would at least have set foot on the Isle of Man. Communication is not easy, Shipping lines go out of business or on strike, they seldom if ever keep to their schedules. Planes fail to take off or fail to land, flights are continually cancelled, they are diverted to Manchester or Philadelphia or Frankfurt and one has little hope of reaching one's intended destination. It is amazing that anyone, in this day and age, gets to the Isle of Man at all, since it is impossible, of course, to reach by train or bus, car or bicycle, and private launches are relatively rare. Thomas Brown himself had a very nasty crossing in November 1896, from Liverpool. Islands tend to be inaccessible. In bad weather, islands are even inaccessible to each other.'

I could no longer see myself reflected in their eyes, the lone diver poised to plunge. I wished to God I had time for reflection; to remember what it was I had intended to buy; what was missing from my life. I clasped my hands together, hoping to feel my hands in my hands. I stood heavily, searching for the supporting boards through the soles of my shoes. The truth rasped out of me; my accent was foreign.

'I go so far as to say with complete assurance that nobody has ever travelled from the Isle of Man to Roxburry, and that nobody, at least over the last two billion years, has made the return journey. Roxburry is not attractive; no one, not even the most desperate, would resort to it. During the time I was there it displayed few, if any, signs of life, except for the laurel bushes, which were unaccountably sturdy. My mother's seeds, plants and cuttings mostly remained below ground. Birds, it's true, did perch on it from time to time. Butterflies, though God knows where they came from. Presumably they were migratory, perhaps on their way to Iceland, which is one of the few countries in the world, if not the only country, to have no resident butterflies. The *Deiopeia Pulchella* moth has been seen wandering about a thousand miles from home, and clouds of *Pyrameis Cardui* have been reported far, far out in the ocean, with no place to rest but on the winds and currents of air. They landed on Roxburry but didn't breed there. I never, in my early childhood, saw larvae or caterpillars. This was one of the many deprivations of which, not knowing any better, I did not feel deprived. Love, of course, was another. Newspapers, chewing gum, electric trains and live animals were totally outside my experience. I lived in this way until I was eight years and seven months old. If you consider how long eight years and seven months is, the difference between twenty-two and thirty, forty-nine and fifty-seven, you must agree that it is perfectly valid to call it a lifetime.'

I shuffled the blank pieces of paper. I felt more confident. The word 'lifetime' was good—positive, confident, giving them something to look forward to. At some point during the evening I might dare to do a little dance on my board. Sing, even. The Chairman was quiet. My balance was not sufficiently good to risk turning to see if he was still there, so I pinned the paper with my right forefinger and, supported by the forefinger, moved my head cautiously and looked down out of the corner of my eye. He was slumped with hands loosely latched across crumpled stomach; beard on chest, offering his bald pate to the light. Asleep? Dead? If the former, then still suffering; if the latter, not.

The audience also was quiet. People were running pencils down the spiral spines of notebooks, squeaking in their clothes, breathing lightly. The sneezer had either recovered or left, taking his paroxysm into the hall outside, the men's room, the street. By now he was in some distant part of the city, perhaps already embarked, passport stamped with the sudden, indelible sound of his own sneeze, his moment nearest to death, when I had blessed him. I felt a pang of love, pain from a severed limb.

'Educated—if I may call it that—on an island, one falls back on the belief that air, whatever its pollen count or degree of humidity, is, to say the least, prevalent; that the atmosphere, however varied its composition, however polluted, or heady with ozone, is the only matter to be shared, at the same moment in time, by every animal, vegetable and mineral on this earth. One also—and very early on—learns that islands are surrounded by water, in which there is no air as we know it, and in which it would be impossible to sneeze and survive. I merely throw in this thought for your consideration. It is easy to overlook.' I picked up the pencil, weighty as a pole but unbalanced, since it had a bulbous eraser on one end. I noticed that the pencil was hexagonal rather than round, and had the curious word 'Mongol' printed along one side. I bounced the pencil on the eraser a couple of times, showing off, and replaced it in its groove on the lectern.

'But I digress. As I was saying, or was about to say: my father and mother had come to Roxbury for a purpose. Their purpose was to live one life, during which, inadvertently or by design, other lives might be created. As, of course, this was a totally impractical enterprise, they failed. To put it rather less simply, their marriage was not a success. It couldn't be. They didn't have a thing in common—height, weight, age, sex, temperament, genealogy, hopes, tastes, memories—nothing. If they had been animals in a cage—even animals on Roxburry—they wouldn't have taken the slightest notice of each other. They were far more dissimilar than a male ass and a female horse which do occasionally, when driven to it, couple. Though you may be saying to yourselves that the result, in both cases, would have turned out to be a mule.'

I waited long enough for the one obedient titter. When it came, it tired me out, the catastrophe of fatigue almost bowled me over. Possibly there might be a dancing and singing time, even a time of loving them; but there would be—unavoidable, even now—cycles of disgust, aeons of lassitude so profound that I would hardly be able to drag myself from word to word, up over the craggy heights of 'inextricable', down the slippery sides of 'delineate', through and around 'authoritarian', bump bump from 'and' to 'by'. I picked up the pencil again and leaned on it, hopelessly remembering my bad back, torn tendon, flat foot, arthritic knuckle: my signs of life. I glared into the light with the bleary contempt I normally reserved for my mirror.

'Marriage!' I yelled, carelessly jumping up and down. 'What *about* marriage, then? What about sex, eh? What about that rare and exotic bird, the female orgasm? What about that fabulous phoenix, risen from the ashes of desire? What about Misses Slap and Tickle, Masters Bump and Grind? Who's got Phil the Fucker's Daughter or Bill the Bugger's Mate?'

I didn't have to look to know that the Chairman was definitely alive. Reactions zipped up out of the mud like pellets, buzzing zig zap across the auditorium, volley after volley of hard little mud-spattered shocks that would have knocked me off the rostrum if I hadn't held on with all my strength. I waited until there was comparative calm, though the surface was still choppy and littered with foreign bodies as I spoke:

'Well. There was none of that on Roxburry, I can tell you. Apart from that one regrettable collision between my father and mother, there was no touch. You understand me? There was no touch. No contact of any kind. No licking of skin, brushing against arm or leg, clasping of hands, fingering, stroking, holding. None whatever. Until I was eight years and seven months old I had no sense of touch: even as far as my own body was concerned, each part of it was remote from and inaccessible to the rest. It's impossible for you to understand this, I know. It is almost impossible for me to remember it. Before we left, or were cast out, my mother made clothes from the enormous leaves of the palm tree, *Lodoicea maldivica*. They didn't last long, and were soon replaced by wool. Do you have any questions?'

They were receding, draining away; they trickled and burbled towards the Exits; they flowed up the aisles. The Chairman was on his feet, making swimming motions; the agitation of his head seemed to indicate that he was opening and shutting his mouth, though apparently without sound.

'*Do you have any questions?*' I shouted. If they weren't there to receive me, what should I do? If I had intended to fling myself onto dry land I could have used any number of convenient heights, the city was full of them. I needed the impact of flesh, however harshly it might be covered. I had known, of course, that the truth would offend them. But I had sincerely believed that my reputation as a liar, the eminence of my deceit, would keep them hoping. The idea of having to continue my life (an idea which I had not considered for some time) was so appalling that I shoved the lectern to one side and stood unprotected, with nothing to hang on to, my legs like weeds, reaching out for support to the light, the haze, the insubstantial air.

'When General Gordon—a British general in the nineteenth century, with which, of course, you are familiar—made a military survey of the Seychelles in 1881—the Seychelles comprise ninety islands in the Indian Ocean, six hundred miles northeast of Madagascar and have a total area of one hundred and forty-five square miles—he stated categorically, he categorically stated, that the Vallée des Cocos de Mer on Praslin Island was the site of the Garden of Eden. Praslin Island is eight miles long and rises to one thousand, two hundred and sixty feet, far larger than Roxburry. I dispute General Gordon's statement! I am trying to tell you, to inform you, to convince you, that God never walked on any island in the Seychelles, or invaded any garden there—no, not in a cool evening, not at any time. What would he be doing there, six hundred miles northeast of Madagascar? What on earth would he be doing there? Would the British, even the British, use God's first invention as a prison, a place of detention for heretics and archbishops? Listen to me! I have told you about islands, and with the help of a projector I could have told you more. I have described Manhattan and Long, Sark, Rumm, Eigg, Muck and Man, all of them isolated and yet bound together by air, many of them hard to reach but all to some degree inhabited. I have disposed of the Seychelles, all ninety of them, but with particular reference to Praslin, whose forbidden fruit is no more than an uncommon coconut which—possibly in a moment of intense longing—roused the lust of an eccentric soldier, long dead. But I have told you about Roxburry, my birthplace, my state of innocence, my genesis, between fifty-five and fifty-eight degrees North and five and eight degrees West—a place accessible only to thought and the arduous, retracing steps of mourning. You want me to dance for you? Teach you? Sing? DO YOU HAVE ANY QUESTIONS?'

'Questions?' my echo asked. 'Questions ...?'

The auditorium was empty. The Chairman climbed laboriously towards me, every exposed inch of his skin expressing concern. I took a deep breath: no need now to hold it, or pinch my nose between forefinger and thumb. I jumped. I landed at the Chairman's side. He reached up to hold me, as a man strains to support a falling elm.

'Are you all right?' he babbled. 'All right?'

I looked around me: this wood, this metal, these electric lights, these doors to pass through, these paths, pavements, passages, corridors, roadways to move along—for ever.

I said, 'I must go.'

'But are you all right? Where must you go to?'

'There's something I need.'

'What do you need? Let me get it for you. What is it?'

'I don't know,' I said, and walked away, each foot following the other.

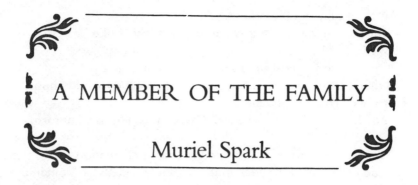

A MEMBER OF THE FAMILY

Muriel Spark

'You must,' said Richard, suddenly, one day in November, 'come and meet my mother.'

Trudy, who had been waiting a long time for this invitation, after all was amazed.

'I should like you,' said Richard, 'to meet my mother. She's looking forward to it.'

'Oh, does she know about me?'

'Rather,' Richard said.

'Oh!'

'No need to be nervous,' Richard said. 'She's awfully sweet.'

'Oh, I'm sure she is. Yes, of course, I'd love——'

'Come to tea on Sunday,' he said.

They had met the previous June in a lake town in Southern Austria. Trudy had gone with a young woman who had a bed-sitting-room in Kensington just below Trudy's room. This young woman could speak German, whereas Trudy couldn't.

Bleilach was one of the cheaper lake towns; in fact, cheaper was a way of putting it: it was cheap.

'Gwen, I didn't realise it ever rained here,' Trudy said on their third day. 'It's all rather like Wales,' she said, standing by the closed double windows of their room regarding the downpour and imagining the mountains which indeed were there, but invisible.

'You said that yesterday,' Gwen said, 'and it was quite fine yesterday. Yesterday you said it was like Wales.'

'Well, it rained a bit yesterday.'

'But the sun was shining when you said it was like Wales.'

'Well, so it is.'

'On a much larger scale, I should say,' Gwen said.

'I didn't realise it would be so wet.' Then Trudy could almost hear Gwen counting twenty.

'You have to take your chance,' Gwen said. 'This is an unfortunate summer.'

The pelting of the rain increased as if in confirmation.

Trudy thought, I'd better shut up. But suicidally: 'Wouldn't it be better if we moved to a slightly more expensive place?' she said.

'The rain falls on the expensive places too. It falls on the just and the unjust alike.'

Gwen was thirty-five, a schoolteacher. She wore her hair and her clothes and her bit of lipstick in such a way that, standing by the window looking out at the rain, it occurred to Trudy like a revelation that Gwen had given up all thoughts of marriage. 'On the just and the unjust alike,' said Gwen, turning her maddening imperturbable eyes upon Trudy, as if to say, you are the unjust and I'm the just.

Next day was fine. They swam in the lake. They sat drinking apple juice under the red and yellow awnings on the terrace of their guest-house and gazed at the innocent smiling mountain. They paraded—Gwen in her navy-blue shorts and Trudy in her puffy sun-suit—along the lake-side where marched also the lean brown camping youths from all over the globe, the fat print-frocked mothers and double-chinned fathers from Germany followed by their blonde sedate young, and the English women with their perms.

'There aren't any men about,' Trudy said.

'There are hundreds of men,' Gwen said, in a voice which meant, whatever do you mean?

'I really must try out my phrase-book,' Trudy said, for she had the feeling that if she were independent of Gwen as interpreter she might, as she expressed it to herself, have more of a chance.

'You might have more chance of meeting someone interesting

162

that way,' Gwen said, for their close confinement by the rain had seemed to make her psychic, and she was continually putting Trudy's thoughts into words.

'Oh, I'm not here for that. I only wanted a rest, as I told you. I'm not——'

'Goodness, Richard!'

Gwen was actually speaking English to a man who was not apparently accompanied by a wife or aunt or sister.

He kissed Gwen on the cheek. She laughed and so did he. 'Well, well,' he said. He was not much taller than Gwen. He had dark crinkly hair and a small moustache of a light brown. He wore bathing trunks and his large chest was impressively bronze. 'What brings you here?' he said to Gwen, looking meanwhile at Trudy.

He was staying at an hotel on the other side of the lake. Each day for the rest of the fortnight he rowed over to meet them at ten in the morning, sometimes spending the whole day with them. Trudy was charmed, she could hardly believe in Gwen's friendly indifference to him, notwithstanding he was a teacher at the same grammar school as Gwen, who therefore saw him every day.

Every time he met them he kissed Gwen on the cheek.

'You seem to be on very good terms with him,' Trudy said.

'Oh, Richard's an old friend. I've known him for years.'

The second week, Gwen went off on various expeditions of her own and left them together.

'This is quite a connoisseur's place,' Richard informed Trudy, and he pointed out why, and in what choice way, it was so, and Trudy, charmed, saw in the peeling pastel stucco of the little town, the unnecessary floral balconies, the bulbous Slovene spires, something special after all. She felt she saw, through his eyes, a precious rightness in the women with their grey skirts and well-filled blouses who trod beside their husbands and their clean children.

'Are they all Austrians?' Trudy asked.

'No, some of them are German and French. But this place attracts the same type.'

Richard's eyes rested with appreciation on the young noisy campers whose tents were pitched in the lake-side field. The campers were long-limbed and animal, brightly and briefly dressed. They romped like galvanised goats, yet looked surprisingly virtuous.

'What are they saying to each other?' she enquired of Richard when a group of them passed by, shouting some words and laughing at each other through glistening red lips and very white teeth.

'They are talking about their fast MG racing cars.'

'Oh, have they got racing cars?'

'No, the racing cars they are talking about don't exist. Sometimes they talk about their film contracts which don't exist. That's why they laugh.'

'Not much of a sense of humour, have they?'

'They are of mixed nationalities, so they have to limit their humour to jokes which everyone can understand, and so they talk about racing cars which aren't there.'

Trudy giggled a little, to show willing. Richard told her he was thirty-five, which she thought feasible. She volunteered that she was not quite twenty-two. Whereupon Richard looked at her and looked away, and looked again and took her hand. For, as he told Gwen afterwards, this remarkable statement was almost an invitation to a love affair.

Their love affair began that afternoon, in a boat on the lake, when, barefoot, they had a game of placing sole to sole, heel to heel. Trudy squealed, and leaned back hard, pressing her feet against Richard's.

She squealed at Gwen when they met in their room later on. 'I'm having a heavenly time with Richard. I do so much like an older man.'

Gwen sat on her bed and gave Trudy a look of wonder. Then she said, 'He's not much older than you.'

'I've knocked a bit off my age,' Trudy said. 'Do you mind not letting on?'

'How much have you knocked off?'

'Seven years.'

'Very courageous,' Gwen said.

'What do you mean?'

'That you are brave.'

'Don't you think you're being a bit nasty?'

'No. It takes courage to start again and again. That's all I mean. Some women would find it boring.'

'Oh, I'm not an experienced girl at all,' Trudy said. 'Whatever made you think I was experienced?'

'It's true,' Gwen said, 'you show no signs of having profited by experience. Have you ever found it a successful tactic to remain twenty-two?'

'I believe you're jealous,' Trudy said. 'One expects this sort of thing from most older women, but somehow I didn't expect it from you.'

'One is always learning,' Gwen said.

Trudy fingered her curls. 'Yes, I have got a lot to learn from life,' she said, looking out of the window.

'God,' said Gwen, 'you haven't begun to believe that you're still twenty-two, have you?'

'Not quite twenty-two is how I put it to Richard,' Trudy said, 'and yes, I do feel it. That's my point. I don't feel a day older.'

The last day of their holidays Richard took Trudy rowing on the lake which reflected a grey low sky.

'It looks like Windermere today, doesn't it?' he said.

Trudy had not seen Windermere, but she said, yes it did, and gazed at him with shining twenty-two-year-old eyes.

'Sometimes this place,' he said, 'is very like Yorkshire, but only when the weather's bad. Or, over on the mountain side, Wales.'

'Exactly what I told Gwen,' Trudy said. 'I said Wales, I said, it's like Wales.'

'Well, of course, there's quite a difference, really. It——'

'But Gwen simply squashed the idea. You see, she's an older woman, and being a schoolmistress—it's so much different when a man's a teacher—being a woman teacher, she feels she can treat me like a kid. I suppose I must expect it.'

'Oh well——'

'How long have you known Gwen?'

'Several years,' he said. 'Gwen's all right, darling. A great friend of my mother, is Gwen. Quite a member of the family.'

Trudy wanted to move her lodgings in London but she was prevented from doing so by a desire to be near Gwen, who saw Richard daily at school, and who knew his mother so well. And therefore Gwen's experience of Richard filled in the gaps in his life which were unknown to Trudy and which intrigued her.

She would fling herself into Gwen's room. 'Gwen, what d'you think? There he was waiting outside the office and he drove me home, and he's calling for me at seven, and next weekend . . .'

Gwen frequently replied, 'You are out of breath. Have you got heart trouble?'—for Gwen's room was only on the first floor. And Trudy was furious with Gwen on these occasions for seeming not to understand that the breathlessness was all part of her only being twenty-two, and excited by the boyfriend.

'I think Richard's so exciting,' Trudy said. 'It's difficult to believe I've only known him a month.'

'Has he invited you home to meet his mother?' Gwen enquired.

'No—not yet. Oh, do you think he will?'

'Yes, I think so. One day I'm sure he will.'

'Oh, do you mean it?' Trudy flung her arms girlishly round Gwen's impassive neck.

'When is your father coming up?' Gwen said.

'Not for ages, if at all. He can't leave Leicester just now, and he hates London.'

'You must get him to come and ask Richard what his intentions are. A young girl like you needs protection.'

'Gwen, don't be silly.'

Often Trudy would question Gwen about Richard and his mother.

'Are they well off? Is she a well-bred woman? What's the house like? How long have you known Richard? Why hasn't he married before? The mother, is she——'

'Lucy is a marvel in her way,' Gwen said.

'Oh, do you call her Lucy? You must know her awfully well.'

'I'm quite,' said Gwen, 'a member of the family in my way.'

'Richard has often told me that. Do you go there *every* Sunday?'

'Most Sundays,' Gwen said. 'It is often very amusing, and one sometimes sees a fresh face.'

'Why,' Trudy said, as the summer passed and she had already been away for several weekends with Richard, 'doesn't he ask me to meet his mother? If my mother were alive and living in London I know I would have asked him home to meet her.'

Trudy threw out hints to Richard. 'How I wish you could meet my father. You simply must come up to Leicester in the Christmas holidays and stay with him. He's rather tied up in Leicester and never leaves it. He's an insurance manager. The successful kind.'

'I can't very well leave Mother at Christmas,' Richard said, 'but I'd love to meet your father some other time.' His tan had worn off, and Trudy thought him more distinguished and at the same time more unattainable than ever.

'I think it only right,' Trudy said in her young young way, 'that one should introduce the man one loves to one's parents'—for it was agreed between them that they were in love.

But still, by the end of October, Richard had not asked her to meet his mother.

'Does it matter all that much?' Gwen said.

'Well, it would be a definite step forward,' Trudy said. 'We can't go on being just friends like this. I'd like to know where I stand with him. After all, we're in love and we're both free.. Do you know, I'm beginning to think he hasn't any serious intentions after all. But if he asked me to meet his mother it would be a sort of sign, wouldn't it?'

'It certainly would,' Gwen said.

'I don't even feel I can ring him up at home until I've met his mother. I'd feel shy of talking to her on the phone. I must meet her. It's becoming a sort of obsession.'

'It certainly is,' Gwen said. 'Why don't you just say to him, "I'd like to meet your mother"?'

'Well, Gwen, there are some things a girl can't say.'

'No, but a woman can.'

'Are you going on about my age again? I tell you, Gwen, I feel twenty-two. I think twenty-two. I am twenty-two so far as

Richard's concerned. I don't think really you can help me much. After all, you haven't been successful with men yourself, have you?'

'No,' Gwen said, 'I haven't. I've always been on the old side.'

'That's just my point. It doesn't get you anywhere to feel old and think old. If you want to be successful with men you have to hang on to your youth.'

'It wouldn't be worth it at the price,' Gwen said, 'to judge by the state you're in.'

Trudy started to cry and ran to her room, presently returning to ask Gwen questions about Richard's mother. She could rarely keep away from Gwen when she was not out with Richard.

'What's his mother really like? Do you think I'd get on with her?'

'If you wish I'll take you to see his mother one Sunday.'

'No, no,' Trudy said. 'It's got to come from him if it has any meaning. The invitation must come from Richard.'

Trudy had almost lost her confidence, and in fact had come to wonder if Richard was getting tired of her, since he had less and less time to spare for her, when unexpectedly and yet so inevitably, in November, he said, 'You must come and meet my mother.'

'Oh!' Trudy said.

'I should like you to meet my mother. She's looking forward to it.'

'Oh, does she know about me?'

'Rather.'

'Oh!'

'It's happened. Everything's all right,' Trudy said breathlessly.

'He has asked you home to meet his mother,' Gwen said without looking up from the exercise book she was correcting.

'It's important to me, Gwen.'

'Yes, yes,' Gwen said.

'I'm going on Sunday afternoon,' Trudy said. 'Will you be there?'

'Not till supper time,' Gwen said. 'Don't worry.'

168

'He said, "I want you to meet Mother. I've told her all about you."'

'All about you?'

'That's what he said, and it means so much to me, Gwen. So much.'

Gwen said, 'It's a beginning.'

'Oh, it's the beginning of everything. I'm sure of that.'

Richard picked her up in his Singer at four on Sunday. He seemed preoccupied. He did not, as usual, open the car door for her, but slid into the driver's seat and waited for her to get in beside him. She fancied he was perhaps nervous about her meeting his mother for the first time.

The house on Campion Hill was delightful. They must be very *comfortable*, Trudy thought. Mrs Seeton was a tall, stooping woman, well dressed and preserved, with thick steel-grey hair and large light eyes. 'I hope you'll call me Lucy,' she said. 'Do you smoke?'

'I don't,' said Trudy.

'Helps the nerves,' said Mrs Seeton, 'when one is getting on in life. You don't need to smoke yet awhile.'

'No,' Trudy said. 'What a lovely room, Mrs Seeton.'

'*Lucy*,' said Mrs Seeton.

'Lucy,' Trudy said, very shyly, and looked at Richard for support. But he was drinking the last of his tea and looking out of the window as if to see whether the sky had cleared.

'Richard has to go out for supper,' Mrs Seeton said, waving her cigarette holder very prettily. 'Don't forget to watch the time, Richard. But Trudy will stay to supper with me, I *hope*. Trudy and I have a lot to talk about, I'm sure.' She looked at Trudy and very faintly, with no more than a butterfly-flick, winked.

Trudy accepted the invitation with a conspiratorial nod and a slight squirm in her chair. She looked at Richard to see if he would say where he was going for supper, but he was gazing up at the top pane of the window, his fingers tapping on the arm of the shining Old Windsor chair on which he sat.

Richard left at half-past six, very much more cheerful in his going than he had been in his coming.

'Richard gets restless on a Sunday,' said his mother.

'Yes, so I've noticed,' Trudy said, so that there should be no mistake about who had been occupying his recent Sundays.

'I daresay now you want to hear all about Richard,' said his mother in a secretive whisper, although no one was in earshot. Mrs Seeton giggled through her nose and raised her shoulders all the way up her long neck till they almost touched her ear-rings.

Trudy vaguely copied her gesture. 'Oh yes,' she said, 'Mrs Seeton.'

'Lucy. You must call me Lucy, now, you know. I want you and me to be friends. I want you to feel like a member of the family. Would you like to see the house?'

She led the way upstairs and displayed her affluent bedroom, one wall of which was entirely covered by mirror, so that, for every photograph on her dressing table of Richard and Richard's late father, there were virtually two photographs in the room.

'This is Richard on his pony, Lob. He adored Lob. We all adored Lob. Of course, we were in the country then. This is Richard with Nana. And this is Richard's father at the outbreak of war. What did you do in the war, dear?'

'I was at school,' Trudy said, quite truthfully.

'Oh, then you're a teacher, too?'

'No, I'm a secretary. I didn't leave school till after the war.'

Mrs Seeton said, looking at Trudy from two angles, 'Good gracious me, how deceiving. I thought you were about Richard's age, like Gwen. Gwen is such a dear. This is Richard as a graduate. Why he went into schoolmastering I don't know. Still, he's a very good master. Gwen always says so, quite definitely. Don't you adore Gwen?'

'Gwen is a good bit older than me,' Trudy said, being still upset on the subject of age.

'She ought to be here any moment. She usually comes for supper. Now I'll show you the other rooms and Richard's room.'

When they came to Richard's room his mother stood on the threshold and, with her finger to her lips for no apparent reason, swung the door open. Compared with the rest of the house this was a bleak, untidy, almost schoolboy's room. Richard's green pyjama trousers lay on the floor where he had stepped out of them. This was a sight familiar to Trudy from her several weekend excursions with Richard, of late months, to hotels up the Thames valley.

'So untidy,' said Richard's mother, shaking her head woefully. 'So untidy. One day, Trudy, dear, we must have a real chat.'

Gwen arrived presently, and made herself plainly at home by going straight into the kitchen to prepare a salad. Mrs Seeton carved slices of cold meat while Trudy stood and watched them both, listening to a conversation between them which indicated a long intimacy. Richard's mother seemed anxious to please Gwen.

'Expecting Grace tonight?' Gwen said.

'No, darling, I thought perhaps not *tonight*. Was I right?'

'Oh, of course, yes. Expecting Joanna?'

'Well, as it's Trudy's *first* visit, I thought perhaps not——'

'Would you,' Gwen said to Trudy, 'lay the table, my dear. Here are the knives and forks.'

Trudy bore these knives and forks into the dining-room with a sense of having been got rid of with a view of being talked about.

At supper, Mrs Seeton said, 'It seems a bit odd, there only being the three of us. We usually have such jolly Sunday suppers. Next week, Trudy, you must come and meet the whole crowd—mustn't she, Gwen?'

'Oh yes,' Gwen said, 'Trudy must do that.'

Towards half-past ten Richard's mother said, 'I doubt if Richard will be back in time to run you home. Naughty boy, I daren't think what he gets up to.'

On the way to the bus stop Gwen said, 'Are you happy now that you've met Lucy?'

'Yes, I think so. But I think Richard might have stayed. It would have been nice. I daresay he wanted me to get to know his mother by myself. But in fact I felt the need of his support.'

'Didn't you have a talk with Lucy?'

'Well yes, but not much really. Richard probably didn't realise you were coming to supper. Richard probably thought his mother and I could have a heart-to-heart——'

'I usually go to Lucy's on Sunday,' Gwen said.

'Why?'

'Well, she's a friend of mine. I know her ways. She amuses me.'
During the week Trudy saw Richard only once, for a quick drink.

'Exams,' he said. 'I'm rather busy, darling.'

'Exams in November? I thought they started in December.'

'Preparation for exams,' he said. 'Preliminaries. Lots of work.'
He took her home, kissed her on the cheek and drove off.

She looked after the car, and for a moment hated his moustache. But she pulled herself together and, recalling her youthfulness, decided she was too young really to judge the fine shades and moods of a man like Richard.

He picked her up at four o'clock on Sunday.

'Mother's looking forward to seeing you,' he said. 'She hopes you will stay for supper.'

'You won't have to go out, will you, Richard?'

'Not tonight, no.'

But he did have to go out to keep an appointment of which his mother reminded him immediately after tea. He had smiled at his mother and said, 'Thanks.'

Trudy saw the photograph album, then she heard how Mrs Seeton had met Richard's father in Switzerland, and what Mrs Seeton had been wearing at the time.

At half-past six the supper party arrived. These were three women, including Gwen. The one called Grace was quite pretty, with a bewildered air. The one called Iris was well over forty and rather loud in her manner.

'Where's Richard tonight, the old cad?' said Iris.

'How do I know?' said his mother. 'Who am I to ask?'

'Well, at least he's a hard worker during the week. A brilliant teacher,' said doe-eyed Grace.

'Middling as a schoolmaster,' Gwen said.

'Oh, Gwen! Look how long he's held down the job,' his mother said.

'I should think,' Grace said, 'he's wonderful with the boys.'

'Those Shakespearean products at the end of the summer term are really magnificent,' Iris bawled. 'I'll hand him that, the old devil.'

172

'Magnificent,' said his mother. 'You must admit, Gwen——'

'Very middling performances,' Gwen said.

'I suppose you are right, but, after all, they are only schoolboys. You can't do much with untrained actors, Gwen,' said Mrs Seeton very sadly.

'I adore Richard,' Iris said, 'when he's in his busy, occupied mood. He's so——'

'Oh yes,' Grace said, 'Richard is wonderful when he's got a lot on his mind.'

'I know,' said his mother. 'There was one time when Richard had just started teaching—I must tell you this story—he ...'

Before they left Mrs Seeton said to Trudy, 'You will come with Gwen next week, won't you? I want you to regard yourself as one of us. There are two other friends of Richard's I do want you to meet. Old friends.'

On the way to the bus Trudy said to Gwen, 'Don't you find it dull going to Mrs Seeton's every Sunday?'

'Well, yes, my dear young thing, and no. From time to time one sees a fresh face, and then it's quite amusing.'

'Doesn't Richard ever stay at home on a Sunday evening?'

'No, I can't say he does. In fact, he's very often away for the whole weekend. As you know.'

'Who are these women?' Trudy said, stopping in the street.

'Oh, just old friends of Richard's.'

'Do they see him often?'

'Not now. They've become members of the family.'

ANOTHER SURVIVOR

Ruth Fainlight

He's fifty now, but the day his mother and father took him to the railway station with the one permitted suitcase, clutching a satchel crammed with entomological collecting equipment he refused to leave behind, that chilly, too-harshly-bright day of a windy, reluctant spring, was in 1938, and he was twelve years old. With the other children lucky enough to be included in this refugee group going to England, and their agitated and mournful parents, they moved to the far end of the platform in an attempt to make themselves less conspicuous. Rudi recognised two of the boys from last year at school. Since the holidays he had been kept at home: Jewish students were no longer acceptable; nor were they safe. A few children had begun to cry, unable not to respond to the tears their parents tried so hard to repress. The entire group emanated a terrible collective desolation, unaffected by any individual attempt to put a good face on matters, or hopeful talk of a future reunion. For all of them, it was their last sight of each other, their last goodbye. Sharing a stridently upholstered couch with three men as withdrawn into their separate worlds as he is, staring unseeingly at other patients moving restlessly around the crowded day-ward, Rudi's face is still marked by the same appalled expression which had settled on it that morning so many years ago.

His parents belonged to families who had lived in the city for generations. Though Rudi was an only child, there had been many houses and apartments where he was welcome and at home, many celebrations to attend and cousins to play with. The family ramified

174

through the professions: doctors, lawyers, academics, architects: one of those cultivated, free-thinking manifestations of Jewish emancipation whose crucial importance to the European spirit only became apparent after its destruction. His father had been a biologist, his mother a talented amateur pianist. At night, in the dormitory of the school he was put into by the same kindly people who had organised his rescue, he tried to make himself sleep by seeing how many themes he could bring back to mind from the music she had played. He remembered their apartment full of the sound of her piano, and himself creeping up behind her, steps deadened by the soft Persian rugs whose silk nap glinted like water in the mote-laden beams of afternoon sunlight coming through creamy net curtains, hoping to reach the piano stool and put his hands over her eyes before she even realised he was home from school.

That was the picture he had kept on the iconstasis of his mind during the years when there was no news of them at all. That, and another one—walking in the country one Sunday with his father. Even now, through the distractions of hospital life, he distinctly remembers the surge of pride and intellectual excitement when he suddenly understood what his father was explaining about the particular structure and composition of the hills around them—a lesson in geography and geology; and he remembers, also, how he called upon that memory to sustain him through every boyhood crisis.

Though he mastered English quickly and did his schoolwork well, the only thing that really interested him was the prospect of taking part in the war and adding his energy to the battle against Nazism. But he never managed to see any fighting or even get onto the continent of Europe before it ended. And then, after seven years of suspense, of great swoops between optimism and an absolute conviction that he would never see his parents alive again, the camps were opened up and the first reports and pictures began to appear. The effort he makes, even now, is to shut off parts of his mind, to push all that information away. Nightmares, day-mares— black, white, bleeding, disembowelled, flayed: Goya-esque mares with staring, maddened eyes had been galloping across the wincing terrain of his brain ever since. But he was not able to stop

175

collecting facts; nor stop imagining how every atrocity he heard or read about might have been suffered by his parents.

Then he calmed down, came through it—another survivor. So much time passed that he could even acknowledge how privileged and fortunate he was, weighed in the balance of the global misery. Every morning over breakfast he could read in the newspapers stories of war, famine, torture, and injustice, and be no more affected by them than the newspaper readers of that time were by the catastrophe which engulfed him and his family. He was healthy, prosperous, successful. His wife had not left him. His children were growing up. His work presented no real problems. It was just that now, after more than thirty years, he was overcome with a most intense yearning for his mother. He felt as though he were still a boy of twelve, gone away from home for the first time: the adoring son of a proud, doting mother (that identity which in truth had been his, which had been waiting all this time for him to admit to and assume) who cannot be diverted by promises of even the most fabulous pleasures if they will keep him away from her one moment longer. And the strength of this feeling made him aware of how much he had repressed when it had really happened.

For the first time he was able to remember what his mother had been like before the war. During the intervening years, memory had been blotted out by imagination, which is always stronger. He had only been able to imagine her as a victim, not as a woman at the height of her vigour and self-confidence. This release of memory from the prison of fear had brought about her resurrection.

Twenty years ago when Rudi and Barbara found their house, the streets between Camden Town and Primrose Hill were neither fashionable nor expensive. They had lived there ever since, while houses around them changed hands for ten and twenty times what they paid. It had been fixed up and periodically redecorated but basically retained the style of the era when they moved in: austere and utilitarian, student-like; with white-walled, charcoal-grey and neutral coloured rooms intended as the background for rational living. He had been attracted to Barbara because she seemed so rational. Nothing about their house reminded him of where he had lived until the age of twelve. The two interiors were entirely different.

Barbara had never been interested in how the house looked. Since the last of the three children started school she had trained and qualified as a social worker, and was out for most of the day and quite a few evenings. Rudi, who had become an accountant after the war, found he was bringing more work home, and often spent whole days at his desk in the big open all-purpose room on the ground floor. There was nothing wrong with his corner—it had been especially planned so that everything necessary was within reach; but sitting there one early winter afternoon he looked around and wondered how he had lived for so long in this bleak, characterless environment. At home, he thought—and became aware that home was not this house at all—everything had been so much prettier and more comfortable; more comforting, too; gratifying to the eye and the spirit in a way the room he now sat in gave no indication of understanding or allowing for. He had a strong, momentary hallucination of his mother as she must have been in 1933 or 1934, perfumed and elegantly dressed to go out for the evening, walking a few steps through the door and glancing around. He had become inured to and then unaware of the frayed, stained upholstery they'd never bothered to replace after the children had outgrown their destructive phase. Through her slightly slanting pale blue eyes, he saw the muddy, formless paintings friends had given them years ago which remained the only decorations, and watched them narrow with distaste and incomprehension before she disappeared without having noticed him.

Walking home from the tube station next day, Rudi was surprised by how many antique shops had opened in the district. A lamp on display reminded him of one in the dining-room of his childhood home. It had stood on the right-hand side of a large, ornately carved sideboard, and he had loved the winter evenings when its opalescent glass shade glowed like a magic flower. Antique shops had always made him feel ignorant and gullible, but he forced himself to go inside. The lamp was more expensive than any comparable object he had ever bought, and as he wrote a cheque he was sweating as though engaged in the commission of a fearful, dangerous crime. Standing and lit on his desk, the lamp made everything in the room seem even more nondescript. He could not stop looking at it.

'Oh, that's new, isn't it?' Barbara remarked as she hurried through the house between work and a meeting, tying a headscarf over her short blonde hair. 'I forgot some papers,' she explained, 'or I wouldn't have come back. I've left something for supper for you and the children.'

'That's really beautiful. I'd like to do a drawing of it,' Faith said. She was the elder of the two girls, and had just become an art student. Though circumstances had made him an accountant, Rudi often wondered if he had betrayed his potential. He thought of himself as an artist manqué. Faith was the only one of the children who took after him. It would be hard to tell that Mavis and Tony had a Jewish father. They were much more like Barbara's side of the family.

Most fathers he knew would be more likely to spend time at the weekend with sons rather than daughters. But Tony had never given him an opportunity to develop that sort of special relationship. When not at school the boy was always out somewhere with friends—an eminently social being. Mavis, the baby of the family, had been her mother's girl from the start, and so Rudi and Faith had been left to make their own Saturday excursions. Visiting museums and galleries with her, combined pleasure and anguish. He was grateful for the opportunity to view paintings or statues which had excited and drawn him back to them over and over again as a young man, but which he had not seen for years. It was wonderful to watch Faith's knowledge and appreciation increase, to witness the development of this lovely, perceptive creature. The anguish came when he remembered visiting museums with his mother; when he recognised the inherent sensitivity of Faith's responses, so similar to what his mother's had been; when his pleasure at her responses made him aware of what his mother must have felt about him.

Often they would set out with no particular destination, call in at bookshops or wander around street markets. Now, Rudi had an aim, and they would search for pictures, rugs, china, bits of furniture—anything that reminded him of the comfortable bourgeois home he had grown up in. Faith thought it perfectly natural to buy so much—while he found it much easier to spend money in the company of his pretty, auburn-haired seventeen-year-old daughter than when when he was alone. He had loved her from the first sight of her hour-old face. What had touched his heart so profoundly, though he had not known it at the time, was an unmistakable and strongly marked resemblance to his mother. The echoes and parallels and actual duplications between his daughter and mother incremented like compound interest once he began to look for them. Because of this, he felt he had to do whatever he could to help her, as though the years torn from his mother's life could be made good somehow if Faith were happy and fulfilled.

The difference between his recent acquisitions and the rest of the furnishings gave the house a hybrid quality and disturbed them all. Rudi began to be irritable and dissatisfied, suspecting that he would never manage to achieve a convincing reproduction of his parental home. It was becoming harder to summon up his mother's image with the same marvellous tangibility. The lamps and rugs and little tables were useless magic. And yet even the memory of her first, vivid return as the person she really had been instead of only the dehumanised victim which was all he had been able to imagine since the war, was enough to change his relationship to everything.

He found it difficult to believe that he and Barbara were actually husband and wife. She was so calm, so settled and busy and mature; like a kindly, abstracted nurse. He'd had a nursemaid rather like Barbara, when he was about six years old. Apart from commenting on the amount of money he must be spending, she seemed benignly indifferent to the transformation of the house. In bed, though, when the light was out and he took her warm, silent, acquiescent body into his arms, he could not stop himself from imagining that she was his mother. Frequently, he felt about to burst into tears.

The sight of his glaring eyes and pale, tense, puffy face in need of a shave, repelled him when he caught sight of it in the bathroom mirror.

Rudi had avoided talking to the children about the war, the camps, and how his parents died. He had never even managed to give them any explanation about their connection to Judaism. Now he felt it was too late to begin, and was bitterly ashamed of his cowardice. Of course his mother would have wanted her grandchildren to know everything. Perhaps that was why she had come back, and, because he was not fulfilling his duty, the reason for her withdrawal. This thought put him into a deep depression for several days. But that Saturday afternoon on the Portobello Road with Faith, he saw a dress very like one his mother used to wear, dangling from the rail of an old-clothes stall. It gave him an idea. If his mother would not appear of her own free will, dressing Faith in similar clothes might force her back.

Faith was delighted with the dress and hurried him home so she could try it on. The others were out and the house was empty. When Faith came down the stairs Rudi was astounded by the uncanny resemblance. This was not a fantasy or hallucination, but a solid, breathing figure of flesh—a revenant: his mother even before he had known her, before his birth, when she had been a young girl. He was awestruck and terrified. Unaware that she was being used for conjuration, his daughter had innocently assumed the identity of a dead woman.

He had succeeded beyond his imaginings. His mother was in the room—but how many of her? There was the young girl incarnated in his once more recognisable daughter (recreated in any case by the natural laws of genetic inheritance): the two of them fused into this touching being for whom he had been trying to make the appropriate setting with every object purchased; and another—the one he had not wanted to meet again ever.

It was the victim who had haunted him for years. Perhaps those lamps and rugs had not been bought to lure back the girl and untroubled woman, after all—but to ward off this one. Gaunt, dirty, cowed, huddled defensively near the foot of the staircase and wearing the threadbare clothes of a camp inmate, she glared with sick, unrecognising eyes towards him. The sight made him want to die. He could see them both at the same time, they were only a few feet apart, though inhabiting separate universes.

'Take off that dress!' he commanded. 'Go upstairs and take it off right now!'

Faith stared with amazement. 'I don't want to take it off.' The concentration camp woman vanished at the sound of her voice. 'I like it. I want to wear it all the time. It's lovely. The girls at school will all want to have dresses like this.'

'You look stupid in it,' he said desperately. 'You look ridiculous.'

'I don't think I do.' Her expression was defiant and challenging.

The only way to control his fear of breaking down was to stiffen his spirit with anger. Faith could not understand what was happening. 'Take that dress off immediately or I'll tear it off.' She knew he would, yet refused to obey and stood her ground.

He had crossed the empty space between them in less than a moment. The cloth was soft and old and gave easily. She screamed with shock and fear. The turmoil of his emotions was sickening. He thought he would lose consciousness. She was in his power and he was tormenting her like a camp guard who could not resist exercising that power; as though she were his specially chosen victim. There must have been someone who singled out his mother in the same way.

She pulled away from him, clutching the torn dress together, and ran up the stairs. 'Fascist!' she shouted, her voice thick with tears. He opened the front door and walked out of the house.

It's dark and cold, but he walks rapidly ahead, with no plan or choice of direction, completely indifferent to where he is going, his mind quite empty. After a time, the emptiness on all sides makes him realise that he must have crossed the road and climbed Primrose Hill. He tries sitting down on a bench, but the moment he stops moving, he is swamped by such self-contempt that he cannot bear it, so he starts walking again. He knows that if he goes back he will break into Faith's room and probably beat her to death. His stride lengthens. He is walking down Park Road now, down Baker Street, crossing Piccadilly, crossing the river; a tall, thick-bodied man unable to stop walking. He is going to keep walking until a car knocks him down or someone fells him with a blow, until he reaches the end of his endurance and drops in his tracks.

THE ELEPHANT MAN

Susan Hill

It was on the same day that they drained the Round Pond, for the first time in forty years, that Nanny Fawcett met her Friend. And in all the time the three of them spent together afterwards, she never gave him any name in front of the child, he was always My Friend.

William had asked anxiously about the Pond, what it would look like, how big it would be now?

'The same size as always, won't it? *That's* a silly question.'

'Just with no water in it?'

'We don't say "with no" we say "without any".'

'Yes. How big will the pit be?'

'What pit? There won't be any *pit*, will there? Lift your arms up.'

The stream of lather came trickling around both sides of his neck and down his pale chest. At the edges of the bath, the scum was grey, when the water moved. He struggled to imagine the Round Pond, to which he went every day, empty of its expanse of water, rippled across the centre by the wind, but he failed, he could not picture it and was alarmed by his ignorance of how it might be.

'If there won't be a pit, what *will* there be, then?'

A grip fell down into the bath out of Nanny Fawcett's coiled-up red hair, as she bent over him.

'Mud,' she said sharply. 'Stand up.' There was a line of sweat-beads along her upper lip. She retrieved the grip impatiently. Wary of her moods, which came unpredictably, and then hung about her, thickening and tainting the atmosphere or rooms, he did not ask what would have happened to the ducks. He imagined them, kept in individual, waterless cages, and fed by keepers with broken bread, and later, hung in rows by their webbed, pink feet along the steel rail at Murchison's, Butcher and Poulterer.

Nanny Fawcett began to rub him with a very dry towel.

At the beginning, there had been another Nanny, about whom he now remembered only a smell, and an air of weariness and loss of hope. 'I was trained in the old school,' she had said, on arrival, 'I am only used to the best type of home.' And she had been firm in her demands for Sole Charge and no sweets of any kind and the sacking of the cleaning woman who used bad language. 'But then she is so reliable and decided,' William's mother had said, sipping a Manhattan in the oyster-grey drawing-room, 'everything is so nice for me, so straightforward.' Though, in truth, she felt a little guilty that this was so, believed obscurely that it was not altogether natural to have a nanny who gave simply no trouble. So that it had been almost a salve to her conscience when that Nanny had, abruptly, died, and the problems of finding someone new and suitable began. William was three and a half.

He could not now imagine how it had been before Nanny Fawcett came to the house, he saw the world entirely through her eyes, all his experience of life reached him filtered through her. Nanny Fawcett was Irish, she was in her middle thirties, she came from a good, Protestant family in Dublin, she was moody. Her breasts were too large and concealed a heart filled with prejudice, most markedly against men, and against the Republic of Eire.

William's mother had some weeks of anxiety. 'I do hope we have done the right thing, she did *seem* the most suitable, though it is clear to us all that Nannies are not what they were. But I am afraid that I suspect Nanny Fawcett of dying her hair. That red is so unnatural.' She spoke as one of some distant generation, but she was not old-fashioned, merely true to her breeding. She spoke in a high-pitched, nasal, slightly whining voice. But she felt, too, a little more comfortable with Nanny Fawcett, felt secure in her own position as mistress of both house and child. It was only what one expected, to have to put up with some quirks, in a Nanny.

When they visited the house in Cadogan Square, William's

maternal grandmother sat among the fringed sofas from Peter Jones, the skin beneath her eyes most carefully powdered and asked, 'What about this Nanny Fawcett?' 'But I think, you know,' said William's mother, when they had discussed it, 'that she is *all right*, I think that everything is as it should be, on the whole. Of course, I would never entrust William to just anybody.'

They could feel their duty done, then, and dismiss the child's welfare under Nanny Fawcett from their minds.

To William, the only realities of which he could be certain, the only truths he knew, came to him through Nanny Fawcett. Everywhere else was the territory of strangers, the ground upon which he walked, in company with his mother and father and the Cadogan Square grandmother, was insubstantial. He sensed that he could never have survived, permanently, in their atmosphere. From Nanny Fawcett he learned that there were 'Irish *and* Irish', and that the Protestants of good family living in Dublin kept themselves very much to themselves, they had their own clubs and dances and private schools.

'A trained Nanny,' she said, over and over again, 'is not a servant. This a profession. I am not a *maid*, you know, nothing of that kind.'

He learned about the spoliation of Dublin's Georgian buildings and about the low character of the feckless Southern Irish, Roman Catholics and working class, who came over to England and gave their country a bad name. He learned about the winning ways and loose morals of the colleens who worked as waitresses in Lyons Corner House and conductresses on buses of the Green Line. He learned about the integrity of the Unionist party and the reign of terror by bigoted priests among the peasants of Eire. He learned that Nanny Fawcett's grandmother bred Irish setter dogs, and that her family had always been 'proud'. Above all, he learned that most of the trouble in the world, and all the troubles of women, could be laid at the door of men.

'You'll be a man,' she said, laying his checked Viyella shirt out on the chair. 'You'll be as bad as all the rest.' And he had felt suddenly ashamed, knowing that his days were strictly numbered with her. He wished that he might do something to change his sex, to grow up or in some other way escape from the general mantle of male guilt. He was uncertain how he stood with Nanny Fawcett, what she truly thought of him. Her eyes, upturned slightly at the corners like those of an Oriental, flitted over him and gave him no reassurance, nothing more than a casual, spasmodic approval for some point of manners remembered or temptation not succumbed to. He planned ways to ingratiate himself with her, so that he might perceive some definite sign that her commendation would last for ever. But always, the eyes swept quickly over him, and he despaired. There was only the immediate chance of an hour, or day, of favour to cling to, he learned to live his life in these small snatches. They were like stepping stones, below which ran the dark river of her moods.

And so, he was surprised, the first day they met the Friend. It was January, slate-grey, a cold wind cutting across between the trees at their legs. He began to trail behind Nanny Fawcett up the slope, anxious about how the Round Pond would look, of how he might cope with getting to know it all over again, the unfamiliar.

'Don't scrape your shoes, you've only just this week had a new pair.'

Today, her hair shone redder than before, and the coils were more elaborate, gripped under the navy-blue hat. She had said, 'You're to behave yourself very nicely and not to be a nuisance, you're to make a good impression.'

'Why?'

'Because we might be going to meet someone, that's why. And you're having a jumper on under that coat, the wind's enough to cut you in half.'

He wondered who it was that they might see, if it was not the other Nannies, beside whom she would sometimes sit, on the green bench. Though, more often than not, she ignored them, neither sat nor talked, preferring to keep herself apart. The others, she had told him, had nothing of interest to say, or else they gave themselves airs, or were in charge of unsuitable children.

'Who might we see?'

'Never you mind, you'll find out in good time—and that's something else, you're to be quiet and not to go pestering with questions like you do, and "I want this, I want that", every five minutes. *We* want a bit of peace and quiet to ourselves, my friend and I.'

He gave up trying to imagine what kind of friend Nanny Fawcett might have. At the top of the slope, he walked forwards a little, and then stopped. The Pond was huge, it had spread and spread, with the exit of the water it seemed to him that he would never be able to walk as far as the opposite edge, he could barely see it. It was mud, thick and stiff and sculptured into lines of thin waves, towards the rim, as though the water had coagulated. He noticed the boats, beached on the mud and larded with it, so that their shape was disguised. They had been there for years, he thought, since before he was born, they had been there forever.

'Don't stand staring at that, it's only a basinful of mud, and thick with germs, I shouldn't wonder, there's nothing to see.'

But he could not take his eyes off the landscape of the pond, the craters and pits, the branches of trees and the abandoned boats picked out on it, he wanted to step down and walk across, poking and digging, to get into the centre where no one could reach him, not even the men with long grappling hooks, who sometimes had to bring the boats in, when the wind dropped.

Nanny Fawcett caught his hand. 'Did you *hear* me?' He went after her, away from the Pond and up towards the bandstand on the edge of the trees.

For a long time, nobody came. He went away from her and down between the horse-chestnut trees, mashing the old leaves with his feet. He found an almost straight stick and held it like a lance. No other children were here, only, some yards away, a woman in green with a dog. From the beginning the afternoon had been strangely different, this place was not like the gardens to which he usually came, to rush about and sail a boat, while Nanny Fawcett looked on. The whole landscape was changed, everything was coloured differently, and the trees were a new shape. The Pond was dry. They might have been in another country. He was excited by it, and a little alarmed.

From far away, down the pleached walk came the shouts of boys, high and thin in the wind. He began to poke about in the leaves again with his straight stick.

When he looked up, he saw that Nanny Fawcett's friend had arrived, they were sitting together beside the empty bandstand. Nanny Fawcett touched her hand now and again to the coils of hair underneath the navy-blue hat. After a moment or two, William went nearer. The fact that her friend was a man completed his sense of strangeness, everything was suddenly out of joint in his view of the world and of people, if Nanny Fawcett, who despised men, could be so publicly friendly with one, nodding and smiling on the green bench.

He looked, William thought, as though his clothes did not belong to him, as though he were used to wearing something quite different. Though they were ordinary, a grey tweed overcoat, rather long, over grey trousers, and an egg-yellow scarf. And his face, the shape of his head and the set of his flesh across the bones, seemed not to fit with the rest of him, he was like a figure out of the Crazy Men game, where you moved a row of heads along, fitting them in turn to a row of different bodies underneath, and none of them seemed exactly to belong. Something in the man's features was constantly changing, as though he were trying on new expressions, toying with them and then discarding them, he smiled and grimaced and frowned and formed his mouth into a little, soft, pursed shape, and the flesh of his forehead slipped up and down somehow, under the shelf of thinning hair, the skin of his neck was loose.

William thought that he was old—and then not so old, it was hard to tell. He had a lot of very long teeth, and a tiny chin, and very pale, gloveless hands.

He moved the stick about on the grass at his feet, and Nanny Fawcett saw him.

'Come here now, you're not to go off too far into those trees by yourself–come right here. This is him, this William—stand up properly, child—Now, *here* is the person I told you we might be going to meet.' She was talking much faster than usual, and every now and then, her hand went up to the coils of hair. William took a step nearer the bench, and the man leaned down and put out one of the pale hands, smiling with all his teeth, as though it were a joke, that they should be so formally introduced. William thought, he is not a very old man, but he is older than my father. He said, 'They've emptied the water out of the Round Pond. It's just mud now.'

'Ah!' said Nanny Fawcett's friend, and the expression on his face slipped and changed again, and now he looked secretive, he put a tongue inside his cheek and made it swell out a little, as though he were sucking a toffee. 'I daresay you wanted to sail a boat, didn't you? I daresay that's the trouble.'

'No, I didn't, I like it empty. I want it to stay like that. There are boats that have sunk, you can see them. And twigs. There are ...'

'Off you go,' Nanny Fawcett said, suddenly impatient. 'Don't chatter so, about nothing, off you go and run about and don't wander too far off into those trees, do you hear me?'

He saw her turn a little on the bench, so that she was facing the Friend, saw a bright expression come into her face, as though everything he had said and would say were all that could interest her. The man turned his back, so that there was only the dark grey tweed and the line of yellow scarf below.

William moved away, chilled by the abrupt loss of their attention, and wandered about on the path by the trees. His hands were cold inside the woollen gloves. He wanted something to happen, for the day to become familiar again. Above his head, and stretching away into the distance, the sky was uniformly pale, and grey as brains. The woman in green, with the dog, had gone, everybody was going, out of the January wind.

Under one of the horse-chestnuts he found a conker, and although the green pulpy case had blemished, and the spines were soft and rotten, inside the nut was perfect, hard and polished like a mahogany table. He scooped it out and held it, feeling it slip, shiny, between his fingers. When he disturbed the leaves, the soil and moss beneath the trees sent up a cold, sweet stench.

He heard nothing, only saw the feet and legs in front of him. Very slowly he straightened up, holding the stick. It was another man. William glanced over to Nanny Fawcett, sitting with her friend on the park bench, wanting reassurance. Their faces were turned away from him.

'Nice,' the man said, 'that's nice.' His eyes were sharp and vacant at the same time, and he had a tall head. William stepped back. 'I could give you another. I could give you a lot.' And suddenly his hand shot out from under the mackintosh, and in the open palm lay eight or nine conkers, huge and glossy. 'I might give them all to you.'

'That's all right, I've got my own, thank you,' William was afraid of not being polite enough to the man, touched by the offer of the conkers, yet uneasy, not liking him to be there. When he looked again, the conkers had disappeared, and so had the man's hand, back into the pocket of the raincoat, so that he wondered whether he had seen them or not, and the man stood, smiling at him. The collar of his shirt was stiff, and shiny white.

'What's your name?'

'William.'

'That's nice. That's what I like.'

A gust of wind came knifing through the trees, stirring the dead leaves, and rattling down a loose branch. Abruptly, the man turned and began to move away, slipping round the grey trunks until he had vanished as quickly as the conkers had vanished. William stood, remembering the way he had come there. He dropped the conker into his coat pocket and kept his fingers tightly round it.

'Men,' Nanny Fawcett had said. 'There's always something that's not right about men, always something.' Now, he felt betrayed somehow, left alone among the trees with a stranger who offered him conkers, while she went on talking to her new friend.

On the way home, he asked if they would see him again.

'Oh, now, that all depends and don't little boys ask a lot of questions?'

They were walking very quickly, everyone was leaving the gardens and going off down the concrete slopes to tea, it was too cold for snow, she said, and he was out of breath now, with trying to keep up to her.

'But we might, and then again we might not, there might be treats in store, we might be seeing him somewhere else.'

'Where else? What sort of place?'

No answer.

'Doesn't he go to work?'

Nanny Fawcett rounded upon him alarmingly. 'Of course he goes to work, don't all honest men go to work, what do you take me for? I wouldn't have anything to do with any layabout, any idle man, you needn't imagine that I would.'

'No,' William said.

'But if we were to go and see him at work—well now, we might and that would be something!'

'What does he do?'

'Oh, something that would just surprise you.' Nanny Fawcett gripped his hand as they crossed the road at Kensington Gore. 'Something you'll never have heard of, and never would expect.'

'Tell me about it, *tell* me.'

'You'll find out soon enought, I daresay you will find out.'

Her face was flushed, set against the wind, and he dared not ask now, how her friend was different from all the rest, how he managed to escape her blanket condemnation of men. He had not looked any different. But perhaps he might learn the trick from him, if they met again, perhaps he could listen and watch, and discover the secret of Nanny Fawcett's favour.

He had tea in the oyster-grey drawing-room, with an apricot Danish pastry brought in by his grandmother from Cadogan Square.

'We're not going to the Park today, we're going somewhere different. It's to be a treat.'

He was being dressed in best trousers and a white shirt, his mother had gone out. 'Mum's the word,' Nanny Fawcett had said. He wondered what to expect, dared not ask.

Outside a hotel, they stopped. Nanny Fawcett bent down to him. 'You're to enjoy yourself,' she said, pumping his hand up and down to emphasise her words. 'You're not to be a trouble. You go with my friend and do as you're told, and remember just how lucky you are.'

He looked up at her, prepared for anything at all. Nanny Fawcett laughed. 'Cow's eyes!' she said. 'You'll be the death of me. It's a *party*, isn't it?'

They walked up the wide, white marble steps of the hotel and through the revolving doors, and inside everything was hushed and softly lit from chandeliers, the carpets were rose-red on the floor. Nanny Fawcett held hard on to his hand. It was some minutes before her friend came, looking more than ever strange, in shirt sleeves, and with his hair combed flat back, as though he had been disturbed from a sleep, or in the middle of some job, up a ladder. William wondered if he lived in the hotel. He made a curious face at him, screwing the flesh up around his eyes and nose, and then letting it collapse again like a pile of ash, looking blandly at Nanny Fawcett.

'Well,' he said. 'It's all fixed up, you see, all arranged.'

'I wouldn't like to think that it was not,' said Nanny Fawcett.

He brayed with laughter, showing the long teeth.

'*We* were not coming to the back entrance,' Nanny Fawcett said.

The friend's hand shot out and pinched William's cheek, and he danced a little, on the balls of his feet.

'Time presses,' he said. 'We'll do well to be getting off, getting this one settled and so forth. Well, now ...' He winked.

'Get *along* ...' Nanny Fawcett gave him a little push in the back, 'and you mind your manners, I'll be around to collect you later, won't I?'

The friend waved his arm in the direction of a deserted lounge, full of green and gold armchairs. 'What about getting settled,' he said, 'having a nice tray of tea, what about you going and putting your feet up, and I'll be down directly.'

He took William's hand.

He had thought that the upstairs corridors of hotels led only to bedrooms, but when they emerged from the left, there were tall cream-painted pillars, and huge, fronded plants, and gilt mirrors, and they walked towards another lounge.

'Going to enjoy yourself?' the friend said.

William frowned.

192

'Well, don't have a lot to say, do you? Don't have much of a tongue in your head.'

He leered down horribly, the rubber face contorting itself and seeming to flush and darken, until a grin broke it open like a wave, and everything was different again. William wondered if the face changed in sleep, too.

'Where am I going?'

They stopped. The friend banged him lightly on the back. 'Well, to a *party*, aren't you? You're going to a party.'

'Oh. Is it your party?'

'It is not.'

A door swung open ahead, letting out voices.

'All you've to do, you've to mind what you say, then you'll be nice and dandy, you see, and nothing to do but enjoy yourself.'

He did not explain further.

At Christmas, there had been four parties, and none of them was at a hotel and all of them had terrified him, each time he had prayed that there would never be another. Now, he stood back behind Nanny Fawcett's friend, looking upon the room full of strangers, other children, in ribbon and net and velvet and white shirts under tartan ties, and his stomach clenched with dread. He did not know why he had been brought here.

'Well now, how very nice!' said the woman in mauve, bending down to him, 'How nice, dear! We were expecting you.' And she turned to the other, beside her. 'Our entertainer's child!' she said, and both of them laughed a little, and looked about the room for someone to take charge of him. 'His name is William,' she said.

He had thought that always one met the same people at parties, his cousin Sophie and the Cressett twins and fat Michael, but he knew nobody here at all, their names confused him and he hung back on the edge of their games.

'We've been told to be nice to you,' a boy said.

William stood, thinking of Nanny Fawcett and the friend, far away down all the carpeted stairs, eating tea in the empty lounge.

As it went on, it became like all the other parties he had known, the terrors were at least familiar, the awful taste of the tea and of trifles in little, waxed paper cases and the staring of the bigger girls.

193

There were games which he did not win and dancing for which he had not brought his pumps. The woman in mauve clapped her hands and laughed a lot and changed the records on the gramophone, and from time to time, she took his hand and led him closer into the circle of the others. 'You are to look after this little boy.'

But then, suddenly, one of the hotel waiters had drawn the curtains and they were all made to sit tightly together on the carpeted floor, squealing a little with apprehension and excitement. Then the music began. Oh God, Oh God, make it not be a conjuror or a Punch and Judy, William thought, pressing his nails deeply into the palms of his hands. But it was not, it was something he had never seen before, something worse.

The area ahead of them was lit like a stage, with a high stool placed there, and then a figure came lumbering out of the darkness. From the shoulders down it was a man, his costume all in one piece and wumbling as it moved, like the covering on a pantomime horse. But it stood upon only two legs and the legs were three times, ten times, as long as human legs, and oddly stiff at the joints. Above the shoulders, the huge head was not a man's head, but that of an elephant, nodding and bobbing and bending forward to the music and waving its disgusting trunk.

William sat and every so often closed his eyes, willing for it to be gone, for the curtains to be drawn again and the ordinary January daylight to flood the room. But he could still hear the music and when that stopped, the elephant man spoke and sang, the voice very deep, distorted and hollow, booming away inside the huge head. He opened his eyes and did not want to look, but he could not stop himself, the square of light and then the lurching animal man drew him. It was dancing, lifting its huge legs up and down stiffly, clapping its hands together, while the head nodded. From somewhere, it produced a vividly coloured stuffed parrot, which sat upon its shoulder and answered back to jokes, in a terrible rasping voice. Then the music started again.

'Now, children, now what about everybody doing a little dance with me, what about us all dancing together? Would you like that?'

'Yes,' they yelled. 'Yes, Yes!' and clapped and bounced up and down.

'And what about somebody coming up on my shoulder and being as high as the sky, what about that? Would you like to do that?'

'Yes,' they screamed. 'Yes, yes!' and rushed forwards, clamouring about the baggy legs, clutching and laughing.

From the gramophone came the music for a Conga, and the elephant man set off with everyone clinging on behind in a chain, prancing about the room, and first one, then another was lifted high up on to its great shoulders, swaying with delight, hands touching the ceiling, swinging the chandelier. William stood back against the wall in the darkness praying not to be noticed, but when the line reached him, he was noticed, the woman in mauve clucked and took his hand, putting him in with the others, so that he was forced to trot on one leg and then the next to the music. And then, suddenly, he felt the elephant man behind him, and he was lifted up, the hands digging tightly into his sides, and he could neither scream nor protest, he could scarcely breathe, only dangle helplessly there, near to the cream-painted ceiling, and see, far below him, the upturned, mocking faces of the others, hear the blast of the music. Through the slits in the elephant head, he could see eyes, flickering like lanterns in a turnip, and he looked away dizzy, praying to be set down.

At the end, the lights did not go on immediately, he could slip out of the door and nobody noticed him.

The corridor was silent, everything closed and secret. The music faded away as he ran, and found a flight of stairs and climbed them, not daring to look back. Here the passages were narrower, the carpets dark grey and thick as felt, so that his feet made no sound. There might have been nobody else in the building.

He had thought that he would die of fear, high up in the clutch of the elephant man, but he had not died, and now he must remember it, he could still hear the music and the shrieking of the others, pounding in his ears. He came up to a long mirror at the end of the corridor and was terrified by his own reflection, tense and white-faced. The elephant man could be following him. He began

to run, back down the stairs, but on the lower corridor heard voices
and imagined some punishment inflicted upon him by the elephant
man, or else by the hotel porters and maids, and the woman in
mauve. He pushed open one of the grey doors in his panic. When
the voices and footsteps had gone away, he would run again down
to the lounge where Nanny Fawcett was having tea with her friend,
it would be all right.

'Well, now!'

He spun round. It was a bedroom, with draped curtains and a
light switched on over the long dressing-table, and reflected in the
mirror, he saw the elephant man, arms up on either side of his head.
He could not move, only stare in terror as the hands lifted off the
grey head, up and up, and then down again, until it rested on his
knees.

'Master William the party-boy,' said Nanny Fawcett's friend,
and the face creased in sudden, wicked mirth, trembling and
quivering. On a chair, William saw Nanny Fawcett's navy-blue
coat and hat, and the sensible handbag. 'All a bit of a romp and
a treat,' said her friend, 'blowed if it isn't!' His face crumpled into
sadness and mock-weeping. 'Poor old elephant!'

William saw the two images separately, the face of the man, and
that of the elephant on his lap, and then the reflections of them
in the glass, he was surrounded by the terrible faces. He gave a
sob, and put up a hand to shield his eyes, groping for the door-
handle. It would not yield, something pushed him back, and then
there was Nanny Fawcett, straightening her skirt, he was forced
to go back into the room, while her friend the elephant man
laughed until the tears ran down his cheeks. Outside in the corridor,
the voices of the others, leaving the party.

'You didn't collect your present,' Nanny Fawcett said.

Because it was raining and the hotel was not near home, they went
on a bus.

'You never would have guessed it, I know, never in a million
years,' Nanny Fawcett said, her face flushed with pleasure. 'He used
to be in the pantomimes and circuses, my friend, he's a very high
class entertainer.'

The lights of the cars swept down Piccadilly in a row, like an army advancing through the rain.

'You're the lucky one, aren't you, there's plenty that would envy you, I know. Going to a party and not even knowing the person! Well!'

He realized that he had not discovered for which child the party had been held.

'You've gone quiet,' she said, making him walk too quickly round the Square. 'If you ate too much, I shan't be very pleased, shall I, after what I told you?'

He thought of the dreams he would have that night.

'Mum's the word,' Nanny Fawcett said, turning her key in the latch. For he must say nothing about her friend and nothing about the party.

He woke in the darkness to find his pillow, and the well of the bed below his neck, filled with vomit.

'The *next* time, you learn to hold back,' said Nanny Fawcett, stripping off his pyjamas. Her hair was twisted into curious plaits about her head. 'Your eyes are bigger than your stomach, so they are. The next time you just curb your greed, thank you very much.'

He stared into her face, and did not dare ask about 'the next time'. 'He's a very nice type of man,' she said, rubbing the cold sponge briskly about his face. 'Not at all the sort you would commonly meet, so mind your P's and Q's in future and play your cards right and you'll be going to quite a number of parties, I shouldn't wonder.'

Lying in the dark again, between stiff, clean sheets, he knew that since the day they drained the Round Pond, everything had surely changed and would never be as it was, and felt afraid, wishing for the time past, when Nanny Fawcett had despised all men.

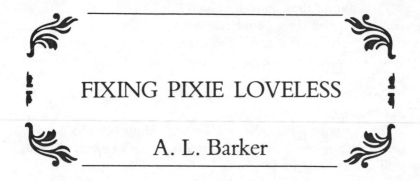

FIXING PIXIE LOVELESS

A. L. Barker

Lumley was fretting about the girl. She was on his mind, she was on all their minds, but Lumley fretted. Fish asked if he was scared of her. 'Scared of a little kid—six, seven years old—are you?'

'I'm a thinking man, Goldy, which you're not. Thinking requires something up top besides hair.'

Fish shook his yellow curls out of his collar. 'Then tell us what you thought when you thought of bringing her here.'

'I thought she'd hang the job on us.'

'She can't hang anything on me, I've never been in trouble.'

'Trouble?' Lumley went into a bronchial paroxysm of laughter.

Fish couldn't bear the crackling and curdling of Lumley's chest. It revolted. He screamed at Lumley and stamped his foot. Lumley was expiring with laughter but they both stopped immediately Ritter told them to.

'I'll finish the two of you, so help me God!' But Ritter, they knew, wouldn't need God's help.

Lumley had stuffed the inside pockets of his coat with money, such a wad of banknotes that the coat stood off from his chest. 'I put my hand over her mouth and then what could I do? She had her breath all drawn up ready to yell.'

They wouldn't forget. They had each been working, each doing his part, with just a chip of time to do it in, knowing they couldn't depend on a minute more or be sure that they wouldn't have to manage with a minute less. And it was going well they felt in their bones, not needing even to nod to each other. They worked as one, solidly and sensitively, and as one they looked up and saw the girl. Their three skins crept, it was the last of their solidarity.

She had been in the manager's office all the while, curled up on a shelf—what a place to be, between acid-flasks and an old foam fire-extinguisher!—she had a blanket and pillow and was watching them, chin in hand. Who had put a dark-faced kid halfway up the wall?

They had seen her actually decide to cry out. As if she had been waiting to get their attention first she pushed herself into a sitting position, filled her chest and opened her mouth. It was like watching a juke box go into operation after putting sixpence in.

'There was no time to gag her.'

The job was finished, they were on their way and the guard was on his, checking every door as he came along the passage. Lumley had done the only possible thing in the circumstances.

'We couldn't know he had his kid with him. It's against the security rules. He's going to have to own up. When they find the money's gone he'll have to tell them the girl's gone too. I wouldn't like to be in his shoes.'

They could afford to smile. The job couldn't have been better done if they had been professionals. They went into the place and did what they had to do and each thing latched on to another so neatly that they had felt—feeling as one—that it was history already.

Then Lumley said, 'We'll have to fix the kid.'

'Fix her?'

'Or she'll talk. She's had a good look and she'll know us again.'

'How do you fix a kid?'

'How do you fix anyone?'

Fish had already made up his mind about Lumley. He didn't need to ponder Lumley's motives, they were all of the same colour and there was no need to keep on being shocked. But Fish was shocked just the same, he had not learned to conserve his emotion.

'Get yourself life if you like,' said Ritter, 'but not while you're working for me.'

Lumley's ears went back. He tapped the money in his chest

pocket—the first thing it had bought him was nerve—'I'm working for Edgar Lumley and no kid's going to put me inside.'

Ritter went to the window. The other two, jumpy, had been constantly moving about, pacing to and fro, brushing round the four walls like flies, but this was the first time that Ritter had left his seat. Alerted, they watched him. On this moonless night, with nothing familiar for even their minds' eyes to place, they were willing, and eager, to believe that he could see farther than they could. Ritter had arranged everything, told them where the money was and how much, and what they must perform to get it. They had performed as he had said and they had the money as he had said. They waited now for what else he would say.

'We'll leave her.'

'Leave her! To talk?'

'She can't talk about us.'

'She can't? She can't tell them it was Bill Ritter, Edgar Lumley and a strawberry blond called Fish that blew B. J. Riley's safe on Thursday night?'

'She doesn't know us from Adam and there's nothing to connect us,' Ritter said patiently. 'The only danger is that if she talks right away she could put them on our tail. So we'll leave her where she won't be found right away.'

'At the bottom of a well?'

'It'll be light in a couple of hours so that's how much time we've got.' Ritter turned from the window. 'Get the car, Edgar.'

Lumley went out to the shed. He tramped through the snarled grass that had grown unchecked all summer, the money in his pockets pressed like two loving hands on each breast. He had never done a job of this importance before and was feeling inspired. He foresaw a bright future, against the slabs of dark it was very bright and very private.

The shed was padlocked, a precaution they had taken although this girl couldn't walk out. 'Someone could walk *in*,' Ritter had said, 'like a tramp looking for a place to sleep.' He believed in taking care of eventualities. Lumley was for cutting them off short. He shone his torch into the back of the car.

They all knew that the girl couldn't walk, her crutches had lain beside her on the shelf and had been left there, but Lumley's stomach turned over when he saw nothing on the back seat, only the blanket they had wrapped her in. He snatched open the car door and the blanket heaved and she looked out from under it. She did not blink, her eyes were two guns aimed at his head.

He hastily switched off the torch. 'What are you doing?'

She didn't care for the dark she said, and wrestled with the blanket, tutting her annoyance. 'It comes so *close*!'

The blanket or the dark, Lumley didn't care which—he got into the car and slammed the door. He had reasons for backing out without lights: so as not to risk attracting attention from the road, and so as not to let her get another look at his face.

'I cried and cried. Didn't you hear me?'

'Crying? You should be ashamed of yourself.'

Lumley had lifted her down from the shelf and carried her, dodging cylinders and trolleys and things that he needed both hands to advise him of in the semi-gloom. She was what he had carried out of that place—his prize! Lucky for him that Ritter and Fish were there to bring the money, lucky for them that he was there to bring the girl.

'Are we going home?'

He asked would she like to be and she said scornfully that he must be joking. Damned kids, he thought, they're not grateful to their parents.

'Are we going somewhere nice?'

Lumley had found her surprisingly heavy. She was as solid as a cricket ball but her legs dangled as he ran and her heels had struck his shins. Carrying her was painful.

He enquired, 'What's wrong with your legs?'

'They're paralysed. Where are the other men? Where's the one with the pretty hair?'

'Shut up.'

'Why did you bring me here if you don't like me?'

'To keep you quiet.'

'I wasn't going to make a noise.'

'You opened your mouth like a church door. We saw you.'

'I wouldn't have screamed. Sometimes I breathe in and out my mouth to stop my back aching.' She leaned on the seat behind him and blew into his ear. 'Like this. It lets the pain out.'

He was reversing out of the shed at that moment and would have struck her if he'd had a free hand, perhaps it would have done them all some good.

'You'll be sure to tell them what you saw, won't you? Every little detail? Don't you forget any,' he said viciously. 'Details are important.'

'I don't always tell people what they want to know.'

'Suppose we made it worth your while to keep your mouth shut?' Lumley wheezed with laughter. 'What's your price?'

'Why does your chest make that noise?'

'Would a fiver satisfy you?'

'I don't want money, I've got bags of money, all the money in the world.'

Lumley's face stiffened, his chest roared and crackled, but not with laughter. The noise of his chest was harsher than the steady purr of the engine.

He had to switch the headlights on to see where he was in relation to the yard gate. He also saw the first rain for days slanting on the dark. That's all we need, he thought, tyre and foot-marks for them to get their callipers on.

'If you promise to take me for a ride every day I won't tell. I do so like riding in cars.'

'I wouldn't give you car room.' Lumley fell out and slammed the door and shouted 'Rag legs!' through the window.

Ritter jumped on him as soon as he got into the house. 'Dead quiet I said! What are you trying to do? Advertise us?'

'Cars have engines, bits of metal making crap, crap, crap—a car won't go dead quiet.'

'I'm not talking about the car, I'm talking about you.'

'The thinking man,' supplied Fish.

'That girl's got no morals. She tried to get me to bribe her. Me!' cried Lumley. 'If we don't fix her she'll tell everything she knows and a lot more that she doesn't. She's got to be fixed before she fixes us.'

'Or before you do.'

Lumley kicked Fish's bottom and Fish lashed out with his kitten-stroke at Lumley's jaw. Ritter went between them and with a chop of his hand knocked up first Lumley's and then Fish's long bony nose. Fish cried out with shock and pain.

'Now listen. You're going to take that girl where she won't be found. You're going to run the car into the woods, right in under the trees and lock it and leave it.'

'Who's going to?' cried Lumley. 'Who are you looking at?'

'One of us. We'll draw for it.' Ritter took out a wad of banknotes and snapped off the elastic that held them. 'The lowest number gets the job.'

'We're all in this, we all stand to lose if she talks.'

'There's no point in multiplying the risk. Take a note.'

Lumley grumbled but he took a note, so did Fish, then Ritter. Fish drew the low number.

'The girl will be pleased.' Lumley grinned. 'She fancies you, Goldfish.'

Ritter held out his hand as Lumley was about to pocket the note he had drawn and told Fish, 'Three miles from here, a mile the other side of Hy Cross, a track runs off the road. Follow it till it forks. Take the right and run in under the trees as far as you can. There's a bank and a sharpish slope into an old clay pit. Get out of the car, take the handbrake off and let her roll. She'll settle at the bottom out of sight.'

'How long for?'

'Long enough.'

'And the girl?'

Ritter had red pockets under his eyeballs and sometimes looked like a spaniel. 'The girl can't walk.'

'I shouldn't have to do it, Lumley should. He brought her, let him do it!'

'Get clear as fast as you can and don't thumb a ride afterwards, walk across country to the Junction and take a train home.'

'I've left home. I'm going away.'

'Where to?'

'That's my business.'

'I must know, Derek,' said Ritter, 'for all our sakes. I may need to get in touch.'

'Some touch. I'll be in Vietnam.'

'Vietman!' Lumley's voice cracked. 'What the bloody hell for?'

'To help the bloody children!'

There was a silence which Fish endured, stiff in every hair with rage. The idea leaked into the corners of the room, then Ritter sighed, unregretfully blew out his lips.

'You'll have to go home, Derek.'

'I'll do as I like.'

'You'll have to go home just as if it was any other day and you'll stay there until you hear from me.'

'Home?' cried Fish. 'What's the good of the money at home?'

Lumley picked the strap of Fish's rucksack off his shoulder. 'You won't have the money if you don't cooperate.'

He had seen Fish stow his share away in the rucksack. Fish had climbed a fifteen-foot gate and crept on finger and toe-tips along a narrow ledge. They couldn't have got inside the factory without him but as all he had done was climb they gave him the smallest cut. He had told them, 'I'm the one that risked his neck', but they wouldn't allow him a penny more and they watched him like uncles while he put his share away.

He tried to pull the strap of his rucksack out of Lumley's grip but he merely pulled it off his back and he and Lumley were left holding a strap each.

'Let go!'

'You don't get paid till you've finished the job.'

'I have finished it!'

'Not till you fix the girl.'

'You'll get your money back later,' said Ritter and took the rucksack from them. 'We're in your hands, Derek.'

Fish didn't feel his age, he had that uncles feeling about Ritter and Lumley and he felt like a child.

'Give me that rucksack or I'll—I'll——' What could he do against wicked uncles? His rage was a head of steam which had been getting up all his life. The world was full of Ritter and Lumley and hope was the reason they succeeded, silly bloody hope that people just couldn't be like that. 'I could fix *you*—I only have to say one word, I'd get off with probation but they'd put you away for years.'

'The money's yours and you'll get it when you've fixed the girl.' Ritter hung the rucksack over his shoulder. 'You have my word.'

'What more do you want?' Lumley winked.

Fish's rucksack hung like a hump under Ritter's neck and all Fish could say was, 'My pyjamas are in there.'

'You've got his word, you won't need money if you've got that.' Lumley's chest rustled with laughter. 'And you won't need pyjamas, men don't wear pyjamas——'

'I don't give tuppence for a dictionary of his damned words!' Fish could have wept but wouldn't, he would never forgive his tear ducts if they operated in front of Ritter and Lumley. He made the worst gesture he knew, twice—once in each of their faces— flung the door back on its hinges. Ritter, who insisted on caution, sprang after him, but Fish ran out willing someone to see the light and come to investigate. 'Please God, please Jesus, make them get caught–*now* if there's any justice—or be a Fraud for ever and ever, amen.'

The darkness was thick enough to taste and it tasted like mud. What had he done to deserve this? He had sweated along a two-inch parapet above a fifty-foot drop into a cast-iron vat: gashed himself on barbed wire, jumped when he was told to jump. Justice shouldn't be for him only, if he tasted mud those two should eat dirt. Now that he could weep in private his tears remained unshed. Who could he trust—with Ritter and Lumley at one end and the Holy Damned Fraud at the other? He walked into the side of the car and collected a cut lip.

The girl had managed to climb into the front passenger seat. She was supposed to be completely immobile—at least Ritter and Lumley supposed so and now Fish liked the thought of their being wrong, it could be the beginning of justice for them. He could of course have walked away and left them to it. And to his share of the money. It would be a miracle if he ever got that. He licked his burst lip. 'Work a miracle, you Holy Damned Fraud!'

As he slid into the driver's seat the girl said, 'It's you. I'm glad.

I like you. I like your hair, I can just see it. My father says only bad boys have long hair.'

Fish would have liked her to be dumb as well as lame. She was his very bad luck, fate could hardly have organised worse for him. He started the engine and revved it to a scream, he also switched on the headlamps and punched the horn as he roared out of the gate.

'Where are we going? I'm glad those men aren't coming, it'll be lovely on our own. It's a lovely car. Make it go fast. You can't go too fast for me.'

Fish had done no wrong until now. Climbing a gate and entering locked premises wasn't a crime, not when it didn't profit him, when he was actually the loser by it. His life had been only average blameworthy because it took effort to collect blame. Now he was being made to make the effort.

'Did you see me at the factory? I saw you, I was watching you all the time. I thought you were a girl.'

He was going to be sorry–not about her, what finally happened to her was all the same to him. It was the principle that mattered— that was calling it names, perhaps, dignifying a practically shapeless conviction about his part, what his part ought to be. Not a hero's part, nor a saint's, nor anything the Holy Damned Fraud would own, but a contribution just the same, a plus by virtue of its being minus—Derek Fish's estimate of what was generally not needful. This thing he was about to do came under that last heading, in his estimate there was more than enough of this already.

'I was glad when you came. It gets so dull at the factory and I can't sleep. I'm a half orphan, my grandma lives with us but she's gone to hospital. My father took me to work with him and put me on the shelf so I could hide if anyone came. He says he'll kill me if I show myself and make him lose his job.'

She moved with difficulty in her seat, using her arms to work nearer to Fish. 'I'm glad you're not a girl.'

Fish trod on the accelerator. Driving into the glare of the headlamps was like driving into the horn of a gramophone. The black fields yawned after them and somewhere the black figures of Ritter and Lumley were running away with Fish's money. His nose prickled with pity.

She latched her little sharp chin on his shoulder. 'What's your name, baby?' The car, bucking out of his grasp, threatened to roll over. He clung to the wheel as if it were his mother's arms. 'You *are* shy. You needn't be, I shan't eat you.'

He might have known he would have to go through it as well as through with it. This was only the beginning, she was going to make herself felt and he was the one who would have to feel. He had this genius for feeling and the crime was against him. Ritter and Lumley, the criminals, were forcing him to feel it all.

'Your hair's natural, you don't dye it, do you? I'll tell you something, I didn't even look at those other men, I was too busy looking at you. Anyway, I know your name, I heard it.'

That was marvellous. Here he was, the only one to risk his neck, the one who had to finish the job, who had to feel and who got the smallest cut—and the only one positively identified.

'You're called Goldy.' With an effort that made her gasp she hauled herself across the seat and leaned against him. 'Where are we going?'

Fish had no idea. The road was unhelpful, providing none of the landmarks he could have recognised. Also, it had gone on too long, even allowing for his feelings there was too much of this road. He peered ahead, looking for Hy Cross.

'You're taking me to a dance and I'm wearing a beautiful green dress. When you first saw me in it you said I was like your wildest dream.'

'You're only a kid!'

'How old am I?'

'Seven, six—how do I know?'

'Oh you!' she cried lovingly. 'Remind me to smack your face when we get home and I've taken off my beautiful dress. I don't want to crush it.'

Sight of the village relieved him, he was glad to be on a map, any map. He'd be thankful to be pointed on any pin. Hy Cross, between the moor and the fells, wasn't much of a place, so he took comfort from looking to the west where the twenty-tonners twinkled along the trunk road.

She said soberly, 'Why did you take the money?'

'I didn't.'

'I suppose you want to get rich without working. What are you going to do?'

'I haven't got the money. The others have got it.'

'I expect you'll spend it and then you'll have to steal some more. Will you?'

'No.'

'My father will get the sack. You don't think of that.'

'He should look after the place, that's what he's paid for.'

'Why don't you go to work and earn some money? If you're not clever enough to earn much you should save. I've saved five pounds.'

'Five pounds!'

'Well,' she said, brushing her shoulder where she had leaned against him, brushing off his sin, 'I'd rather have five pounds of my own than five thousand of someone's else's,' and Fish was so angry that he blew the klaxon and bounced the noise to and fro in Hy Cross's main street.

'Tell me what you're going to do. What are you going to buy? Will you buy everything you've ever wanted? Will you go away? Will you take me with you? I don't care how fast you go, I can never go fast enough. And I don't want to come back. Let's buy a red, red car and drive like devils!'

How could she be righteous one minute and ready to sin the next—at her own father's expense? She was sickening.

'Where I'm going,' he said, 'where I *was* going, was Vietnam. I had to have money for the fare.'

'What were you going there for?'

'To help. You'd think I'd be allowed to do that!' He saw the track which Ritter had described and turned into it. The car at once began to wallow in and out of potholes. He gritted his teeth as he hauled at the wheel. 'In this world you can't do good, by stealth or any other way.'

'Where are we?' She peered through the windscreen. 'We're in a wood.'

'It's a short cut.'

'Where to?'

'Never mind.'

The track was terrible. Ritter must have meant to fix them both, he meant the car to run into a bog and sink wouthout trace. Or go over the edge of a quarry. Fish recollected hearing that the old workings, under a crust of earth, went down for miles. Coming to these woods long ago on a school treat Fish had discovered that the best treat was dropping stones into a shaft and counting down the splash. Why hadn't he recollected that earlier? Oh little lamb, who made thee to hang on the hook?

'You'll do it,' she said.

'Do what?' He stopped the car, pulled up the handbrake.

'You'll go to Vietnam if you really want to.'

'I just might have,' he said bitterly, 'if someone else wanted me to.'

'Why have we stopped?'

'I'm not going any farther.'

'You're such a baby! Aren't you a baby?' Her white china face looked up at him, in the darkness he felt her smile. 'Anyone can do anything. Don't you know that?' Years ago, when Fish was still bigger than this girl, someone had to convince him nightly that the swarming creatures on the floor of his room were but shadows of the tree outside. 'You've only got to want to enough.'

'Don't give me that!'

'I tell you, anyone can do anything——' and then she sat still and he naturally thought she had paused to except herself but she hadn't. She suddenly and vigorously began to nod, saying, 'I shall walk when I really want to.'

'Can't you see what that makes you? It makes you the can-carrier.'

'I keep trying but I can't do it yet because I haven't been able to altogether want to. It has to be altogether, you see, but every time I try there's something else going on—my hand's itching or my ear's burning. When I really get down to it it'll only take a minute. It isn't much to do anyway—walking,' she said scornfully.

'It makes you solely responsible for the whole Kibbutz. Can't you see that? Jesus God!' cried Fish, 'it makes you Jesus God!'

'I'm not responsible for you, silly baby.'

Fish wanted to enlighten her for her own good, as someone should have enlightened him when he was her age.

'If you're praying, don't. No one's listening, there's no one up there except the Americans and the Russians. Do you think they care whether you're fully prayed-up?'

'What are you talking about? I hope you know, I hope the wind's not wagging your tongue.'

'I'm trying to educate you. There's no nice old Gentleman watching out for you, so save your breath. Get up off your knees— if you've got any knees!'

That was her own fault. She had no right to talk like a woman. Her head did not reach his shoulder. She wasn't a woman and she wasn't a child, she was just a living heap.

He told her, 'You make me say things I'm sorry for.' She leaked sorriness. Another day of it and he would crawl into a corner, another week and he would be too sorry to live. 'You ought to know better, the way *you* are you ought to know better than anyone.'

He sat knocking the gear lever in and out. It was time for him to go. He had come as far as he could and the minute anyone sane would have left, anyone with due concern for his skin, had already passed. What was he waitng for? Two courses were open to him, either he could get out and run or he could stay in the car and drive on. Just sitting was not a course, it was lunacy.

Her face broke out of the heap like a whitish flag. 'How you talk! It doesn't impress me one bit.'

'Do you think I'm trying to impress you?'

'I have knees, Mr Goldy, and I can kneel if I want to. But I shan't because it's such a job. I have to lie flat on my stomach and pull my legs round and get on top of them. And if I don't prop myself I fall on my face. Also I get dizzy on the floor. So what with one thing and another I wouldn't be wanting altogether if I knelt and it wouldn't work.'

'If you think wanting will work it, you're a fool.'

'Oh you! You want everything easy. You've got to help yourself because no one else can give you exactly what you want. No one else knows what you want.'

'Isn't that what I've been trying to do—help myself?'

'Oh you!' she said again, with anger that dwarfed his, 'you helped yourself to the money.'

And their scorn, which had been separate items, melted into one disgust. They sat stiff-necked, despising each other and the world. It seemed there was no other emotion left them, whichever way they turned. Fish even despised himself. She probably didn't go so far, she was very young and had to learn. They sat with the windows shut in their car-shaped scorn.

A tapping on the roof shook them. She fell against Fish in fright and he was hemmed between her and whatever was outside. He expected it to be Ritter, Lumley, or a monster. But when he rubbed the steam off the glass a patrol policeman looked in. He signalled to Fish to roll down the window.

Fish tried to start the engine. He stalled it and the patrolman opened the door. The patrol car slewed across the track behind them, turned up its lights and revealed every bristle on the man's chin.

'Now then, what's going on?'

He would be no wiser if Fish told him. It would take the gift of tongues and a wide-open mind and this man wore uniform to show that his mind was properly boxed. He shone a torch, travelled it over their faces and bodies and over the inside of the car. The beam waited longest, and well it might, on the girlie photographs stuck to the roof-lining. The patrolman looked at each picture and sighed.

'Nothing.' The word was croaked, Fish's mouth had dried but the palms of his hands were wet. A fierce white worm in the bulb of the policeman's torch turned scarlet, indigo, black.

'Come on now, what are you doing?'

What would Ritter have said? But Ritter wouldn't have stayed talking to the girl, he would have driven her into a ditch and left.

'This is a dangerous place at night,' said the patrolman and she chirped up, 'Dangerous?' She was over her fright, Fish could feel her opening out in all directions.

'There are some old pits round about, most of them unfenced and easy to run into in the dark.'

'We'll get back on the road.' Fish pulled the starter. The patrolman put his knee in the door.

'Is this your car?'

He must know that it wasn't, he must already have its number as a stolen vehicle. Next he would ask for Fish's driving licence, knowing that Fish did not have one. Policemen liked their little game.

'Fancy you bringing me to a place like this!' She reached up and pinched Fish's cheek. She told the patrolman, 'When he gets an idea in his head he doesn't stop to think.'

'What idea did he get?' The torch shone into Fish's nostrils.

'We wanted to be alone.'

'Alone? What for?'

She said in her smiling voice, 'What do two people want to be alone for, officer?' and Fish curled up inside. He heard the frizzle as his last legitimate feeling curled up and died.

The patrolman leaned into the car and turned his torch on her. She was cuddled under Fish's elbow.

'Why, you're only a kid!'

Fish had to laugh although he felt nothing, certainly not amusement. The action started in his stomach and he sat and quaked with laughter until the patrolman dragged him out of the car crying, 'Damn you, she's only a little kid!'